The Back of the North Wind

Also by
NICOLAS FREELING

Fiction

Non-Fiction

NICOLAS FREELING

The Back of the North Wind

The Viking Press   New York

Copyright © 1983 by Nicolas Freeling
All rights reserved
Published in 1983 by The Viking Press
40 West 23rd Street, New York, N.Y. 10010

LIBRARY OF CONGRESS CATALOGING IN PUBLICATION DATA
Freeling, Nicolas.
The back of the North wind.
I. Title.
PR6056.R4B3   1983   823'.914   83-47994
ISBN 0-670-14398-7

Printed in the United States of America
Set in Times Roman

To Roland:
for, among much else,
taking me up Eggardon

The Greek historian Herodotus refers to a people 'living at the back of the north wind'. This reference is sometimes held to apply to prehistoric Britain.

The Back of the North Wind

A man went on holiday to England. He had set foot there only once before; forty years ago; the times had not been normal. An exotic time, and he had behaved in eccentric fashion. In fact emotional: he did not count himself an emotional man. A European war was then still a notion to stir the blood, at nineteen years old. Things would be very different now. Things and times were very different now: today's nineteen-year-old could scarcely grasp the concept of a war between peoples of the peninsula that is Europe. We amuse ourselves now with war-games about wine or mutton ... Landing in England again produced sensations that he could laugh at or shrug away: he did neither. He was alone, and no attitudes were needed.

He wore a dark blue jacket, at once raincoat and parka: it would in Brittany be recognisable as officers' issue of the Marine Nationale: a corps he had nothing to do with. Perhaps in a sense it was a disguise: he was generally seen in tweed jackets, neat, a bit countrified, and bow ties. The detail has no importance, there being little to mark out this quiet greyish man, neither tall nor short, with regular features scarcely to be called handsome, carefully shaved and, despite many years of desk-work, straight-shouldered, and no slop around the waist. A Frenchman sixty years old, of the northerly or Frankish type with the long head, the narrowish chinny face, hair that has been fair, and pale grey eyes.

His luggage was on his back. It was early enough in the summer for there to be fewer tourists. He hoped to eat and sleep in country pubs. The food would be indigestible? – he would pay no heed. It would rain a great deal? – his jacket was of excellent quality. He spoke little English? – he would understand what was said to him and had little to reply. He was a solitary man. Much devoted to his wife, and if she accompanied him upon journeyings he was content, but if she chose to stay at home then not malcontent. The weeks of his holiday would be

7

well spent in listening and in looking. In this land of the Hyperboreans – strange and secret island – he might catch scraps of voices within himself, glimpses of a man he knew little. There were discoveries to be made. He knew the countries of peninsular Europe well, was attached to them, but of these close and yet far-away neighbours he knew little. Concerning one another both French and English had strange misleading notions, preconceived, arrogant, and quite ridiculous. Among ourselves, is it not much the same? This person we have lived with for a varying quantity of years, we imagine we know and understand well; but leave aside habit, sloth, the wish for comfort, and we find that vanity and fear, the twin powerful motors of our thought and action, blind us to reality. This man, to close acquaintances, to neighbours, to colleagues at work was a little-known and somewhat mythical figure. Was he not his own closest neighbour and oldest friend? He had gone on holiday, come here, with the wish to search, to find out. Leaving aside that absurd militarist adventure of forty years ago he had been for more than those forty years a police officer. He had risen towards the top of his profession, would rise no further. What he had done might be thought enough to satisfy a man. Now he was past sixty it no longer satisfied him or his wife, dark and little-known woman.

He was Adrien Richard, a Divisional Commissaire of the French National Police. The chief of a regional service of Police Judiciaire. Not counting Paris there are sixteen to cover the national territory and his responsibility carried one of the largest districts and one of the ten principal provincial cities. It needs a little explaining. In the country-side one finds the Gendarmerie, a paramilitary force whose officers hold army ranks. It is more like a fire brigade; the separateness is felt. An urban centre has its municipal force, the larger ramifying into many specialised groups. Defined with a deliberate lack of precision (a notion of checks-and-balances is at work somewhere) the PJ has authority both in town and country; is a body suspect of élitism; puts its nose into everything, does not wait like Scotland Yard 'to be called in' though it is the same type of skilled and trained body whose work is criminal investigation.

One is a cop, under orders; going where sent at wish or whim of government. One may end in Paris commanding a well-publicised sector (television appearances, a star . . .) or in the island of La

Réunion at the head of four drunks and a worn-out jeep. It's all according. And an able officer, because of inertia and inbred conservatism, may well be left where he is for many years. Richard had begun his career in urban brigades, been promoted to C.I.D. for being bright, and for a 'good war record', risen to command, and been given 'a good province' for being a good administrator. And then been left there.

He might have expected one of the final plums of his service but for lacking an essential quality; the ability, and wish, to ingratiate. Despite many turpitudes (only the worst cop, thorough-paced pig, has a saintly conscience) he remained his own man. A quality that displeases the mighty: they may respect it; they will sanction it, leaving you a little pointedly in the ditch that you have dug. Richard could feel content at not having been banished to Martinique, at having many years of continuity in a serene senior post. Perversely, he was discontented. An illogical, even asinine comportment. Could this be analysed? It was among his purposes, here.

He had got on the ferry and this was Southampton. England: to the average French person (remaining exactly as Stendhal described him with acidity in 1837) here be sea monsters. It seemed now oddly a scruffy, turbulent and rich-smelling place. It seemed now oddly placid; sad, and even pathetic: well, he was much the same himself. Nothing to feel surprise about. He took a railway ticket to Dorchester (had looked in the atlas at home, Made Plans). The train was full of jolly persons from London, going for a day by the sea. They were friendly, and talked: he smiled, made himself small. The French believe the English to be stiff: the definition applies – as in France – to a humourless and self-important bourgeoisie; not to real people.

English faces, bumpy, irregular, brim-full of feature: most peculiar. Marked eccentricity of dress and behaviour. Some very odd old ladies got out at Dorchester. As he walked away from the station he passed a middle-aged gentleman of mild, even academic aspect, fierily clothed in parachute overalls, corduroy trousers with holes in embarrassing places, a walk as though wearing spurs. Richard was pleased. In this island lived an exceptionally tiresome people of knobbly and madly dotty sort, such as he could get on well with, reconciling him to his shortcomings.

He felt better still in his first pub, amid a collection of what the

English soldiers of his youth had taught him were lahdidah accents. Expensively dressed young men of loutish aspect, superannuated pederasts, a woman with immense goggling eyes and no chin whatever: plainly, inbreeding flourished as in the deep of the Dauphiné and he felt quite at home. The beer was not warm, tasted delicious: myths were crumbling about him. Allegro assai; he had shed a skin of egoism such as chills and hardens the heart. In rain and wind and sometimes sun he hoped to peel away more: was he an onion? What was at the centre?

The tourist hereabout is grockle. Hard for the French mouth to compass, since the English l occurs somewhere at the back of the throat instead of the tongue on the teeth, and he said 'Grocko' several times like a demented cockyollybird, to the entertainment of grinning natives. Their feelings towards this breed were contemptuous but not spiteful. It seemed to him that he had known too little that was not mediocre.

A countryside suiting this people, sudden and secret. From the bare chalk escarpment one plunged into the watervalley, streams tinkling along through cresses; toy millrace, tiny weir, enchanting series of miniature landscapes seen from narrow roads so crooked between their thick hedges that one scarcely saw a hundred paces before one. Disconcerting. The striding spaces of France have amplitude, and often majesty; often too aridity. The French, said Stendhal furiously, cannot see a beautiful tree but they must cut it down for the sake of two miserable louis. This is like the bocage, thought Richard, the back-country of Normandy. Peopled likewise by sorcerers and spellbinders, faith-healers laying on hands? – quite probably: it was not at all long since witches had been burned in Dorchester. He worked his way along, like an earthworm.

He climbed hills. Like Maiden Castle: he had expected a great robber stronghold, massive and terrible like Coucy or Château Gaillard. He didn't have the right kind of imagination. Very large, yes. Colossal ditch and rampart exceedingly remarkable, yes. Thousands of people with antler-picks or whatever working at that damned hard chalk reminded him of Egypt: pyramids yes, and monstrous temples. All exceedingly boring. In the pub they tried to frighten him, telling him to go up there at night. What – he'd been a cop for forty years: thistles and cowpats are the same at night.

10

It was a different sort of hill altogether that changed his mind –
steep, vicious. A flint axe flung at his head, rearing above valleys of
sinister woodland, dark and close. Wouldn't want to get stuck here in
winter, thought Richard: snow in your eyes and you'd die of exposure
in half an hour. Challenged, he had to go to the top. The summit
curved, wicked as a scytheblade from the blunt end to a precipitous
spur, appalling him. It would not do to fall off here: those splinters
might be only chalk but looked razor-sharp. Dangerous as hell; a puff
of wind would take you over. If a fog blew up. . . not at all a place to go
up at night. Or by day either, not even this one, in a soft southwest
breeze and the haze off the friendly, not too distant sea wrapping the
sky in a madonna-blue veil. The place stinks of violence: get off quick.

Instead of getting off he sat down; lit – his head under his wing like a
damned seagull – tobacco; thought about violence. There should be
nothing a forty-year cop does not know about violence. When man-
made. Mean and silly, senseless and futile. And bloodshed is mostly
farcical, a grand-guignol, like most obscenities.

There was very little here that one could find comic: a place of
sacrifice. Ordinary human violence diminished here to a burned-out
match. Rasped upon an abrasive surface the human being catches fire,
burns a moment. Everyone understands the simple chemistry of the
match. And nobody understands the nature of fire, which is metaphysical. A moment of violence, enough for pipe or cigar as for rape or
murder. Leaving a twist of carbonised fibre. But have I lived this far,
thought Richard, and understood no more? A whole career. I have
done here and there some small good, perhaps, and everywhere much
harm. And it all seems very little up here. Was that what I came to
find? That the violence of nature is noble and just, while the violence
of man can never be anything but ignoble and base? Hastily, before
this led to theology, he scrambled off this frightful hill.

Halfway down and slithering he met a kindly, serious Englishman;
seriously and kindly involved in flying a large model glider: it effaced
vertigo.

"What is the name of this place?"

"Eggardon," he was told politely.

And in the pub they went on again about Thomas Hardy, of whom
he had already heard too much: a looming local presence as great a
bore (he felt sure) as Dostoyevsky. Only artists understood crime, and

11

violence, as he never would nor could.

"Fuck Thomas Hardy," thought – and said – Commissaire Richard.

"Great strides altogether," – in every pub there is an Irishman – "your man does be making with the basic English." Yes, perhaps he had acquired a scrap or so of useful knowledge...

Commissaire Richard had gone on holiday. Castang, likewise, was On Holiday. One had little choice in the matter: half of France was O.H., so that administratively speaking it was the quietest time of the year. Serious crimes do sometimes get committed during August; a great mistake, for judges are also away, and the committer finds himself clappèd in jug by shorthanded and thus cross policemen and left there (totally forgotten) for up to two months.

Castang did not want to go away. Meeting fellow citizens in great numbers on the beach is even worse than meeting them at home. Greased bodies lying, be they prone or supine, are vile. Where had Richard gone? Nobody knew. On foot, wearing peculiar clothing, vanished. The general feeling, that Richard was an impenetrable enigma, was enough. There are things it is no use trying to penetrate.

Richard had been ruthless: Monsieur Castang would please take off. The PJ would survive, animated by the serious-crime senior inspector, with as regent Richard's adjunct, the Person from Pau: neither Castang nor Richard had heard of the Person from Porlock, but both would have said fervently they knew him.

Castang had a remedy for not going away: moving house. A cottage had been found on the city's outskirts, where remnants of village life could sometimes be seen: semi-ruinous, with crabapple trees in what had once been an orchard. The obstinate old lady living here died at last: her one surviving grandchild lived in Montreal. Saving this property from the claws of speculative builders, financing the purchase without recourse to usurers, winning necessary permissions for repairs and alterations from the bowels of municipal administration – this would occupy long and boring pages to describe.

The holiday month was passed thus by Richard wandering about like Wotan in a Wagner opera, and by Castang digging out layers of antique filth, making crude repair of the more obvious dilapidation. Frightful job, but how else would it have been cheap enough to buy? September arrived as it does, with brilliant weather so that everyone who has been on holiday in August comes back cross. Richard reappeared, tanned. Castang tanned, despite tales of a month spent in a damp cellar. The person-from-Pau went on holiday, and the chief of the Economic-crimes, and Fausta. There were no very urgent matters afoot: just as well. Nobody who had come back had any zeal. It takes a month in France to recover from anything as strenuous as holidays. The city recovered from tourists: ancient, historic, occasionally beautiful, the city attracted many tourists. Grockle, said Richard. Most of them were gone by the end of August, but a long and involved governmental directive arrived (this was a year of socialist new-brooms) and all about delinquency. One would almost rather tourists.

Castang, appearing in Richard's office upon a brilliant, sunny morning, found the divisional commissaire studying statistics. He looked up and said "Agitated." It could apply to Castang, to the authors of this prose; not, surely, to himself. Was there an interrogation point, or did the slight rise in intonation betoken only a slight reproachful emphasis?

"Violence," said Castang in much the same voice.

"I'm reading about it. They're worried. I am to be worried, meaning you will be much more worried. According to the figures for last year, violence – in criminal terms of reference – cost this country eighteen hundred million francs. Do you find that a lot?"

"Yes."

"I thought you might: so did I. Until I got to the bit saying that non-violent, generally termed economic crime, cost this country during exactly the same period seventy thousand million. Putting things, I should hope, in proportion. However, you didn't come here just to say you were shocked, did you?"

"No. The great outcry is about the delinquence being so very juvenile. I – ," Castang's valuable conclusions on this subject were interrupted by two telephones ringing at once. Numbers of people (sounding agitated) saying it would be a good idea to get there quick, meaning before *France-Soir*: a crime, he was given to understand, of violence.

Richard had already put his phone down.

13

"Well Monsieur le Commissaire," said he pleasantly, "I'd better not delay you."

"You already? . . ."

"Yes, that was the Substitute."

"You don't propose? . . ."

"I'm too old to go running round scenes of crime. This sounds anyhow an unenviable example. You'd better take everybody you can get." That 'you aren't getting me' was apparent. It was nothing abnormal. Richard was a person to lift a large file off his desk and hand it across, saying, 'Haven't looked at this. Don't propose to.' Do something silly and he would cover for you; at least in public. The subsequent private interview with him would be something else again.

Castang went to review the troops, found Orthez struggling with paperwork about delinquency, and Liliane, the senior inspector, talking to a small female delinquent and getting small thanks for that.

"Sorry," said Castang, "I need you."

An underling removed the delinquent and Liliane said, "Don't be sorry" in a heartfelt way.

"We've a smelly one by the sound." The banditry service was all out. Too many people were on holiday. He collected a few cooks-and-non-combatants and climbed into the car.

"The woods at La Charité, Orthez. The Substitute will be waiting by the bridge." The word is accurate, he reflected. Not just meaning ersatz coffee. The Public Prosecutor, a mighty man, does not displace himself to the scene of smelly crimes. The law states that he must, which is why his aides are called substitutes. Just so. Richard sends me. I am also a substitute. Sounds even worse than understudy, or stand-in.

Ordinary mid-morning traffic, but even with lights on, the winker on the roof, siren going, and the coxswain-at-the-wheel (Orthez was a rally driver) it took twenty minutes. The woods at La Charité are outside city limits. They are interesting in a number of ways, but no time for that now: Castang would have to put all that in writing.

The bridge in question lay upon a narrowish country road and in an S-bend; a hazard to late-night drunks. The woods on either side had been cleared enough to provide parking space to people who come for a walk or whatever, because the area is a lung: protected green space. Two or three official cars were already there, and a few morbid sightseers held at bay by a gendarme. The Substitute, a youngish lawyer, whom Castang knew and liked, would be considerate and unpompous. He opened the car door.

"I'm afraid this could hardly be worse. Outside the city, the gendarmerie is spread thin with traffic and tourists, we've a large tangled area, it's a hot day . . . we've bits of a chopped-up body. Priority, find the rest. Sorry, Castang," shaking hands, "good morning."

"Orthez, collect our boys, what help there is from gendarmerie, forester service . . ." It was not enough; he turned to the legal official. "Could we get some CRS?" Auxiliary police, crowd-control types.

"I'd have to ask the Prefecture – use your radio?"

"Orthez, concentrate on getting every unauthorised person out of it. Liliane, organising a search, you're the administrator; see the forester, get a map. We may need it all cordoned, chessboarded, marker-flagged . . ." The prosecutor got out of the car.

"Yes, that's all right. A busload and more if we need them."

"So if you'll coordinate that, Lil, I'll see what we've got and join you when I can."

"What about the water?" The river splits around here into four separate streams. There are ponds, gravelpits – where people would be swimming, this time of year . . .

"God yes. River brigade and underwater team if need be but pray that – where was the first bit found?"

"The marshy area, the bit they want to make a bird reserve." Castang made a face. "Quite; nasty! That's how the forester . . ."

"He found it, did he?"

"And sensibly did the proper things. Which is how I – " making in his turn a bad face. "We'll have to bite on the bullet."

"IJ will be here any second." Identité Judiciaire is the technical team, which collects, measures, photographs, examines evidence.

"Here they are now." Not pleased either. "Doctor here yet?" We will also need forensic pathology.

"Place is full of mosquitoes."

"Talk about a bird sanctuary – whole goddam zoo in there. All we need is lions."

"One moment, I've gumboots in the car." Birds singing. Insects – a tremendous amount of life. Death is a biological balance.

15

"I'm not going back there," said the forester. "Threw up all I have already. Take you to within sighting distance. My job is woodland, mate. Animals at a pinch."

"He's done all he can," said the prosecutor sympathetically. "I'd rather a courtroom myself, frankly." He could not stop a shudder while thanking those gods as are recognised by the legal profession that he'd never had to attend a public execution: it was to be hoped, now never would. "There are going to be smells . . ."

Castang got back to his office with no thought at all about lunch. Sat, bleakly; went to his cupboard, found some whisky, had a drink standing up. The cupboard held clothes, objects handy in emergencies. These included an electric razor, eau de cologne: he poured some on his hand and smeared that across his face. The mixture with whisky was odious, but there were worse smells: he sat a moment breathing in deeply. He went to look for a typist: they'd all gone to lunch. He dragged out the dictating machine, put in a spool, put the mike on his table, let out three breaths with a moaning cowlike noise. Got up, poured a second drink, found cigarettes, wished Fausta were here; she might have made him some coffee. Make your own; possible. Make a start on this first. In an hour one of the girls will be back. He put his notebook and pen before him on the desk and switched the tape on.

"Voicelevel, nous n'irons plus aux bois, les lauriers sont coupés." Or, if you go down to the woods today you're sure of a big surprise . . .

"Preliminary, usual copies to Richard, Proc, instructing Judge etcetera. Usual heading, Castang; homicide. Present time, thirteen seventeen. Origin time, eight fiftyfive. In accordance etcetera; pursuant to, etcetera. Accompanied by Liliane, Orthez: see reports and daybook. Text follows: don't let's have the judge being sarcastic again about spelling. OK, paragraph.

"The lands of the former La Charité estate, cap and quotes, lie outside city boundary but are municipal property. A large area is now a park, with paths, benches, picnic areas. E.g. the physical fitness circuit, wooden frames and stuff for gymnastics. Point to make: joggers, bicyclists, walkers frequent this area at all times attracting no attention. Same applies to parked cars. The weather has been fine and warm and even at night the area attracts numerous people. Paths are

16

sanded, in places beaten earth, pine needles and stuff. Paragraph.

"Behind this area is a further large stretch bounded by a stream, accessible by three footbridges; also by riverside path past disused gravelpits. Swimming not officially allowed due to some bacteriological hazard, but at this time of the year tolerated. Blind eye extends to cars which are forbidden access to path, but no adequate barrier exists and infringement is frequent. We see that access to the wild area is easy and attracts little notice. Within it walking is difficult due to thick undergrowth and numerous boggy patches. At this season this delta area is infested with mosquitoes discouraging the tourist or stroller, but we may remark numerous incursions from fishermen, birdwatchers, people with innocent aims. It will be important to recall that the area gives shelter to a large animal population including muskrats and numerous small rodents. Paragraph.

"What I term the wild area is designated as nature reserve and bird sanctuary. It is in the care of the State forestry service but pending decision patrolling is slight and superficial. Since the matter has been ventilated in the press this is common knowledge locally. Paragraph.

"A forester in fact made discovery, his attention caught by unusual activity of small animals and insects. A plastic carrier bag had been torn open and contents scattered. From the skin areas these appeared to him human. It is understandable that he made no effort to collect or protect, but did promptly alert authority. The presumption of homicide being immediate, little time was lost. The area was isolated, divided into sectors and searched with the aid of a squad of CRS. Six other plastic bags were recovered, from which the doctor was able to reconstitute the bone structure. Results point to human female of North European origin with fair hair and skin and probably around twenty years old. Detailed dismemberment and subsequent loss of blood, enclosure in plastic bags. Hot moist conditions made difficult any of the usual observations or tests for time of death. Decomposition did not seem far advanced. Specimens of insect life present were kept and may prove helpful. Pending expertise the working hypothesis is a moment between twentyfour and thirtysix hours before discovery. All findings have been brought to the Pathology lab and Professor Deutz notified. His interim report is awaited. Measurements, photographs and such findings as IJ have established should be available this evening. Paragraph.

17

"Brief summary of observations follows. One, a strong hypothesis of local knowledge in the author. E.g., the choice of area and plastic bags of supermarket origin. Two, careful planning. E.g., detailed dismemberment for easy transport and concealment. Attempts to bury bags over a widely scattered area in boggy ground. Note in passing that the soil type varies abruptly from hard dry going to fluid mud and no satisfactory footprint has been identified. The presumption is that the author counted at least upon rapid decomposition and even upon prolonged concealment. He showed little understanding of wildlife habits, which points with some strength to urban background. Three, all soft tissues were greatly mutilated and traces of bruising or throttling etcetera imperceptible. Cause of death thus unknown pending detailed pathological exam. The same applies to hypotheses of struggle, sexual assault, ligatures and indeed all circumstances surrounding death. Four, review of missing persons is at best approximate pending exact parameters for height, weight, etc. Mutilation of features very considerable and identification may depend upon dental record. No—" Ah: there was a girl back . . . at last.

The Substitute had not found it easy to get back upon even keel, and had had recourse to literature. Castang himself had not been overstable in his emotional responses.

"I suppose," he said unhappily, "that the soldiers of '14–'18 would have found all this a boring commonplace. I mean bits and pieces lying about; plus a perpetual stink; plus rats, crows and other nasty animals; plus mud. I'm not quite sure about the mud" – he was talking a great deal and hurriedly while hunting for something that should look like a hand–"Passchendaele I know about but it was autumn no? – and cold mud. What I dislike is hot mud. Up there in the mining country the hot weather would be mostly dry – sodomise these mosquitoes."

"You ever read Conrad's *Secret Agent*," asked the lawyer, perhaps tactfully assuming a lot about police tastes in reading.

"No" irritably monosyllabic: lawyers . . .

"There's a chap blown up by a bomb," determined, "and a conscientious English copper gathering up small pieces. Inspector Whatnot examines the trove. It was watching you brought the phrase into my mind – I paraphrase – 'looking over the byproducts of a butcher's shop with a view to choosing an inexpensive Sunday dinner.' "

18

Castang was grateful for being able to laugh.

"Party dinner for small mammals. Beuh – bluebottles. Entomological interests for Deutz. What d'you make of this disjointing?"

"I don't make anything, leave that to Deutz: you mean was it a butcher or what?"

"I don't mean much. I'd think any countryman would have a sharp knife and could make a rough job of jointing a sheep or a deer. But a countryman would know about weasels and things. Wouldn't bury stuff that wasn't going to stay buried. Unless in panic and I see small evidence of panic. Not an axe or saw . . . I really meant, anything legal."

"Come, you know better than to ask me that. Calm, collected, handy with a knife; that's still no real evidence to state of mind . . . if he worked in the town he'd have a problem with blood, no?"

"If it was me," said Castang nearly losing a gumboot, "I'd strip, do it in the bath, and then get under the shower. One would get quite neat with practice."

"And acquire the habit," said the Substitute dryly.

"Mad scientist. Mad black magic man. Full moon werewolf."

"Madman seeking headline in *France-Soir*. I'll look after the press, shall I?"

Could it be a woman? Castang was thinking. He had had three cups of coffee and was dictating to an anaemic typist. Why not?

"In conclusion; a rapid identification of the victim could lead to termination of enquiry within twenty four hours just as the slightest disturbance of fortune could suffice to make the whole picture negative. Rapid retrieval has been the initial key and will continue to be so – I'll be in my office when you've got it ready."

Monsieur Richard (his second given name was Gabriel but he had suppressed this, having been, he remarked, rarely the bearer of good news) had simply gone off to play golf. This was not as frivolous as it seemed, because he had experience enough of suitcase murders, and did not need any preliminary report from Castang (anyhow a competent investigator) to tell him the conclusion. You do mostly get them within fortyeight hours, because they are a snip for the Scientific Methods. What was worrying him much more was being the chief of the first criminal-investigation team to turn up a suitcase-murder whose author would be a little girl of twelve. For the definition of iuvenile delinquency had been meaningless for years. In the public mind – like every mind extremely slow to grasp or accept any new idea at all – it still meant a raid on the ice lolly stall, intervention by the fatherly neighbourhood copper, a magistrate's clip over the ear and a talking-to. The children's judge, of all legal functions the least enviable, had the exceedingly unpleasant task of worrying whether an adolescent should be treated as child or as adult and in what proportion. In Western Europe the legal threshold is still the eighteenth birthday. Suggestions have been made to lower this to sixteen. As though that would help!

The crime against the child (the problems of the legal and judicial professions were not thank-heaven his) is the policeman's worst nightmare. The crime by the child runs a close second. For traditionally the child's offence is against property. In fact children were now increasingly signing their names to crimes against the person. Not very long ago Castang had had a married woman raped by three fourteen-year-old boys . . . During the holidays there had been a homicide, so far unresolved. The urban brigade had another, now two months old. They'd been sitting on it, and keeping their mouths shut. This morning Liliane had come to him with an uneasy theory that the two were linked, and she wasn't happy . . . She didn't know that he wasn't happy either, because Fabre, the Central Commissaire of the urban brigade, had circulated a confidential report suggesting the same thing, and his final paragraph . . .

Golf . . . there are very few golfclubs in France, and those exceedingly flossy. Quite openly, indeed officially, membership is a symbol of successful affluence, to be noted on your individual tax declaration, in the same breath as ownership of a yacht. You mix only with the notables, and you are expected to fit in. Richard did. It was expensive, but having neither children, mortgage nor mistress, nor even an extravagant wife, he paid his subscription and bar bills in the spirit of a man making a good investment. As for actually playing golf – idiotic pursuit – it sufficed to concentrate. He was regarded as an acceptable partner, and a man worth being polite to. Cultivating, a little, from time to time. One didn't have to be assiduous. For notables have a feeling that being friendly with a senior police authority is a sheet anchor. Just in case . . . One should hear too ('getting the drift')

20

what kind of instructions may be filtering down from his political masters in Paris. Almost as good as a chap high in the Prefecture. This was naive of them, but businessmen are naive. Vanity prevented them noticing that he listened more to them. Talk in the golfclub is less guarded than in most places.

Thus, he was a pleasant companion in the bar. Made jokes. There is in Paris a sort of intelligentsia-ghetto where they make jokes, but nobody in provincial cities makes jokes, least of all the notables. The downfall of the giscardien régime could in part be attributed to its utter humourlessness: one might never laugh at King DongDong. Socialists are mostly very gloomy folk too, but with them at least there is less likelihood of being Deprived of your Civic Rights on account of laughing. Golfers need jokes too: they get very intense, given to braining folk with the three-wood.

There was nobody much around today. Businessmen were on holiday, or transferring their personal fortunes to Switzerland. Others would be indulging their cardiac or digestive troubles. Laying their secretaries. Whatever. They would arrive later, telling about the hard day. There were a few fat old ladies in Bermuda shorts, who golfed with great strenuousness. That was all right. Richard wished to walk about, think a little, push a ball in front of him to aid concentration.

As a change from Fausta's food – Judith too was for ever making him eat things like muesli – he went to the bar for a self-indulgent moment with a sandwich. There was no restaurant here, but the notables, for whom La Bouffe – Grub – is never far from the mind, insisted upon a meal-thing. The barman, adroit fellow, hired a woman, and made a sophisticated sandwich. You wouldn't come in here and say 'Ham'. There was a smoked loin of pork today, just underdone enough to be juicy. That pink was a good colour, unlike the pink of that biddy's scarf, which was that of a marzipan pig.

"Muscadet? A nice beer?" He carried his plate to a corner, away from a gang of old dears drinking just-a-sip of still champagne: you could have a bet on the moment they'd be back for a second bottle. He retired into his thoughts.

Thought parted suddenly like rain-curtains: he saw a face in the alcove on the other side, of a man alone like himself. It took him a moment to recognise, although perfectly familiar. One of the shining lights of the last government, so downfallen one would say 'finished', but that is never very prudent in France, where only the tomb is a finish. They would all have wriggled into safe jobs. This one had not been a minister; more rarefied and less shopworn than that dozen or so of faces perpetually on view being cued by a television-lackey. Still a mighty personage. A face going with slow, academically precise voice, dispassionate smile, air of intellectual distinction lightly carried, honours lightly worn. Interesting person, for one would have thought him too civilised and too detached to have tied his wagon quite so tight to that appalling band: it was less greedy a face than the others.

However, with that peculiar insensitivity that affected them all he had stood for the National Assembly. Perfectly safe seat; smallish town (some sixty kilometres off, thought Richard; he's far from home) of which he had been mayor, a sound political base. He'd been tumbled by some unheard-of boy. Many more had suffered the same fate in a landslide but this had been among the least expected.

"I fear, Commissaire, that I am intrusive." He must have been staring!

"By no means."

"But you are preoccupied."

"I confess to a personal interest in meeting you – do sit down – but I wasn't aware that you knew me."

"We knew one another's faces," smiling. "The truth is that I am far enough from home to know few, hereabout – might I simply say that I felt lonely?"

"Golf is a new passion?" smiling.

"Too early to say. Like driving a car myself, a thing I haven't done in years." Put lightly; he'd had an official car and driver. "A new way of concentrating the mind? I thought I'd learn. An old dog should learn new games."

"We can play."

"I shouldn't dream of inflicting a clumsy and boring beginner upon yourself."

"It's not a game I take solemnly enough to accept your description in any context."

"Then with the greatest pleasure. Shall we have some coffee? – may I go and order for you?"

How does he know me? wondered Richard. It was of no great

22

consequence. His curiosity was to know how this friendly and easy person, writer moreover of distinction (whom he had not read: memo Fausta, get book by Aldo de Biron), matched with a coldblooded, reactionary politician, known to have been the real author of a particularly appalling piece of social legislation now in line for repeal. The polished language was over-exquisite but there was more to him. In the Academy? – a bit crude, that (too many people nowadays notice that the Academy is the unreadable writer's last refuge) but perhaps the Institute of Moral and Political Sciences? (Fausta: look it up). Monsieur de Biron had made a discreet visit to the lavatory and arrived with the coffeecups.

"I was spending too much time in Paris, as I have recently learned – in severe but salutary fashion. Our town is small – do you know it at all? Not much to recommend it – a few scraps of good architecture."

"It's in 'my district'. I have probably been there on three official occasions which I have totally forgotten."

"I am not in the least surprised."

A pleasant afternoon. A man not wearisome and Richard hoped the same would be thought of himself. No politics, no books, no golf was spoken about. Trees, wild flowers, grass, birds: Richard knew nothing about any of these things, but instruction came without a shadow of pedantry.

"My awkwardnesses have not been over-oppressive? I find you more patient a teacher than the professional. You are a natural stylist; probably it is the case in all that you do. I have enjoyed myself. I look forward to more such meetings, but would not wish to impose myself by these clumsy flatteries."

"Haven't we perhaps earned a drink before going home?" asked Richard.

There was a hook. What it was, why it should be, he could not tell; but the shadow (however minute) of a fly being danced over his head presaged something. Wondering about it was in vain – but worth a little homework.

He would have to look in at the office before going home. Castang knew very well where he was, despite pretences to the contrary, and would have rung in the event of a snag, but prudence must overcome sloth. In the inner ear a voice could be heard, speaking in the gentle treacly tone of a defence counsel on to a good thing. 'And where was the divisional commissaire during these goings on? Ladies and gentlemen of the jury . . .' Shaking hands with Aldo de Biron in a friendly fashion Richard made a note: think about him – but a little later.

Castang had stayed to do a little work on delinquency, but had no intention of hanging about until somebody came up with a problem. Enough was enough.

Each new day you start from scratch. Each day you know nothing. Learn something. You got up in the morning and made the coffee: it was a new page in the notebook, white and clean. You began neatly, writing legibly. Through the day the page got steadily dirtier, stained and scribbled: the phone numbers in margins, the balloons containing 'Thinks', and the balloons surrounding 'He Says' – generally meaning don't-believe-a-word-of-it. Mysterious drawings made by the un-conscious while Holding the Line. Dirt accumulated. Bits got torn off, bits crossed off: bits of lives, and much of that his own, nibbled away. The end of the day was dogeared and greasy: enough was enough.

He got out of the car to open his gate. He rode a bicycle less often now that he had further to go. Or because now that he was a Commissaire bicycles were below one's dignity? The house was a bit below dignity too. Among the nineteen-hundred-odd police com-missaires in France he knew a few. They lived in wealthy residential quarters, in apartment blocks that had Standing. It was needful to rank, like the privileges.

It was as Richard had said: 'What's the use of rank unless you can pull strings?' and this latterday Godfather had demonstrated. Phone calls were made to people who later made other phone calls. Difficulties melted; the magic of La Magouille the Big Fiddle, the Arrangement. Papers were put before him and people said 'Sign here' – like so many confessions of crimes . . . which they were. Let people do you little favours and they will expect little favours done for them. One learned.

Building materials . . . Vera had been horrified, having innocently gone to the supplier's yard with a long shopping list and come back aghast. 'They ask one five francs for a brick'.

24

"My poor girl," said Orthez, who was fond of her, "if you insist on building in a workers' district, got to do it their way. Can't just ring up and say knock off fifty per cent as if you were a toff. Leave it to me." And sinister people appeared in filthy station-wagons with anything Castang wanted. 'Five hundred. To a friend three-fifty. Cash. Right here.' It was all stolen. He had heard Orthez say quite openly, 'Don't tell him, you silly prick', to that young idiot Lucciani, the electrical maniac, who turned up with a car full of cable and switches. Tools were 'borrowed'. Diogenes would please not light his lantern to look for an honest workman.

"I was brought up to be honest," said Vera, much shocked. "I know now why capitalists say the proles do no work and even if you watch them like hawks they steal you blind."

"Bullshit," said Orthez comfortably. "Ask them where we learned to steal, and how to do it without getting caught by no cop on the gate neither."

"I know," unhappily. "When we went Communist at home it was exactly the same."

Corruption everywhere. What isn't for sale? We aren't, said Castang. It isn't 'up to a point' – it's once past that point.

The great snag about living here was simply that it defied convention. You could do this in Paris but the stamp of the provincial is that like herds with like. Live in a bourgeois quarter and nobody asks questions. People here will not enquire what you do for a living: their own, too often, would not bear looking into. The petty functionary wants to live on a street with his fellows – they will understand his little ways. Thank God this town has doubled in size over twenty years – but in this villagey survival from another era people like to know who you are. He was matey with people in the pub. A certain tolerance had been established. But be prudent, said Orthez. Put a notice on the gate saying Chien Méchant. A sheepdog sort of beast got from the Animal Protection people, it was not in the least vicious: Castang wouldn't have had it around Vera and the child if it were. It was just a prudent measure . . .

"Prudence!" said Vera disgustedly. She wanted to change the world, and was fed up with prudence. She was right too, Castang supposed: prudence no longer sufficed.

He parked the car in the yard and went back to lock the gate. 'Build

25

your little fortress', had said Vera cattily. 'Allow nobody inside. French thinking! . . . I want to go out; meet people, talk to people; I've been paralysed long enough'.

It wasn't her awkward legs she was talking about. Or yes, it was, thinking was at a standstill. Everything in society was blocked, everything was breaking down. The mechanisms were worn out. A change in government was no more than cosmetic, superficial, inadequate. There was no new thinking. And what were we going to do about that?

Castang didn't know. She would have his supper for him shortly: there was time to do a bit of carpentry. Later, there would still be light enough for some paintwork. He had a homicide investigation on his back and that was enough job to be going on with.

He had patience with her Cassandra passages, but sometimes they made him sigh. Prophecies of gloom were cheap, he thought, and she was so wholesale.

'Our world is seized up. Familiar lubricants like Jesus or Buddha don't work any more. And things will get worse: it won't be just forest fires or the black tides from oil spills. Volcanoes that have been ten thousand years dormant will erupt – are, already. Earthquakes . . .'

Castang shrugged; it was very possible. And meantime, another homicide to work at.

There was a note from Professor Deutz, in his fine old fashioned handwriting, legible and disciplined. Dated the previous evening.

'A lot of work here, Castang, and it will take me another twentyfour hours before my good-lady is ready to start typing up voluminous notes. There is much of interest, and if you have a suspect, it would be as well to come and talk to me before questioning him – it is a him; there was sexual interference. I think after death as well as before: I am not yet sure. I say this only to warn you.

'The life cycle of the bluebottle presents no problem, and you will get fairly exact timing.

'For the moment you have an identity problem. I have thus made you a brief schema on separate sheet. The mensurations will be exact to the centimetre. We will of course be deprived of a great deal that is normally most informative. I have had plaster casts made of the dentition and am sending these across. That will have to do for now. The most recognisable features (ears, eyes, lips) are as you inferred too far gone'.

Signed simply 'Deutz'. The abrupt formal monosyllable (the single gruff bark of a dog, said Richard, before it recognises a harmless person) was highly reassuring. The Professor of Pathology at the University Hospital was one of the very few people known to actually mean what he said and who moreover did not sign things unless they said what he meant.

And 'passport information' . . . How far could you get with height, weight, age, when your photograph was of someone suffering from advanced leprosy? The teeth are the clincher if, nowadays a largish if, the subject has been regularly treated by the same dentist over a number of years. And to arrive at that stage you need a virtual certainty to which only formal proof of identity is lacking: you do not send plaster casts to all the dentists in the world or even in New Zealand, saying 'Recognise these?'

Deutz would not have sent the teeth unless he thought them useful: Castang opened the cardboard box. A few fillings were marked with ballpoint on the white plaster, nothing much. Girl of twenty; she'd had good teeth: and then? . . . But there was a note tucked underneath.

'The upper jaw was too large for the lower, and at early teen age she had four teeth extracted to make room, and the front uppers braced: skilful professional work by orthodont specialist. This condition, taken with the modelling of the skull, points to a Scandinavian origin'. Better; but you don't, alas, find Swedish blondes in Sweden alone. Even if you include North Germany, England, and the State of Minnesota. It could still perfectly well be New Zealand. The trouble is that Europe is full, and most of all in high summer, of young girls milling about. And if a twenty-year-old from Fairbanks, Alaska, is a casual postcard-sender it may take months before anybody even concludes she is missing.

If you have a photograph, then you can superimpose an X-ray of the skull, and if that fits . . . this was like saying if we had eggs we could have bacon-and-eggs if we just had some bacon.

"Orthez," said Castang down the phone. Orthez was not exactly Professor Deutz, but they had this in common: give them an instruction; it would be meticulously and tenaciously carried out with absolute accuracy as to detail.

"It's as we thought, there's no feasible reconstruction of features. So telex to Interpol: they're a broken reed but it's got to be done. I'll dictate; you boil it down to suitable text.

'Facial characteristics being too far obliterated for comparison, identity can only be sought by cranial features using x-ray superposal technique'. Subject female, age twenty, height one seventy-six, weight sixty-four, build well-developed, uh, athletic. Type Scandinavian, I hate that but it's the best we can do, hair straight and fine, natural cornblonde, undyed or altered, over shoulder-length. Teeth large, white, regular, prominent but corrected by successful orthodontic treatment: that's probably the most hopeful thing we have – people do notice teeth!' "

"Since most people's are bad," said Orthez colourlessly: his own were splendid. Castang's were like a public building before Malraux had it cleaned, or so Vera said – a sort of ochre . . . "Do I send the photos we have?"

"Of course or we'll be drowned in rubbish. The full face and profile from IJ."

"We'll be drowned in rubbish anyhow."

"Correct, the computer can't digest stuff like that and every cross-eyed loony in Paris will be sending us their version of Swedish blondes. We put up a large-screen transparency thing, I'll get the cranial X-rays from Pathology, I'm going round there anyhow, and I want Liliane to set up a team for comparing every single one we get. Looking ahead, I want a national television flash for the midday news and the evening one too. Those buggers will change the wording but let's get it as foolproof as makes no matter. Let's see. The national police make the following appeal to the public. A girl has been assassinated in conditions of such brutality as to make her face unrecognisable. She was twenty, tall, well built, and had long fair hair and noticeably fine white teeth. Her nationality and origins are unknown. Will anybody who has been in the company of such a person or who thinks he may have seen her please lose no time in reporting the facts to the nearest police station. And that of course on our computer for every gendarmerie post: air-sea-land frontier control for what use that is – but blanket. She may have been hitch-hiking."

"They're not going to like it."

28

"Neither will Richard like it and he's got to approve it and I'm going to see he does."

Monsieur Richard, however, only said "As long as I don't have to go on television. Has Interpol no tall blondes? – astonish me."

"Don't be ridiculous – trillions of them in every imaginable guise from photomat miniatures to soft porn in blurred focus and Exquisite Pastel Tints. Liliane is snowed under."

"Then why not eliminate them first? Who knows, you might even get a positive."

"Waste time and the fish goes stale. What's the chance on an Interpol signal – hundred to one against? How many girls are floating about the country in August and haven't written home for six weeks – if they've got a home? If we get a corpse, floater or whatever, decayed beyond recognition, how old is it? Six months or so? Whereas this isn't more than fortyeight hours old right now. Friends or acquaintances may be still in the district." Richard nodded, accepting this reasoning.

Professor Deutz had just finished dictating to his secretary (who instead of being the expected elderly female of forbidding aspect was a highly pleasant-looking young girl) all about the egg-laying cycle of the bluebottle fly.

"Here's another," he said without animosity, when Castang entered: the girl got the giggles but gathered up her pad and went off to the typewriter.

"I got the impression you'd something more interesting than maggots for me," said Castang.

"I have indeed. You aren't interrogating anyone yet though?"

"Good god, we haven't even an identity for her yet – you didn't see the midday news?"

"I never look at television, except of course when it's Commander Cousteau."

"Politicians being pathological specimens and you've enough of those. Sport of course the same."

"Stop fooling about then. So now we're quite well equipped. We've got beyond the sink in the corner and the chipped enamel basin. We've good lighting, and we've an expensive Japanese camera with several lenses. So have you, you'll say. I've nothing against your IJ photographer – we aren't looking for the same things. Annie, where are those photos; you didn't put them away? Here we are. This is her buttock."

29

"Recognisable, if barely."

"Yes, it's supermarket butchery. Now since all the soft tissues of the flesh areas were extensively nibbled, your photographer quite naturally assumed all the mutilations were due to the same cause. Whereas the analogy of a roast being made ready for the oven – a leg of missionary, say – caught my eye."

Castang was used to the old boy's robust view of pathology. Live surrounded by cancers, and you learn to see their comic side. Criminal-brigade cops, and especially the anti-gang brigade, themselves bandits to a man, had a violent sense of humour. Why else are so many medical students rugby-players?

"There's something hairy about missionary," he objected, – "smells of old goats. Roast haunch of blonde looks better on the menu."

"Now you're getting somewhere," turning the photo around and clicking the magnifier up to ten-power, "and give me your opinion now on this." At first it looked like the Gobi desert after a sandstorm. Large parallel ridges in sharp angular planes.

"A knife," he said triumphantly.

"Right," said Deutz. "Watch a really skilled butcher slicing ham and it looks perfectly even. But when an amateur like you or I goes to carve a leg of lamb – your knife is shorter and less sharp. Your pressure on the downstroke is heavier, and each upstroke alters the angle and direction a wee bit. Bitemarks, no matter what the animal, never look like this. Whether you seize or tear, or whether you have the large sharp incisors that scythe away – here, look at these under the high power. You've a cannibal, my boy; you're in psychopathology."

"He ate her?" asked Castang. Disbelievingly wasn't quite the word: what other possibilities are there?

"He didn't want her skin for a lampshade. Whether he had a nice sizzly barbecue is outside my province, but when you get him look for his knife, and I'll fit it for you to these grooves."

Fifteen years now, pretty near, in the business, and nigh on ten in the criminal brigade, and he knew this much: anything goes. They'll call any criminal a psychopath nowadays. The word has become so worn

30

down as to be nearly meaningless. If we'd ever been taught any Greek, said Vera sadly, we'd be less sloppy in our thinking. If Americans had ever been taught any Greek (she went on logically) there'd be less meaningless scientific jargon. Pathos is a root and means suffering. By extension – and erosion – you get meanings like illness, and even just 'feeling'.

"What is pathology?" he asked Professor Deutz.

"The study of maladies, their causes, their effects – the definition goes back to Claude Bernard," said Deutz crisply, addressing the first-year student on the first day.

"So – any abnormality at all?"

"Loosely – you're getting dangerously near the position held by Doctor Knock."

"Who's he?"

"You never saw Louis Jouvet as Doctor Knock? 'There's no such thing as a healthy person: there are only people who are ill and aren't aware of it'. The finest actor, boy, of my time. Why? – because you couldn't find a more abnormal person – I knew him well."

"I saw Jouvet," said Castang, "as a boy, playing the old cop in 'Quai des Orfèvres', and it was that which put me in this business."

"Incomparable psychopathologist," said the old man.

He went back to the office and took down the dictionary. Psychopathy, Monsieur Robert's dictionary told him, is mental disease, in the original meaning, now obsolete. Hm, I am obsolescent if not yet quite obsolete. Modern sense: a constitutional mental deficiency characterised by impulsivity, instability, and an incapacity to adapt to the surroundings, leading to antisocial conduct. Long, that, and fairly clumsy, but reasonably lucid and mercifully free of jargon. Psyche: soul? – same page. Ha: the sentient soul. That is cautious of Monsieur Robert. The sentient soul is just about anything outside physiological definition. The Greek word phusis, dear boy, means nature.

That's one thing about holding a senior position. And having an office to yourself. You've time to think, as well as looking up words in the dictionary. A junior police officer, with the uneducated person's traditional distrust of words, would say 'What you doing then? – looking up cunt to see what it means?'

'You're a stupid cunt, Castang'. Richard was fond of saying.

'Stupid connasse' he had said one day to Vera, when cross. She had flown into the greatest rage he'd ever seen her in.

'It is all there, everything is in that. All the denial of women and contempt for women since history began. The woman's sex is the perfect synonym for everything stupid, idiot, imbecile. Go on, ask yourself why, and tell yourself the truth for once in your life'.

Orthez, Liliane – the whole damned brigade that wasn't on holiday – were working their tiny heads off, and he was sitting there with a dictionary. Psychopath. Why not pathopsych?

Put a television flash on the midday news, and you'll get an incredible amount of psych, and all of it path. There were a lot of lost girls. There always are. In just about every police station of the world are photographs. You don't have to bother any longer with the old belinogramme transmission systems: the Sony Corporation will do it for you much faster. There are people still with a low opinion of commercial television broadcasts? Who remark acidly upon vulgarity, vapidity, crass imbecility ? – they should try linking their receiver to a friendly computer.

The mistake was in using the word Scandinavian: the machine insisted pedantically that it understood this area to be that served by SAS Airlines. After a struggle Lucciani said, "Look, just give me blondes all right?" and started getting them from Japan and the Gold Coast.

"I'm bloody well drowned in blondes," he complained, sneaking out for a cup of coffee.

"Isn't that the death you've always longed for?" asked Liliane acidly. She was trying to cope with the replies to the broadcast appeal: there were eighty, not counting the frivolous, the obscene, the lunatical, and the deliberately false-just-for-the-pleasure-of-annoying. Fifteen of these were in the district and had to be checked by someone with time, patience, experience; commodities in short supply.

Some came in person to the doors of the PJ, and further. The downstairs office is really only a clearing house for everything else: communications, dispatch, messages – there is a little sliding window for enquiries. The filter hereabouts is bound to be crude: Arabs and clochards, the poor and the inarticulate will be received with a courtesy that can only be called scanty. Saying 'tu' with no courtesy at all has been put down by the new Minister but the old habits die hard.

The obverse of this still also applies: a person well dressed, apparently educated, or clothed in a little brief authority, will be treated with some unction and forwarded to the Secretary upstairs. He was on holiday: the job fell to Castang, because there was nobody else.

"Please sit down. Your name?"

"François Somvieille. With an em and two ells." Mm, a fussy person, and selfimportant. Late twenties, prosperous, smartly dressed in a summerweight suit.

"Your address?"

"Sixtyfour Rue d'Ypres."

"And your profession?"

"Cadre d'entreprise." Mm. Business executive. "Savempo, we make packaging materials of a specialised – "

"That won't be necessary." Some indignation, at being interrupted.

"And who am I speaking with, if I may enquire?"

"Commissaire Castang: I am directing this affair, about which you have information as I understand."

"Good, I don't want to waste time with subscrubs. I don't have information; I have the solution. That'll be a relief to you, no doubt."

"It will indeed. I am listening," politely.

"I killed her. Temporary insanity of course, and I'll have to see what advice my psychiatrist has to give me. My advocate will know how to deal with it. I thought it best to come to you first, and directly, in order that innocent persons should not be unjustly exposed to suspicion."

"I see," said Castang, tempted to say 'and the door is behind you' but one must follow certain formalities. "What was her name?"

"Vanessa. I never learned her other name."

"And where did you meet her?"

"I picked her up along the road outside the city. In my car." That explained everything. It was probably a fancy car.

"And you killed her."

"Yes. I had sexual intercourse with her, which of course she welcomed, and then I killed her. I strangled her."

"Why?"

"She was not satisfactory to me."

"I see. And what did you do then?"

"I ate her."

Castang was taken short aback. It was not a detail that had been published.

"You ate her," he said levelly. "Well. You wouldn't mind giving me some details."

"How, details?"

"With a knife and fork? No I'm not trying to be funny. You didn't just crunch her up like a shark."

"I just – . . . "

"Yes? Go on. Explain to me."

"I bit," fiercely. "I bit pieces out of her."

"Very good," getting to his feet.

"You're putting me under arrest?"

"I'm placing you in preventative detention; it's not quite the same thing. Garde à vue as it is named – at the disposal of justice for twentyfour hours." He picked up the interphone and said "Send me someone." Stayed standing: these people could be unexpected. "You are ill, Monsieur Somvieille."

"Temporarily. Temporarily."

"How ill it is not within my competence to say. I ask in these cases for an independent expert opinion. The agent here," a sturdy figure appeared in the doorway "will accompany you. Down to Sainte Anne," laconically to the wooden-faced cop. The mental hospital serving central Paris is the synonym in police jargon for 'psychward' in general. The cop knew what to do. There is one like this a week on average. "Restraint where needful." The cop produced handcuffs: Castang sat and wrote on a form 'delusion of homicide. Barely contained violence. Committal on my authority. Give me a ring. Castang, crim-brig'.

"This isn't good enough," the man burst out.

"Perhaps not, but it's the best we can do."

"Easy does it," said the cop.

The next was still worse. The interphone rang and a puzzled voice said "I've a woman here, chief. American. Far's'I can make her out she thinks she knows who the girl is. I think it's bullshit but she's making a hell of a row."

"All right; I'll handle it," said Castang, who spoke enough English to protect himself from getting eaten. Because this one looked fit to eat boys and girls alike, just as they came. He could hear a ripe, rich

California accent from his doorway all the way down the stairs.

She came up them like a deer, stood a metre away from him, her hands on her hips, highly aggressive. Not panting, not sweating, nearly as tall as him and twice as strong: an athlete in hard condition. Clean bronzed; bright clear blood glowing in the warm skin. A superb, magnificent thing.

"You in charge here?" She was; would be, everywhere.

"That's right. Sit, why don't you? I am Castang, Commissaire – that is uh, captain, I will help you. If I can, all I can." It would get better with practice. Have to rub the rust off, first.

"All right, Captain. Pleased to know you." She held out a hand with a grip. She didn't introduce herself. She assumed everyone knew. She wasn't far wrong; he knew her face. Tennis-player. Would go for the most impossible shot – get it most of the time too. Scream out 'Fuckit' if she missed. If she hit a rabbit shot, the next would always be a winner.

"What is on your mind?" He took a cigarette from the packet on the table, and then the lighter didn't work, which spoiled the effect. He held the thing up against the light. There seemed to be plenty of gas in it: what was wrong with the stupid thing? He'd had an electronic one for his birthday – never worked either.

"I'm playing at Monte Carlo." Spoken abruptly; she had sat abruptly, anyhow, finding a flat space behind her and throwing herself on it. "I heard – I was told – I took a plane." She needed no more in the way of explanation but he wasn't much the wiser. "You have a girl here and she's dead. I have to see her." No point in putting gloves on here: this was bare knuckle.

"It wouldn't help. If I allowed it, which I won't. She's not fit to look at."

"I tell you, it would. That's crap. She's all cut about, they tell me. You think that'll make me heave up, that I'll get hysterics – you don't know me."

"Tell me, Miss – "

"Never mind the Miss, piss on all this beating round the bush and show me."

"Just tell me why you think you know her." Great sombre Indian eyes bored into him. She had that splash of blood. It might be only one thirtysecond, and it comes out pure in the face. You can obliterate us –

35

what's another massacre here or there, in Spanish America? – but you won't get rid of our blood. "What's your name? – I can't remember it."

"Matilde. Last night – before I knew about this – I saw her. I dreamed. I saw her. Her head was cut off. She was all blood."

"If that was all there was I'd show you. He buried her in a swamp. There were animals – carnivorous. She's chewed. She's got no eyes. No mouth, no nose, no ears." She put the strong brown hands over her face and bent down, her face in the skirt between her knees, her long hair falling forward to the floor. "You want water? Whisky?"

"No. Leave me alone." He understood. She had lost a set, was recharging her battery. One has to play against these goddam baseline queens, who never take a risk, who put the ball machine-like back in your court however hard you hit it. They don't beat you, but they're adept at making you beat yourself. Suddenly he understood more.

"She was your lover?" She straightened up, put her hands between her shining knees, squeezed hard. Sat bolt upright, composed herself, looked him hard in the eye and said "Yes."

"She walked out on you?"

"I threw her. I was cruel. I was . . . disgusting."

Castang got up and walked around the room a couple of times. He went over to his cupboard, got his bottle of malt, looked at the level in disbelief – it had been punished, the day before – filled the glass, drank some.

"Would you recognise the angle of her jaw? The orbits of her eyes?"

"Mister, I'd recognise every inch of her body and I'm not trying to be dirty." He refilled the glass, pushed it across to her and said "Drink."

"What is it?"

"Never mind what it is, it's good." He opened his file, shuffled through the stack of photos, found the one he wanted and put it straight under her face. She stared levelly, took the glass with a steady hand, tasted, drank it slowly, her eyes never leaving the print. She put the empty glass on the table, looked up at him at last. The eyes were no longer dead: there was hope in them.

"It's not her," he said.

"It's very like her," she said, "but it's not her." She clenched her teeth and shuddered so violently she nearly fell off the chair; her hands in a double fist, biting down hard upon it. The magnificent thing.

36

There was nothing he could do: nor she, any more than if she had been in orgasm. She got her feet together and made them grip on to the floor. She had her hair bound on the two sides with ribbons. She undid one unnecessarily and did it up again. She got to her feet.

"Thank you," she said. "I'm sure sorry to have troubled you." Suddenly a spasm took her: she bent as though hit in the stomach and said "Where's the john, quick." He took her by the elbow and brought her into the passage. There was nobody there, mercifully – she simply took her skirt in both hands and plumped herself down. No nonsense about shutting the door. Castang walked to the head of the stairs, ready to repel boarders. All that was needed now was for Richard to come sailing out. A commonplace. Happened to him too.

Nobody came; he went back into his office and lit a cigarette. The lady washed lavishly under a loudly running tap and came sailing back in like Anna Karenina at a formal ball and looking twice as good.

"You have a tremendous collection of jewellery – I read about it in the paper." She nodded silently, looking for her handbag which she'd left on the floor. "Why don't you wear it? – you'd look even better than you do now, if that is possible."

"I wear it at home." She smiled suddenly, opened the bag, shook two earrings out on her palm, held it out.

"Are they emeralds?"

"They're worth a hundred thousand dollars apiece. Or nothing. Depends how you look at it."

"Put them on." She did, while Castang thought that two hundred thousand dollars lying on his office floor – and a girl sitting on the lavatory in the passage ... "You're worth more," he said. She laughed but her face was still tense.

"Or nothing. Generally nothing." He put on a very solemn expression, lifted a portentous finger. She shrank away suddenly.

"Don't think evil, girl. Sure. You've heard the joke too often." Her nipples were harder and bigger than the emeralds. "I mean only – it's the worth you put on it, that counts. So go home. And win your match. And the one after that."

"One for me and one for you. And whoever did that – you get him, you hear me. You get him."

"I will. It'll take a day or two longer, that's all."

"You're all right," she said, turned lightly, went down the stairs the

37

way she'd come up, two at a time, floating. Castang felt oddly lifted. There weren't many men who were anywhere near all right, in her book.

At six o'clock he phoned Vera. Went in automatically, to see if Richard were still there. He'd be gone long since. Fausta was gone. No of course, Fausta was still on holiday. Where did Fausta go, for holidays?

Extraordinary thing, Richard was there, sitting at his desk doing nothing. Thinking, perhaps.

"No golf, today?"

"No luck, today . . . Take you out for a sundowner? Or is your girl waiting for you?"

"I phoned her. But I don't want a drink."

"Good, because neither do I. This'll crack though – I feel it."

"Been chasing hairs, all day. Or hares meaning mad. As long as there isn't another."

"It's not that sort." Richard knew he meant another death.

"What do they do, in England?" It had become known, that Richard had been in England. Odd thing of him to do, but he was getting increasingly odd.

"They set up what they call a murder room. Feed everything into it. Quantify everything. File on every last tiny detail. Very efficient. Very serious. Remarkable people."

"And it hangs up on some tiny little human error factor. They plan, we improvise. Works out the same."

"They're more disciplined. We are the sloppiest and least disciplined people there is. Tell ourselves we make up for it by being brighter than the others. Which is crap. We are, about one per cent of the time. It isn't enough."

"We can't be like the English. It isn't in our character."

"In antiquity there were legends about them. Mentioned by Herodotus or someone. The Hyperboreans. The people from behind the north wind. A marvellous place, of wonderful people."

"That's what they've always thought. Hasn't done them much good. Just as vain, as chauvinistic, as idiotic as we are."

"I've been wondering," said Richard. "This land – beyond the north wind – was it England at all?"

"You aren't going to tell me you're an Atlantis-believer."

38

"I don't know. The north is a very peculiar place."

"You mean England's funny, as well as funny?"

"I'm not talking about England. It's an extraordinary mixture, an amalgam of a whole heap of peoples that has made an alloy of very individual character. Saxons and Welsh and Danes and Normans and Huguenots. Brits, and what's Brits?"

"Sounds exactly like us except they've no Corsicans."

"So it is. Less barbarian in some ways, more in others. But they've northerners. Important contribution. Those people don't believe in violence. Whereas us – nothing can be done without violence – oh well. There's this juvenile thing boiling up, Castang, but no use asking you to look at it while you're obsessed with this fellow who cuts up girls with rusty scissors."

"As long as it isn't more girls than one," yawning. "Sorry, I've no mind left over for northerners. The food is so bloody awful" he added as an afterthought.

"That's just the point," said Richard seriously. "They don't have that sort of materialist mind, that thinks all the time about la bouffe." All this melancholy, thought Castang. Look at Richard in a strong light, and you see he's getting old.

Just as the one or the other was opening his mouth to make the classic joke 'Come on then – don't want to miss the beginning' – after the evening news there is always an old film being shown somewhere on French television – the telephone rang and Richard, seeing that Castang was not going to budge, stretched an arm weighted with apathy.

"Castang still there?"

"He is," said Richard, treacherous.

"There are some Germans here," went the downstairs office "with a story to tell." There should be several quick witty comebacks to an opening like that.

"I'll be down," said Castang dully.

"Come up and see me some time," offered Richard, all throaty and sexy.

A young man and a young woman of early-twenties age, unprepossessing. Baggy cotton skirt, pullover with more stitches pulled than there were holding together and a conspicuous absence of bra: jeans and a check shirt, neither boasting any buttons anywhere – the zip was

39

also kaput, creating a medieval codpiece effect. Both had the dolorous ecological face associated with sitting down in front of a truck transporting nuclear effluent. It was this fundamental seriousness that had won the day in the end. The young man hadn't wanted to come at all. The young woman had gone on worrying about her conscience until he'd said 'Gut, then let's get it over with'. He was still inclined to blame Castang for a spoiled evening: one could have been out enjoying the sunset. Hanging about in smelly police stations ...

Summing up this situation, summoning such rags of charm and few words of German he possessed, he set out to convey to them that no, they hadn't wasted their time. As for his ... the story wasn't worth much. But it was a great deal better than anything he'd heard up to now. The whole day, anything even remotely promising had been chased; and every chase had ended in a fizzle.

The young woman spoke quite fluent French and was the spokesman. The boy spoke only patchy phrases, but could follow, enough to correct her on points of detail. Both were students, bright children with minds trained to look at and question what they saw. They didn't like the police at all and kept glancing unhappily about at the surroundings, which one had to admit were forbidding. He got them into his own office, which was at least fairly tidy, more or less clean (and the administration had made efforts recently, even running to curtains, and a carpet on the floor). It was an advantage being French: they wouldn't have been seen dead in any German Kommissariat, of which they had the deepest distrust. Whereas the certain sloppiness and probable incompetence of franzosische fuzz made for a tiny element of human warmth that won the day for him. None of his cherished whisky was getting invested in these ragamuffins, but beginning to need a drink badly himself he sent a cop for beer. The boy accepted a beer and thawed a scrap: the girl said she detested beer but wouldn't say no to that green peppermint stuff.

Pieced together the story was roughly this. Up in the hills, staying in a Jugendherberge they'd met a sympathetic Dutch girl called rather improbably Apollonia, which cheered Castang slightly: there were an awful lot of Dutch girls but there couldn't surely be all that many called Polly. (No, not Polly. Lonny.) They'd got matey. She was a student here in the city. Coming down the hill (she'd gone down the day before) they'd had an arrangement to meet here in the town, and she'd show them around a bit, whatever was interesting. They'd pick her up (where? – outside the cathedral: not very helpful) and have a bite to eat together, because she knew where you could get a bite without getting ripped off, great rarity in France – well (hastily) great rarity anywhere.

Well she hadn't turned up (yes, the timing was more or less right). They'd cursed a moment, hadn't thought anything of it though – all too often people don't turn up. Made an evening of it by themselves, met other sympa characters in cafés, enjoyed themselves. But the thing had stuck in the girl's throat. It wasn't like her. Without knowing the girl at all she was a good judge of another girl. This was a very straight, serious, careful, conscientious girl. When she said she'd turn up at a given place at a given time she'd keep to it.

Between them they made good witnesses – the very unwillingness and suspicion made them good: they hadn't come to tell a fancy tale or to make themselves important – good witnesses. The effort involved, the translation of sights and sounds, laborious into a foreign language, made them more credible. The physical description fitted very well. He brought out one of the very few identity clues he had, a lock of hair. Yes, exactly that kind of hair.

Was this a solid trace, at last? They'd been halfway home, had picked up a paper left on a coffeeshop table, seen that there'd been a horrid happening. There were so many of those they'd not reacted at first. Climbing back in the car her feet had an odd sticky reluctance to leave the ground. Conscience. Yes she Knew – repeating it irritably – she was just imagining things. The boy hadn't been pleased a bit. What are your stupid fantasies getting involved with now? She'd got cross. Just because I'm a woman . . . Back they had come; here they were. Good for them, and good for that hypersensitive German conscience that can't lie down in front of things that are Wrong.

Lonny had been a girl with her head screwed on, and feet firmly on the ground. Perfectly able to look after herself, and – getting picked up by somebody dodgy? – no way.

Now look, said Castang: I'll tell you straight. We have absolutely no means of furthering this investigation until we know who this girl is. Eighty reactions all over France to newspaper and broadcast appeals: eighty tales of girls missing, girls seen doing peculiar things or in peculiar company, not to speak of nasty-looking men behaving in

41

furtive, antisocial ways. As for men, nasty looking or not, being overenthusiastic in their approach to the female sex, well you can just imagine.

You're the eightyfirst and the first that looks responsible. Now I'm grateful; the French government is grateful. It's late, we're tired, I'm tired too. Don't want to spoil your holiday. The French government will stake you to a meal, not maybe an expensive one but a proper one with a proper bottle. And a hotel room for the night. Where's your car? Ah – looking out of his window at the police parking lot, the beetle with its doors tied shut with string – good. It is indispensable that you unwind, feel unhurried, have a good night's sleep. Come back in the morning with every small detail you can meantime recollect of Lonny's conversation, anything she let slip about her life, family, job, pursuits, friends – anything: write a note on a piece of paper – where she'd been, what she was doing. It's gone eight, have a good dinner, I'll show you a good place, you've only to follow my car, and I'll get a hotel room for you right now.

Vera did not say 'You're very late', not being one to labour the obvious. Supper in summer was generally something cold anyhow, not to spoil with keeping, just as in winter it was mostly soup, easy to reheat. Monsieur le Commissaire of the criminal-brigade was not as often kept late as when he was only Monsieur l'Inspecteur, and rank having privileges, it was now much more frequent for him to be back at four in the afternoon, fresh for blowlamp and paintbrush, saw or chisel.

The child was in bed asleep, the house 'tidy' – Vera-tidy was doubtless far short of German- or Dutch-tidy, but she was a lot more relaxed nowadays. The horrid trauma of being Czech was well behind her: the physical as well as mental trauma of having been a bit paraplegic for-a-number-of-years was overcome. She lurched a bit when walking, bicycling was impossible and even a moped, known in her slightly odd French as the moppy-pad, too difficult but she got around everywhere in a small dilapidated car (the Renault Four is nice, because a box, properly Upright: you sit straight and comfortable, instead of lying down peering over the rim of your steering-wheel with your arse an inch from the deck).

It was he who now had traumas. Less than a year ago she had been kidnapped-by-the-fascists right out of her own living-room, and

Orthez, who had tried to protect her, left with a broken skull in a sticky welter on her floor (he had been able to congratulate himself on that thick head everyone complained about). This had been a trying episode to all save, apparently, herself: Orthez being clonked was horrible but for the rest she'd rather enjoyed it. They hadn't kidnapped her daughter, regarding a baby as an unnecessary complication. She'd known we'd get her out. The PJ was not good for much, but not that small-minded . . . in fact the French government in a reaction against overtimidity had been extremely lavish, and taken advantage of an isolated countryside, a private estate in the backwoods, and a merciful absence of pressmen to clonk-the-fascists with a company of para-troops. It was Castang who'd been so worried, and still was. One of the best features in his French eye – it was a very French feature – of the cottage was a large high solid fence in good condition: about the only thing in the cottage that was in good condition. In the middle of the fence was a massive gate. All this didn't just keep the dog in and stop the baby wandering off out. It kept out intruders, prying eyes, small boys' balls and people selling things, in a thoroughly discouraging French way. Nothing the French love more than tremendous fences round the Property: the hell with neighbourliness: the French are not neighbourly . . . Vera said it gave her claustrophobia but the objection had been brushed aside as frivolous. There were altogether too many funny and unfunny characters knocking about, and a Commissaire of police can get himself disliked by several of them.

She was looking pretty. Not tennis-girl pretty. Rather too Slav, hair sometimes scraggy, and tied right now with bits of knitting wool.

That kidnapping – lamentably milksop word – had surely changed her mentality too?

She jeered at any such notion. Milestones, signposts; these were lazy and misleading metaphors. Her mind had not waited upon a melodrama, some event in itself garish but fundamentally unimportant. Seeing the light, upset in some ditch on the road to Damascus, was a typically male phenomenon.

As for the little woman, that other cherished figment of the male imagination, had it ever existed at all? If you treat people, for century after century, as though they were utterly feeble-minded, it is no surprise when they behave that way. With harpy, fishwife-scold and memsahib variations.

There had been an inexperienced and awkward girl who had lived a sheltered life and believed in simplistic ideologies like the rights of man. She'd learned about them quick enough.

Coping with her own awkwardness ('Yes, awkward; it took an exceptionally clumsy and confused woman to fall off asymmetric bars and injure her spine: I think she did it on purpose') had been as much as she could cope with for some years. She had not wanted to know much about the pathological side of Castang's work. He was a state functionary, a pen-pusher. He had to learn to be a human being; difficult and unpleasant task. So did she. As for Castang, he had thought vaguely that the little woman should be spared the squalid side of a cop's existence . . .

Drawing had been her first tool, which came first to her hand, for she'd had some training as a girl, back on the old sod. Drawing had forced her out, even in the wheelchair days, had made her look at things as they were.

There had been the day then, when without saying a word to him she had gone out and persuaded a bemused person in the prison administration that a woman would be some use. Oh yes, that does the women good. 'No I don't want to talk to women, I want to talk to men'.

A long lip got pulled over that: letting a woman into a men's prison would upset the men. Tenacity – Castang had learned a little about her bullheadedness ('and how may I ask are cows bullheaded?') – had prevailed over even the obscurantist backwardness of the prison administration. 'You imagine that I would talk to them about Gahd, or Rehabilitation'?

It had lasted a year or more, until an unusually – well, not unusually – giscardien governor decided that this woman was simply not on. These men were there to be punished. Her permission was cancelled, abruptly.

Deciding to become pregnant, and getting away with it, had been perhaps a result; who knew?

And there she sat, reading a women's magazine. Really – next would be Barbara Cartland.

"Um," she said vaguely. "Why not? If women are so excluded from life that they turn to stuff like that you may as well tell yourself they need all this guff about Royal Marriages. They are pursuing an ideal."

"Want Romance?"

"Oh yes, especially in the north." Oh Lord, like Richard; here was another one chasing the north wind.

"What have you been doing that you were so late?" throwing the magazine aside – where had she got it from?

"A girl got chopped up and buried in a bog. Deutz says he cut bits off her and ate her, I mean them. Not easy to find out who she was. What may be a ray of light only came in when I was leaving, and I was late then."

"Lycanthropy," said Vera, whose reading in his criminology texts was extensive if selective: Reuss and Gross and all those old bores had been snorted at.

"Act of barbarism – article 303 of the penal code."

"The witch turns into the wolf and becomes a blood-drinker."

"A form of madness," said Castang austerely: not his affair thank heaven. There was a pretty little legal point, such as lawyers enjoy – enjoy! . . . Richard had reached at once for the little red book.

'Acts of barbarism – um – must come after twoninesix. Here we are. A murder if accompanied by acts of torture or barbarity will be treated as an assassination. But if you cut bits off after death – is that torture? The proc is going to have a lovely time arguing it'. Castang was not really with all this. If an act of barbarism was committed by a vegetarian did that make the barbarity more barbarian? It could be safely left to the discretion of the tribunal. Weren't they generally inoffensive little men of the Christie type, looking like Peter Lorre?

"The jungle is neutral," said Vera. "If you happen to meet a tiger is that your fault or the tiger's?" But the police are only interested in catching the tiger. Preferably by humane methods.

Commissaire Richard lived in a fine house. Years before – twenty; he had only been 'souschef' then – an enquiry had brought him to a village then twenty kilometres from the city, and still well outside now. Suburban housing estates had crept nearer and down in the valley there was an 'industrial terrain' that gave him no joy, but up here on the hill things were still rural. Farmers held on to their land, and the richer bourgeoisie (such as himself) would do all in their power to ensure that things stayed that way.

He had been in search of a witness who was not at home. It had been

45

a sunny afternoon and he had played truant, leaving the car on the village square and going for a walk. Off the rustic roadway that led down the steep flank of the whaleback and towards the main road there had been a field, enclosed by the high hedges that still existed then before intensive farming got invented. An awkward field, too exposed to the west to be much use for vines, too steep and small to be good for anything else. He had sat in the field and smoked and watched the sun tilting down to the horizon before walking back to a world of witnesses. He had not forgotten that field, and a year later he had bought it, and three years later he had built on it: the bank decided that Monsieur Richard was a reasonable risk, and if he were promoted or even posted away from the region it would be a sellable property: he got his loan on quite good terms. Many years ago. Perhaps banks were less greedy, or less frightened then.

The house had been for him, but more for Judith: next to children which she – or was it he? – seemed incapable of getting, she wanted a safe place of her own. It was a nice house, designed by her, with only one low storey facing back towards the roadway; two, and a big terrace, when looked at from below: it grew down the hill, and clung to it. Very nice. To be sure, disadvantages appeared – so exposed to the west as to be a perpetual struggle against cold and damp (but oil was cheap in those days). And there was the sunset, and the garden Judith set her heart on and there were no damned neighbours: cows grazed on the adjoining fields and the slope ended far below in a jungly undergrowth on both sides of a little stream: nasty little stream though sometimes one could shoot duck there, but it barred incursions. He no longer shot duck, and probably there weren't any: hideous industrial hangars had crept nearer. But the trees, and the hedge, had also grown.

The 'safe place' . . . it had been a house once. Now it was a fort, a heavily armoured place, enclave and bastion of privilege, power, wealth. All French houses were like that. I have come to hate this house, thought Richard. Stop; that is unreasonable, and illogical. Even if true it's the expression of emotion. What's come over me lately? All my life I have been trained to distrust, to disregard, to discount emotional colorations and surges of sentiment.

You are a journalist, his first chief had told him. The street, and everything in it, belongs to you. Look, listen, report. You are an instrument, a magnifying glass. A camera with its shutter open. (This phrase, made famous by some old English pederast in pre-Hitler

Berlin, had not yet reached provincial France in 1939.) Instinct? – talk about instinct, boy, when you have thirty years' experience.

He had forty, now. Instincts he had developed aplenty. He should be able to recognise one when he met it. Was this an instinct, to hate this house? A good house, a nice house.

Judith had not been able to give rein to a Spanish, Moorish talent for weaving together outside and inside, for playing with space and air and sun till one could not tell where the house ended and the garden began: 'Oh these awful northern barracks shuttered and locked away from all light'. The slope of the ground defeated it, and limits on the money one could raise. And the climate, dear girl: this is central France and cold in winter. Your courtyards and cloisters would be impossible to heat. And for nine months of the twelve the west wind blows: up here you've a fine view but you've precious little shelter. (Clever are these English, thought Richard, and civilised. Everywhere gardens, every possible corner used for suntrap and shelter. Trees, they understand trees because they love and value them. Nobody French understands a tree: idea is to cut it down and sell it for what it will fetch. A fact that aroused Stendhal's fury in 1837 – oh yes, nobody suspected it but he did sometimes read a book – madonna, what would the old boy say if he saw France now?) So there'd been a battle for twenty years between Judith's trees and Judith's sunset. Still unresolved.

Judith and her garden . . . How could you do anything about this house, assuming it was a horrible house? The house was the garden and the garden was her life and her passion. She spent all day in it, the whole year round. As now in a dim flowered garment that she called a frock (she was a tall thin woman, flat-chested and bony) and a floppy straw hat with a down-curving brim. When it was wet, and wet generally is cold, in a sou'wester, a huge Tyrolean loden cape, wellies; looking, said Richard, like Sherlock Holmes. 'Who's he?' enquired Judith, by no means sure that this was a compliment. 'People who live in glass houses shouldn't throw stones' he said when the Orangery was built: and 'Who's going to clean all those windows?' She hated cleaning windows. Equally she hated people in the house. Even with the village cleaning woman there was perpetual war; at least a bristly neutrality when they met, as seldom as possible, in agreed areas on no-man's-land: they detested one another. You could not uproot twenty years of Judith's life, whatever instinct said.

47

Simplify. Get rid of all this rubbish. Incrustations of garden had crept into the recesses of the house, from the cellar full of flower-pots, treasures kept from light and moisture to the nursing-homes, convalescent stations, spas and kindergartens where Things, wizened or etiolated, were cherished back to health: even the bathroom was full of them. Sometimes he got cross, nudged with his elbow so that they fell on the floor, assumed bland expressions while Judith mourned, cursed in Spanish – the best of languages for cursing in – and looked accusing.

Only his room was safe: that awful room, she called it. She never touched it, disliked even to set foot in it. Couldn't put a plant here; the cigar smoke would kill anything. It was not called the study, or the den, or the library. She referred to it, if at all, as 'The Place': he called it 'my room'. Nobody came here. The cleaning woman did the floor, dusted round edges, washed the windows occasionally. There was an old-fashioned desk of Third Republic oak to which he gave a lick of wax from time to time. Books, lots of books, browned and foxed and musty-smelling (everything in this house was a bit damp, whatever you did). Shelves of records. He did play them occasionally. You're like an old woman, he told himself, with a linen-cupboard stored with stacks and stacks of sheets and tablecloths – never use any; they're all utterly useless. But gloat over them, count them, be French with them.

At least he had no gold coins. Judith had no diamonds. She didn't want any. She had no fur coat. She had few clothes: she bought as little as she possibly could, and wore that until it fell into rags. 'What do I need clothes for? I never go anywhere. I can't disgrace you'. 'You should be called Daphne' returned Richard gloomily. 'I'm never quite sure whether you haven't turned into a bush'. This had to be explained. 'She fled from Apollo and prayed for her virginity to be preserved and hop là, in the nick of time . . .' Judith saw the point of this, even approved as a vague matter of principle despite saying 'Silly girl . . .', and as an afterthought, 'I might have been a lemon tree, in a previous existence'. But I love her, said Richard to himself; meaning it.

"It's important to get this finished with," said Richard: it was the usual early-morning conference. "Wrapped up while it's still warm is a pious generality, a devoutly-to-be-wished cliché. But it would earn us a good mark, and that would be nice." Nice meant something to set on the credit side because stormy times are coming and we may be piling up a lot of debits. Castang knew this vocabulary. He explained about the German witnesses.

"Good. We should be able to find a trace here. Don't want to say to Dutch police Find a girl called Apollonia, though that shouldn't be too difficult by the sound of it. Sounds like mineral water," ended Richard inconsequentially.

"That's Apollinaris. But she doesn't sound like a tourist. Knew the town. Student." University ... Liliane ... Orthez ... University records are probably badly kept and certainly shambles. But one should be able – meantosay, student cards. The libraries, the canteen: can't do anything without a student card. Trouble is that the administration will still be on holiday: trying to get information from the university in the month of August... Stop creating alibis, said Richard.

These German children, as feared, were no further help. The university said how on earth was it to find anything in the filing system just from a first name: did the police think they kept a register of baptism certificates: all enquiries to the Secretariat would have to wait till the beginning of next month.

"Sauce," said Castang. "Take them by the back of the neck and shake. There must be a register for foreign students: if they haven't a baccalaureate they must show an equivalent. All sorts of info, however meaningless, however buried, but there somewhere. Inscribed, and consequently on file."

"Absolutely not," reported Orthez stolidly. "Not inscribed. Not on file."

With a phone directory they struggled with a hideous list of establishments that might be described as educational. Teachers' training, Conservatory of Music, Decorative Arts. Orthez kept saying 'Eliminated', sounding said Castang like an anticonstipation remedy.

Very well: now all these tiresome places that don't say School but dress it up as something grander. Institute of Macroeconomic Studies.

"Institute of Beauty. Institute no doubt of Thailand Massage. You can be a student of any goddam thing."

"They've all got to be eliminated," said Castang.

49

"You sound exactly like Stalin."

"I am Stalin," from behind Professor Deutz's pathology report, now typed up; depressing reading. "There are also places where graduate students – "

Maybe those Germans made a mistake. Maybe she just called herself a student – kind of a handy password in those youth hostel places. Maybe – everyone was getting steadily crosser.

"If we had anybody called Apollonia – even if Dutch," said the Advanced Physics Laboratory, the Botanic Garden, and Geothermic Research, "we wouldn't be likely to forget it."

"Some of these places don't answer their telephone – don't even exist, quite likely."

"All a red herring anyhow. Those Germans are probably laughing their heads off at us. Free meal and a night's kip."

"You saw them, Liliane: how did you sum them up?"

"The boy maybe: not the girl though. I agree with you. I think there's something in it."

There was a time when we were young, when even Richard was young, when law-abiding people registered at consulates, applied to the Aliens Service for a residence permit, to the Prefecture for a work permit, filled in forms all over the shop. Nobody bothered now. Within the European Economic Community there was free movement. There is brave talk about illegal immigrants but nobody has a notion how many there are. The French look like everybody else, so they look like the French. All the police can do is pester a few blacks – blacks being recognisable – and be promptly accused of racialism. If there get to be too many, move them on. The south coast beaches in August were saturated with people sleeping out. The cops in Cannes, understandably fed-up, in fact chokker, herded up a hundred thousand or so, jerked a good-humoured thumb in the general direction of Marseille, and said 'Git'. People had written indignant letters about the Rights of Man. A lot the police cared about the rights of man – their job was to get the beach cleaned up. Dear People, give less thought to liberty, and a little more to sewage. Castang thought of sending a telex to the commissariat in Cannes asking if they'd seen a Dutch girl called Apollonia. Burst into a snigger. Went home for lunch.

Like every good French citizen he'd built an outdoor hearth of

50

lumps of stone, to barbecue on. Like every good French housewife Vera had bought merguez sausage to grill on it. It was a lovely day. He sat, ate, and was comfortable.

The tiny bright-scarlet insect – a spider? – was it orange? – so tiny a dot and so rapid, ran very fast along the tramline of rusty metal, edge of an old demoted camping table. It didn't like the expanse of (cracked, buckled) skyblue plastic; started in towards the middle a couple of times, rushed back. Why this passion for the peripheries of things? Why was it alarmed to strike in towards the centre? Raced round and round like a demented speedway cyclist. Castang felt much sympathy for this animal. Got up and went back to work. Orthez had just had hamburger, sitting in a metal chair on the grilling pavement. Very much like the beach at Cannes – perhaps slightly cleaner.

"The Opera," said Castang. "It has a sort of theatre school: I don't know what they call it." There was the whole damned Red Faction, the Baaders and the Meinhofs all living openly in Paris, driving the BundeskriminalAmt bonkers, and the French police not knowing a damned thing about it.

"Got her," said Orthez coming back beaming, sweaty, shirt open, scratching his stomach. "Woo woo. Tally Ho. What do the English say?"

"We'll ask Richard. He's forever hunting foxes. Dressed in a red coat. Called pink. Another English mystery."

"Tally Ho," said Richard behind them, "means Il Est Haut."

"Is that French?"

"Does it matter? You've got her."

Lonny van Barneveldt – Orthez had had it spelt letter by letter the way she'd written it. Well yes, they supposed you could call her a student. There was the choir school, and the ballet school – well yes, it was all a bit complicated, but Opera you see is a very complicated business.

Feeling by now a pressing need for concrete, tangible, factual information Castang went to see for himself.

"I really don't know," said an elderly (motherly, sensible) soul. "I just happened to answer the phone. I'm a dressmaker. The Administration's all away still. But your young man said it was important and there was nothing to stop me looking in the office. Hundreds of people work here. There's this big list ..." And if she hadn't been

51

accustomed to taking trouble she'd have said No. Well, he'd deserved a bit of luck.

The office was tidy and organised, and here he found a card index, and the card filled in – it would be her own handwriting, and at last he felt in contact with a living human being. Dutch: a neat, rounded, slightly backhand print. Student status: stage design, second year.

"I expect you want the workshop. I wouldn't know, you see, it's all separate. But we've girls and boys too in costume design. No, I'll show you, it's down in the basement, it's awfully difficult to find anything here, no it's no trouble." Kind old dear. Ariadne in this labyrinth. "They'd rather make pretty drawings but they have to learn to sew – if I get hold of one I sit it down behind the machine and grind its nose, I can tell you. Oh dear, there seems to be nobody here, I expect they've gone out to drink coffee – oh good, there's old Willy, he knows everybody."

Oh yes, old Willy knew Lonny, nice girl, good girl, not perhaps a great deal of talent but steady, responsible. We've too many people with lots of talent and not enough of the bloody other, meaning backbone.

"What I want," said Castang " – first that is – is a photograph. We want to nail down an identity."

"We've photographs enough to fill a bloody storeroom. Should be able to find Lonny somewhere on one of them."

The Publicity was all on holiday, but Willy dived into boxes of rubbish. Took a long time but there at last was Lonny. In overalls, and smeared with dirt, but clear enough. A dress rehearsal – changing that damn rock. Brunnhilde last year. Gave no end of trouble that rock did: how the carpenter cursed. Willy cut her out with scissors: Castang didn't want the carpenter, nor the flaming rock. The photographer had some trouble getting her to fit, but fit she finally did.

It is, and you had better believe it, a considerable satisfaction. Exactly who it was that got chopped is the anxious bit. Once you're that far the rest is fairly routine. The suitcase murderer would not – even the perverted kind of chap who saws firewood for pleasure – go to so much trouble. He (and why not she) has a close connection with the victim; stands to reason, you incline to say, unless like Orthez you persist in the conviction that in this frigging job nothing ever does stand to reason.

They'd been lucky too, because your latterday suitcase murderer is less helpful about leaving useful traces behind him.

So you're left with a circle of acquaintance, and perhaps close acquaintance. Who have to be known, found, interviewed, and filtered; rather carefully. Taking a lot of time, manpower and paper. And the responsibility was Castang's. It can be a tedious job. But at least it's straightforward. This is what the criminal brigade is there for. Above all, there is less likelihòod of the 'coup tordu' or boomerang-effect of finding out that the victim was not after all Mr Bloggs of Berkhamsted but a close friend of Senator McCarthy.

The day was wearing on but the troops must be kept up to scratch.

"Liliane, you and Orthez had better take this theatre crowd and begin by finding out who is on holiday and where, meaning that card index. Who does that leave me? – Lucciani – good, bring a bunch of keys: we'll start with where she lives."

Rue Auguste Salomon. Off the Avenue Georges Mandel. Bourgeois quarter, the Second Empire part of the city. Widish streets with widish pavements, made gloomy and sunless by the weight and height of crowded buildings in Haussmann style, with pompous façades. Castang knew all about these houses: he'd lived in one himself. Nobody knows anybody: the bourgeoisie meet their neighbour by the letterboxes and exchange compassed salutations. Joyless places; artificial smiles. An 'immeuble de rapport' or investment house, owned perhaps by a real person (Castang had had an old and in general poisonous landlady) but more generally by a bank or insurance company. Not at first sight a likely place for a student to be living, but there is an attic storey of servants' rooms, one to each flat, and the tenant has the right to sub-let.

It was very still in the dark dusty hallway. Sour smell of old dirt never dislodged. The cleaning woman does the floor and stairs, but would not dream of going behind a radiator. The letterbox with the neat ballpoint printing 'A. v. Barneveldt IIIa' had a simple lock which Lucciani opened easily. There was nothing in it but the week's bargain offers from a selfservice grocery, and the usual exhortation to subscribe to the *Reader's Digest*. Lucciani made for the lift but Castang stopped him.

"Like to see how easy it is to get in and out unnoticed." A door at the back next that to the basement led to the expected fire stairs. "Check the flat" when they got to the third landing; but the service door was locked and bolted.

"Armoured too – I haven't the equipment to get through that."

"Careful people. Anybody can go up and down stairs." The attic level was open – bare wooden corridor. Nobody was about. Three A had a card drawing-pinned. The door had the original simple lock, no more trouble than the letterbox, but there was a solid bolt on the inside.

It was plain as large print. Exactly as Willy had said. Nice girl, friendly, open – but 'serious'. Everything tidy, respectable, classically 'Dutch' in a way Castang thought didn't exist any longer – framed photograph of Pa and Ma on the step of a neat suburban residence in Hilversum or Amersfoort, and actually holding hands. Read a Dutch newspaper and there are three pages of small-ads for whores and two more of fancyboys. Yeck, the whole damn population is hawking its mutton. Like most things in newspapers this is not quite the whole truth.

Even without the path report – 'I'll go bail she put up a fight' said Deutz – Castang would have confirmed it from looking at the room, which Lucciani was staring at open-mouthed. Book of tickets for the municipal baths, bag of laundry ready for the lavamat, enough cleaning materials to keep the whole building scrubbed. The cheap little handbasin, grudgingly put in together with the radiator by the ownership, was polished and shone: no rim of grime around the taps. Nor on her feet either, muttered Castang. The window was open and the room smelt fresh: she might have left it five minutes before.

There were no valuables, unless you counted a small radio and an Instamatic with three left on the spool – went into the bag. Letters – ditto. No diary. Textbooks, library books, theatre posters, a portfolio of drawings. Clothes of the pullover-jeans sort and a couple of frocks in flowery-floppy style: her winter boots, her winter coat: it was a pathetic collection. Credit notes from the bank in a plastic folder showed the small subsidies from Holland and the small salary paid to an apprentice in the theatre workshop. She did not smoke, she did not drink – or not here – and she took no drugs. It was painfully blameless. There was not even the usual litter of pharmacy and cosmetic. If Deutz was to be believed she wasn't even on the pill.

They were finished inside a quarter of an hour, and had learned nothing. No sign of boyfriend – or girlfriend – or any other person at all. She had dropped out of life and this had left no trace. Even the most unsentimental would have found it touching that she had taken pains to make the bleak little room homely: a handmade wool rug, rather dashing curtains with a pattern of fuchsias. The potted plants were wilting from lack of water.

"Take them with you," said Castang. A girl was dead, but that was no reason to let plants die. Lucciani made a face but obeyed.

"Do you want IJ here?"

"I don't see much point – her prints, possibly, for the file – in case they turn up somewhere else."

"Seals on the door?"

"That, yes." He had been about to say don't bother, and then thought of the parents. They had the right to claim whatever was left of their daughter.

"Home." Lucciani, encumbered by plants and all the technical rubbish he had brought, made heavy weather of the stairs and grumbled a good deal.

"Take the lift back up for the owners' flat."

"Nobody," when he came back. "Could be on holiday, smart enough not to leave a note saying so. Nothing in the box – mail forwarded."

"Memo to send an official form." He put the plants carefully in the back of their car. "We won't get any further this evening, so call it a day. Have those photos in the camera developed, go through the papers. The letters you leave on my desk – note, get a Dutch interpreter. If you find a photo of her have it copied, otherwise copy the one we've got. And write up your report." The boy would grouse at not getting away early: he always did. 'There's a girl outside waiting for Lucciani' had become a standard joke.

Monsieur le Commissaire, having jollied-up the dogsbodies – Liliane wasn't back yet – went majestically home.

Forbidding, thought Vera, looking up at a thorny tangle of hedge and a tall gate faced with sheet metal. You couldn't climb over and there was nothing to see. Inside there might be an enchanted castle of the Beast, designed by Christian Bérard. There was a bellpull. And even a real bell; she could hear a deep jangle a long way in. She waited some time; then a lock clicked, a bolt clonked and Judith peered out looking anxious; a long Spanish face which beamed when it saw her.

55

"Do come in. Bring the car in. Oh, I am glad. Lydia, do you know me?"

"I've had so much work with the cottage. Suddenly I felt all shut in."

"I know exactly."

"I should have telephoned."

"These bells often I don't answer. It's according to the way they ring" – a female reply that was not obscure to Vera.

There was a lot of greenery, and into the walls of the house were set Portuguese tiles.

"Oh, lovely house."

"It's all right, I suppose. Do you want to sit or look at it? Lydia – walk about."

"She'll pick flowers."

"What else are they there for? Have you got lots of time?"

"I'm terribly curious and I want to see everything. I like the hedge all overgrown."

"Makes for quiet," said Judith. "There used not to be so much traffic. And it shelters birds. The French would shoot them all."

"Oh dear yes."

"We can talk. Lots of talk. What the men will call chatterboxing. Comes from being too much alone."

"Fuck the men," said Vera comfortably.

"Exactly." Between Czech and Spanish women there were no communication problems. "Do you like sol, or sombra?"

"Both. Let's sit there where it's dappled. Strange, when men talk all the time. Get into these clubs and yack."

"It is I think a substitute for action. Men want things to be going on all the time. Talking a great deal gives them the illusion. All that noise, saves them thinking."

"Americans say 'talking for birds'."

"I talk to birds," said Judith unrepentantly.

"Meaning silly women like us."

"I likewise talk to flowers."

"They answer?"

"Of course they bloody do."

"It's said that they grow better even if it's not understood why."

"Who needs to understand why? Men are always trying to

understand everything, which is exactly like small children who take things to pieces and break them."

"Lydia's breaking flowers."

"Oh pooh," said Judith, stretching out long legs. "We make tea?"

"I'll help."

The cups were Limoges, hand-painted with flowers like the tiles. Vera 'exclaimed'. Decorative arts were important too.

"I like the tiles," said Judith indifferently. "Adrien collects them for me."

"Good shape, these cups."

"Likewise present from Adrien. A nice husband. Policemen are odd."

"Peculiar. Funny?"

"Not always funny."

"No. There was also an old man. He used to come and talk to me. Often when he was on duty, so I was careful to keep my mouth shut. He got shot then and he had to retire."

"Monsieur Bianchi," said Vera surprised. "I know him too. I go to see him sometimes."

"I also."

"Typical of the old stinker not to let on."

"He doesn't believe in pushing people. Things happen when they're ready, he says."

"You came to see me when Lydia was born. You cared for her when I was stolen by the fascists."

"Now you have come to see me. So we are ready. What must we now be ready for?"

"Well, you know," said Vera seriously, "we have to do something to change policemen's thinking."

Conversation, as it was bound to be, was intermittent.

"You shouldn't give Lydia a good cup; she's bound to bust it."

"I don't pay any attention to her."

"Quite right; the most frightful notice-box as it is. Come here, you."

"Do we contribute?" said Vera, after some time. "Anything at all? To a marriage, to a job?"

"I never have. I had no children either. Adrien doesn't say. He's a kind and thoughtful man. Oh, I try to make the house nice for him . . . He was the old-fashioned type of man who never spoke of the problems at work. Ashamed, you see. All those dirty dishonest manoeuvres. He went away recently to England," said Judith, "and funnily, been more broody, but more talkative, since. Beginning to learn at last. I'm not, you see, quite as dotty as all that."

"Oh stop being pathetic."

"Frustration," in a deep bass voice and hammered Spanish syllables.

"I'm going dotty myself and I had better bloody stop."

"Your man – likewise you – a lot younger. Thus more flexible." Judith drank some tea that had gone cold. "Having some future" emptying fragments of stale biscuit in the bottom of the tin on to the grass at which Lydia, who coveted them, looked indignant.

"Do you remember the telegraph lines?" burst out Vera suddenly. "As a child, in the train? How they climbed. And you wanted them to go on soaring up. And each time the cruel telegraph post came, and snatched them down again."

"Indeed I do."

"I was on my way to the State Gymnasium. I was brought up on the land, you know, among the young animals. It would seem harsh, I suppose, now. The men were often drunk. The women were beaten, sometimes. But that was my first sight of brutality. I saw plenty, later."

"My father," said Judith, "had gloomy fits of rage, in which he withdrew into long hideous silences. I don't recall his ever raising a hand to hit me."

"But on the whole you'd have preferred it if he had?"

"Nothing struck such terror: there was nothing I dreaded more."

"I mustn't leave you with an impression that Henri is brutal; he isn't. There are fits of violence, in which he flings things. Sullen moments, when he complains about the food. And a lovely patient sunniness. He's like a landscape, which is always good."

"How else would they cope, with the horrible things they see, and worse still, I think, those they have to disregard. With Adrien, those appalling silences go on. Born of despair. And there is so very little I can do."

"And if the wives provide dry slippers and clean underclothes and a kiss-up when he's feeling low, will that help, diminishing road accidents, or lessen the fear of hooligans in the Métro – I mean, is it all only negative?" She had raised her voice, she realised, made a horrible face. Lydia, pigging in quiet content, looked up in alarm: she made a kissing gesture, to reassure.

"Reassurance," said Judith. "To let them forget, provide oblivion. A corner perhaps, with a little truth and honour in it. Wives are inglorious things for the most part, and anonymous. Except of course when the men get killed, and the Minister comes, to present us with his posthumous medal."

"So that one never exists as a real person at all?"

"But if you feel like that," gently, "why not take a job?"

"I've thought of it. But what with the funny hours the men keep, and not being able to walk properly, and then that of course," wrinkling a long nose in the child's direction.

"I never dared try," said Judith simply. "I would have been quite happy to go out cleaning; I'm very good friends with my broom. But it wouldn't have done, for the Commissaire's wife. Being Spanish, you see; that's an Arab, in French eyes."

"A Czech is worse still – that's a mitteleuropean pig."

"But an artist."

"Pooh, those piddly little drawings. I haven't enough talent, and I know it."

"The French think themselves the most wonderful people in the world; in fact nobody else exists. Living here, we feel that. But of course the Spanish think exactly the same and so does every stinking nation one has ever met and that's exactly what's wrong with politics."

"You're cheering me up," said Vera laughing. "I'm sorry to have brought all this gloom with me. Shall we be very French and form an earnest association for policemen's wives? Paralytics and loonies especially welcomed. Join the syndicate of cripples, all political tendencies permitted and even encouraged. Come on, show me your garden."

"Oh it's so awful," said Judith, serious at once. "A garden must have water but there is no water: we are too high on the hill. Now we can only get what we pay the village for. Adrien won't allow that; meaningless extravagance he calls that. I want to try to collect rainwater. There's plenty, after all: the gutters empty it into drains and waste it all. Why should I not have it? Without water there is no garden. The Japanese understand this. To hear Adrien you'd think I had left the light on in the bathroom all night."

Vera got home rather late to find a husband slightly startled at this absence, and wondering where the hell she'd been. Conscience-stricken at there being nothing for supper, and one would have to open a tin, she lashed herself into a great rage, demanding rhetorically whether perhaps she should have asked permission.

"I was only wondering what the attractions of the park could possibly be, this late," said Castang mildly.

"I was suddenly bored with that old park and went to Judith on impulse. And it was so fascinating the time just slipped away. She didn't want to go to England, at least she did but said it was the wrong time, you see Kew Gardens – " She became aware that he was not listening. Broody about a murder; it would hardly be fair to blame him for that.

Judith, reflecting that it never rained but it poured, had another visitor, less welcome; indeed disconcerting. She would not have answered the gate but for thinking that Vera, who had been gone five minutes, had forgotten her umbrella or something; opened without thinking and was the more flustered by a person with a soft low voice and over-elaborate formal manners: she could not think what to say.

"I'm afraid Monsieur Richard is not home yet, but I'm expecting him any moment." What possessed her to add that unnecessary second phrase? And he'd wheedled her into letting him in, apologising for her gardening shoes. Exactly the sort of situation she dreaded. Should she telephone? It seemed a terribly important person.

Aldo de Biron had been disconcerted himself by this gipsylike being who muttered scraps of unfinished phrase while staring fixedly over his left shoulder. This was surely Madame Richard, but she seemed disproportionally to lack self-possession. As though taken in adultery, a thought that amused him. However, she collected herself, asked civilly if he would bring the car in – he preferred to leave it outside on afterthought – ushered him into a very pleasant house, sat him down politely enough, and offered him a glass of sherry. Fled then abruptly: he could only suppose that she was embarrassed about the garden clothes. He sipped his sherry, got up and strolled about. There was nothing remarkable about the room, but it bespoke character. He was not mistaken in his man. These pictures – modern, workmanlike, hm: lacking distinction, maybe: conventional enough, on the whole: from the investment point of view they'd hardly make the heart beat faster. Not bad though; improved as you looked at them. He rather liked architectural painting, himsclf. For a commissaire of police they showed taste, and a firmness in that taste. And by no means the sort of trash one would see on the quays or the Place du Tertre. Solid. He strolled to the window and was again taken; sightly view one got from here. Again – it wasn't where you'd have expected a police official to build. He could appreciate the way the eye was led down the garden and skilfully across the valley into the middle distance. Not banal; undoubtedly there is distinction. He'd seen distinction of mind, risking a long shot up there on the golfcourse. His lead of a card here would be decisive: he felt sure, now, that the other would know how to lead back to his suit. Not a man who breaks the china, this Richard. Who entered at this moment, all smiles and bonhomie.

"Well well well; there is an agreeable surprise."

"My dear Commissaire, I feel confusion. I am an intruder."

"By no means: my wife is a shy person. I don't feel apologetic about it." Nobody in the office would have doubted his utter fury.

"I don't mean for a second," shocked "that Madame gave me the remotest impression – on the contrary she supplied me with this very excellent sherry and assured me that you would not be long: my embarrassment is due in entirety to my own clumsiness. I had business in the city and felt a sudden impulse on the way home – I should have telephoned but your number is doubtless unlisted."

"Do sit down," said Richard. At least he'd brought it home to this infernal nuisance. "I think I'll join you in a glass of sherry. None of this is inopportune. I was a little later than usual at the office. Don't feel obliged to make small talk. The Spanishness goes no further than the sherry and we aren't at all formal."

"Then if I may be forgiven this charging in like a buffalo – true, true, I had more upon my mind than I could usefully say, oh, upon a golfcourse. And of disturbing you in your office there would be no question. I am about, in fact, to make you a – suggestion is a little limp; proposal sounds inevitably shady. Prayer, I wonder? Act of faith might be best. As you are aware, I am out of office. An excellent thing, since office too often precludes thought. I have thought much, of what I am about to say. I have decided to share this thought, with some persons known to me, others who are not. In Paris one sees too many people, too few of whom are outside that tight little clan. Can you

61

patter the taal; do you know the passwords? This isn't a time for that. A union of true minds, not merely of people who've gone to school together."

Spontaneous enough, Richard was thinking. There is sincerity there; fire. Passion, even.

He listened, scarcely speaking, for half an hour. Drank two glasses of sherry; smoked a cigar. Said "You'll stay to dinner, of course" with such warmth that even the blunted would have recognised that it had lasted long enough. Biron was not blunted.

"My dear Richard, one can be clumsy twice, but I give no credence to luck in odd numbers. Madame will have forgiven my disturbance, and will forgive my insisting that I now leave. Might I add that I dislike driving at night? – my sight's not what it was."

"No no, let me accompany you. Did you have a hat? You've given me much food for thought. I should like to ponder all this. Take it to heart."

"Rather a mouthful, I'm sorry to say."

"Suppose we make a golf date?"

"Splendid. I'd like to see the nucleus of a study group set afoot before winter. While this lovely weather lasts I'll be making pilgrimage through this lovely country of ours."

"That's a nice handy car," said Richard sillily. "Lunch then, and should I be entangled in an epidemic of assassinations I'll leave word with Trusty-barman-George. Bonne route." And walked back, meditative.

"Supper when you like, Judith."

"That awful man gone? I was afraid . . . "

"True, those highly-intelligent people can be very insensitive. Too accustomed to being the centre of attention. I was properly attentive, I hope. He caught you by surprise?"

"I thought it was Vera forgotten something. She spent the afternoon. I enjoyed that."

"Vera?" said Richard, surprised. "Good. Remarkable girl that. I'm fond of her," surprising himself with the afterthought.

Richard seemed engaged, at next morning's staff meeting, in a boring and interminable parley with Commissaire Salviac of the Bandit

Brigade, and Castang, his mind frankly elsewhere, was frankly asleep when Richard said suddenly "Stay behind Castang – I want you," stabbing with an armour-piercing finger at him exactly like Lord Kitchener. Thus wrenched away from meditation he fidgeted while Richard, at his most tiresome today and wearing a horrible yellow tie, nagged on about the problems of the car pool. Had that famous moustache been of the walrus variety, in popular expression a soupstrainer? Or the kind that divided into two wings like a pilot's badge? Why hold him back? He had a great deal to do. There was also the unpleasant task of conveying horrid news to that girl's unhappy parents. Formally that was done through the local Dutch police, but the next step would be their disembarking on his doorstep with their grief and their bewilderment; it was in some ways the worst part of a homicide investigation. Your victim, your criminal – these are technical matters. But they both tend to have families, and there is a whole new dimension of uncomprehending pain; the disfigurement if not destruction of several more human personalities. The assassin is his own victim – but what of his wife, his mother? What do you call them? The apparatus of justice is a mincing machine. Don't get your fingers caught. Nor your tie. Was Richard finished at last?

There was a long silence.

"Castang, if you were asked to pick out one great symbolic name in French history, to personify unity, a rallying-point – don't say General de Gaulle, he's hors concours – whom would you choose?"

Was it not said – one of those useless items of information – that Lord Kitchener's mind was a lighthouse? Alternating beams of bright light and pitchy darkness?

He hadn't left any grandchildren in France, had he?

"Napoleon?" stupidly.

"No – less uh, bellicose. Less alarming. Less Corsican."

"Jeanne d'Arc."

"She won't do. Inescapably, a woman." Finding this funny. "We're dealing with the blocked male mind," Castang had to stop himself tapping a finger pointedly against his forehead.

"Victor Hugo? Chateaubriand?"

"A writer doesn't make a strong symbol in the pop mind. That's a right pair of windbags anyhow."

"Is this a game?" dully.

"Come now Castang, sharpen your wits; this is serious."

"Cardinal Richelieu."

"He'd do, but for the clerical connotation. One can't get away," coining a phrase with satisfaction "from under the red robe."

"Sorry but the only valid symbol is an artist. Voltaire?"

"Ah, there speaks the civilised mind. Spent half his life cutting the government to ribbons. In the Bastille twice, was it? Living on the frontier ready to nip across to Switzerland if the gendarmerie appeared. A fine one you pick. You pass of course the test. Now put yourself in the mind of a typically manipulative political person, Parisien, centralised. An arid intellectual, sterilised by vanity. And tell me what you think of Charlemagne."

"I know nothing about him. Does anybody, much?"

"Isn't that the whole point? Child's history book. Empire, but unifier, educator, civilisor. Grand Design of the Strong Man. Was a proper bastard in all probability but that vanishes in myth. Pretty good choice. And notice, a memorable name, resonant, easy to say. Forceful disyllable, or at a pinch trisyllable. One more question. You have a political group, say and it's invariably called the Union of this or the Assemblement of the other, making initials or an acronym. Can you tell one from the other?"

"No: just as you begin to get them sorted out they change the name and become something else."

"You wouldn't care to tell me the difference between social democrats and christian democrats, in any country you care to name?"

"One is thyroid and the other is thalamus."

"That's all, and you can bugger off about your business. What are you doing?"

"Having combed out the victim," patiently, "we've now got to look for the assassin."

"Yes, well, that'll be a simple matter," dismissive. "Liliane can be safely left to handle that. You must learn not to confuse your mind with details. Lot of time been wasted," said Richard outrageously, "and I'm setting you to work. Here," picking two quite thin cardboard folders off his desk "see what you make of these, and let me know rapidly. Thank God Fausta will be back next week." Ah; we stand afresh revealed as that drivelling pack of bird-brains.

64

"I've been waiting here a long time," said Liliane icy, with ostentatious flourish of the arm that had the watch on it. "All this confabulation. Ah," the eye falling on the dossiers under his arm, "General Post being played again. Stare at it for three weeks and then pass it on to somebody else. Easy to see Fausta's not here."

"People pull files," Orthez coming in, creating a draught, looking and sounding hot and irritable, which was uncharacteristic, "take advantage of Fausta being away, don't sign them out properly, leave them lying about over the whole building like fucking confetti. That little bugger in the bandits, I'll kick his misbegotten bum off." Castang who had frequently noticed himself becoming alliterative in moments of emotion started to laugh and then said sternly, "The next person to mention Fausta I'll kick his or her bum off." By this time both Liliane and Orthez were laughing uncontrollably. "It's all Richard's fault anyhow – went on and on for three quarters of an hour about Charlemagne, anybody would think she was a witch the way Fausta –"

"Bum bum bum," like a pair of foul small boys in chorus.

"Very well, Liliane, he's stuck me with paperwork, that theatre is all yours, get on with it. Since half these people are not back from holiday it restricts the company she kept and your work is halved. Here," walking into his office and flumping the files on the table, "is the report on the photographs in her camera; I don't want to look at it. Her handbag was gone with the rest of her clothes. Did she have a car? A bicycle? Where did she eat? The neighbourhood shops, Orthez – drycleaners, laundry, hairdresser, greengrocer. A sport, a pastime? She went out to that youth hostel, and the Germans said she was alone there – was that always the case? A careful, meticulous solitary-seeming girl and how d'you read that? Boy friend? Girl friend? – any confidant? I'm getting on to her home and I'll ask if they've letters."

The letters he had were Dutch, but the signature at the end said Mum, a word that is the same in all European languages, and were headed 'Apeldoorn'. He looked this up in the atlas. Good, it was neither too large nor too small: he reached for the telephone and said "Get me the police headquarters at Apeldoorn – all right I'll-spell-that – in Holland; ask for the commissaire and put me on: yes a Kommissar with a k, and they'll probably talk English, so sharpen your wits." Nothing like passing it on to subordinates.

65

The letters were regular, every fortnight to three weeks; always four pages – it's a pity to waste paper; the paper itself of good quality; the writing regular and level. That of a cosy, comfortable person. Maybe I'm reading too much into that, he thought: but this tells me a lot. One doesn't need to know Dutch, surely. Newsy, comfy letters about dogs and neighbours. I met Mrs Chose in the public library and she gave me the latest about Amanda. Hooligans broke the mirrors and antenna off Dad's car. The winding-up invariable: can't think of anything more so that's all for now. I must dash, dear, I've my cake in the oven.

She had kept the letters. She wasn't a rebel who had run away from home – "Yes, right. Commissaire Castang, criminal brigade. Good morning to you too. I've a death notice for you I'm afraid. Apeldoorn is the only address I have but the name is Barneveldt, do I pronounce that right? It's a common name? Given name Apollonia. About twenty, one seventy-five tall, strong build, natural fair hair. Features obliterated, I'm sorry: our identification is from skull photos . . . No, better than tentative: it's pretty sure. We have where she lived and found letters from her mother . . . I'm afraid so; a nasty one. Will you do what is necessary? I can arrange to have the remains sent directly the judge gives permission, but if they wish to come . . . A formal identification won't be easy, and you'd better warn them, highly disagreeable. I would place myself at their service, do what I possibly can. I want to add this: it looks like a local affair here in the city – right, not a hitch-hike thing. They'll have letters from her no doubt, and if she was home recently something better perhaps – yes, absolutely; friends, activities. I'm confident, but it would help narrow things down that much quicker, don't you think? You'll be in touch, will you? – that'll be a help, and thank you." A quiet middleaged voice; a man who would know his job. Always a pleasure to work with the Dutch. Sensible, unextravagant crowd. Dull wasn't the right word. The cliché about still waters meant something there. One supposed they did have violent crime occasionally, but it was a rarity.

What would it be like, to live in a place where non-violence was a norm, instead of an exception? Why do we have to adopt a violent solution to – oh, to everything, it sometimes seems? Even Richard – look what happened last year: kidnapping that woman by force across the German border. Violence bred violence; it had got them into a hell of a mess. A shudder at the bare thought. We barely scraped off with our skins there. The government has changed, and our tutor minister has changed – well for us – but what kind of note has been made on confidential dossiers? . . . stop day-dreaming: work.

The first file had a star telling him it came from the urban police, another saying their Urban Security (Commissaire Riquois, a friendly easy-going old drunk) and a third for criminal brigade, his own opposite number (Maisonneuve, young and pushful, neither friendly nor even drunk). Mm. No star saying 'classified' meaning case closed, though doubtless they'd done their best, because at the top was a peppery minute from the judge of instruction. 'I'm not satisfied with this – too many of these have been staying open but inactive. Refer to Richard at PJ with query and comment'. Flimsy from Richard to judge. 'A suggestion has been made that this may match with our 765/DGV: passed for study and event. verification to Comm/Crimbrig'. Which was him: thanks very much.

Within was the usual ramble, minuted at intervals and marked by stains from wet coffee cups and smears of cigarette ash.

'Mugging railway station query homosexual pickup'

'Milieu investigate'

'Railway red herring? See IJ report'.

'What's this about crushed grasses? Not clear to me, see detail'

'Query mugging anyhow – chequebook/credit-cards?' Oh all right then; start at the beginning: Riquois' absence of zeal – or Maisonneuve's excesses of same – weren't illuminating.

A middle-aged gentleman – businessman of apparently blameless existence and regular habits (see fairly massive family, business and neighbourhood enquiries, performed one would say medium well) had made a trip to Paris and back (first-class ticket, waistcoat pocket, properly cancellation-punched). Found dead in his own car parked station approach (on parking meter) approx 100 meters down the road, relative well-lit area.

Car on meter? Chap who'd spent the day in Paris! They hadn't missed that surely?

Discovery made by patrolling agent station police post (see report).

A good report: fifteen before midnight, man drunk in car? found dead, body cooling though still warmish, alarm given. Car unlocked, keys missing (?) conclusion heart attack, doctor called.

Prelim. medical: *not* heart attack. Cranial haemorrhage heavy blow sandbag-like object. Query possibility slipped and fell – pavement? – medically possible to recover from initial concussion and climb into car before passing out again, this time for good. Post mortem recommended (note: pm. confirms this last ruled out. Sandbagging confirmed.)

Brigadier's report (while accident still a likelihood): no faith placed in accident. Car plainly moved, keys missing, no parking ticket or record from traffic detail. Conclusion of hanky-panky. No sign of violence on or in car. Action: car towed to police compound and signal to criminal detail.

Maisonneuve's boys had been on the job next morning. Technical report on car. No clear handprints bar man's (owner), oily-man's (verification garage-hand), woman's (verif. wife's) but smears & signs of wiping. Initial hypothesis: attempt made to steal car, query interrupted by owner: query signs of struggle corpse. Had he been in the driving seat? Why had no on-spot photos been taken? (Answer, initial conclusion of heart attack: no external sign blood or violence) Recollection patrol agent and doctor; he *had* been in driving seat. Query placed there? Nothing further remarkable about car, save that it had been parked some time within the 24 hrs close to verge of country roadside: traces of grass & weed found trapped in back door.

Maisonneuve had got on to the grass-and-weed, quick enough as his minute showed. The man was a town-dweller; had he been in the country this last day/two? No. Then he – or at least the car – had been somewhere that evening: how fresh is this grass?

Report grass: upon observation two days later grass possibly fresh to that evening, even likely. Grass commonplace verge-side type. Analysis dust, cement & brick trace. Perfectly standard trace suggesting proximity building operations: this in itself inconclusive. Weeds frequent on waste sites all over city and suburban areas.

Post mortem: death from sandbagging medulla oblongata, something soft but heavy (not Professor Deutz this, but sounding quite well trained). Health fair but condition softish and sedentary. No contusion or laceration to indicate struggle; man simply bagged from behind (back seat of car?) Stomach contents consistent meal of buffet (train) type taken about nineteen-thirty hours plus half bottle standard phony Bordeaux vino. No seminal discharge. No conclusive or even highly suggestive indications could be concluded (a standard police tautology,

68

thought Castang). Nothing in the clothing or in the papers (briefcase, wallet, all present) abnormal or a pointer. The man had been to Paris, had a business meeting and lunched (all properly confirmed), gone to the cinema (ticket stub found in outside breast-pocket) and had some supper on the train (SNCF confirm restaurant-car menu). Perfectly good and reasonable work, all this.

It was from there on that it seemed to go downhill. There wasn't anything one could lay a finger on. Nails need cutting, thought Castang, hunting for his little scissors and kicking the wastepaper-basket a little closer. Was there something amateurish about Commissaire Maisonneuve? – he didn't like the man but why? Been promoted much quicker than himself? He could honestly say he didn't feel jealousy on that score. A pushful laddy, a butterer of superiors? The entire PJ thought him a perfect creep but did that mean anything much? He was efficient, all agreed. But following the vigorous pursuit of grass and homosexuals, hotter than the legendary cannon shooting downhill, there was a tailing off. He was too experienced to fall for the sympathy-syndrome, the liking it was easy to take for certain kinds of victim and even certain kinds of criminal – some victims are decidedly antipathetic. Was it fairer to think that this victim had merely been rather boring? Police reports drain the colour from nearly anybody, but it was hard, Castang had to admit, to take much interest in the dead man, a marketing person for a chemicals firm, one of those dreary margin-shavers whose job is to put less paint in the can, and discovering this to be impossible, to expend his entire energies on making the can a farthing cheaper.

Castang didn't like the alternative, which was to suppose that Maisonneuve had a good reason for dragging his feet on an enquiry.

There was a cursory account of criminal-brigade zeal in the railway-station area, designed rather obviously to keep an instructing judge quiet: cracking down on public lavatories, and sluts with pictures of themselves wearing no underclothes.

Finally a half-hearted cover-up by Riquois, describing the whole affair as the 'incompressible' type of crime. Almost certainly accidental, he thought: a pair of clumsy hooligans had tried to steal the car (popular and attractive model) probably for no more than a joyride, been interrupted, clonked the owner, found they'd hit him far too hard, and run off in a panic. Alternative, mugged the owner while he was stooped down unlocking the car: results the same in any case – the absence of robbery was explainable by fright. 'We'll pick them up one of these days for shopbreaking, and they'll admit this homicide but say they didn't-know-he-was-really-hurt'.

The judge of instruction was not content and neither was Castang.

He turned to the other. This was one of their own PJ files, which Castang had not seen simply because it had been opened three days after he had gone on holiday; and it was now in a state of suspended animation because a) the instructing judge had gone on holiday a week later, was not yet back, and had thought of this as something to bother about when he was back (quite enough on his plate as things stood): b) because the investigating officer – Davignon – had gone on holiday the day Castang came back. Liliane, who would normally have gone on working on it, had been dragged away by bodies-in-bogs, and Popers, as Richard called Commissaire Domenech (the Person-from-Pau) had turned it over to her before carting himself off towards the native heath. All quite reasonable.

Davignon, whom Castang knew well, was a quiet unspectacular soul with horn-rimmed glasses and a faintly prim academic manner, but reliable, conscientious, experienced and thorough, and glancing through the file Castang could not see much to pick holes in (nor was there reason to try).

This one had been a middle-aged lady, found in her car (a small economical model) in a quiet residential street of the outer suburbs. Discovered only in the early morning: killed around midnight. The street was dark, people there went to bed early; there'd been no noise or disturbance. The lady had not been missed; she lived alone. Lived moreover in the city and what was she doing here where she knew nobody?

Cause of death sharp blow from behind with stick or club – could be karate chop – breaking cervical vertebrae. Motive presumably robbery – handbag rifled – and though this was not very satisfactory (woman of simple tastes, not likely to be carrying much cash or jewellery) they'd all known of murders committed for under a hundred francs. Just that a great deal of trouble seemed to have been taken. She'd been – alone – to a lecture on cultural subject in a university amphitheatre: would have left elevenish, but no witness had been discovered to this or any subsequent movement. Fine dry weather and

70

no traces in the car, which she had certainly been driving. Davignon had worked away patiently at just about everything but no light had been shed. There could be no justification, Popers had minuted rightly, from holding Davignon back from an overdue holiday.

Castang took hold of his notebook. Liliane had seen 'resemblances'. Points in common: both in a car, both bashed from behind, both at night. Chequebook and credit-cards left untouched. No sign of struggle; both unsuspecting victims taken apparently by surprise. Open whether that pointed to knowledge of the assailant or the exact contrary: more probably the latter since in neither case had the enquiry found the slightest basis for argument, strife, anger or malice. Both were quiet, peaceable and utterly respectable middleaged persons (the woman worked for an insurance company, in a position of responsibility if not of authority, and Davignon had gone through all her affairs looking for a grievance). Pleasant, kind people. Woman unmarried, man married (once) with two daughters.

He set to without much enthusiasm, rolling a single sheet (first draft) into the machine. Confidential: not so much the official 'secret' of an affair under instruction, to which all the girls in the office had access anyhow, but matters involving another department – Castang knew very well how things leaked out, and that anything about Maisonneuve would lose little time coming to that gentleman's ears and creating – certainly – a spiteful atmosphere.

'A "connection" one cannot assume: it would be taken as a hypothesis and might lead somewhere, since both enquiries are as good as stalled. The point in common that strikes me is that both victims were lured somewhere: if the grass-&-weeds means anything it means a waste site, somewhere dark/unfrequented. If robbery was planned prostitution is an obvious pretext: the use of a cosh of sorts implies preparation. Prostitution seems excluded in the woman's case, and the Faculty of Letters an unlikely pickup point.

'In the man's case it is unlikely that he was killed at the spot where he was found; the street is well lit and much frequented. One could suggest that both victims were killed in a quiet spot, that the man was driven back to the station to cover a trace (e.g. this supposed waste space close to the assassin's home); whereas there was no good reason to move the woman's car. An improvement in technique?

'Assuming connection: in the first instance we have a prepared

71

coshing but perhaps undeliberate killing (hit overhastily overhard): in the second a more skilful and more probably deliberate homicide. Again – improved technique?

'The motive in both cases is obscure, for if robbery in both cases then for sums amounting to (probably) under a thousand francs in cash since both carried chequebooks & credit-cards – in neither case touched – the means adopted (hypothesized 'luring') is absurdly over-elaborate. Mais.' suggestion 'to feed a habit' is plausible in first case, possible in second: such people see only immediate satisfaction, and cash in that case, even small sums, is preferable to the eventual or maybe of a cheque. His reasoning that addicts will go to these lengths to secure relief is doubtful, to me unconvincing: I also find it lazy thinking to rely upon narcotics when an explanation is not readily available . . .'

Vera had put a stew in the oven to tick over, been summary with the housekeeping, flung a clean overall on the child, and gone out to the park. Not everyone had a garden like Judith! Her own garden was non-existent, a brambly nettly wilderness full moreover of rotted wood and plaster from the cottage, on which Castang cast a gloomy eye: how to get rid of all the filth by – more or less – legal means was a problem. She liked the parks and had always haunted them: at the time when she had been near-completely crippled, Castang used to dump her and her wheelchair, picking her up on his way home. In the Admiralty she had learned to draw architecture, for here were the massive and moated ruins of the city castle. How can you have an Admiralty in the centre of France, five hundred kilometres from the nearest sea? The answer lay with that painted old queen Henri Third, who had promoted some fancy boy both a duke and Lord High Admiral. 'They tell us that the admiral Is as nice as he can Be' – it was Fred Astaire – 'But we never see the admiral Because the admiral has never been to Sea'.

In the Jesuit Garden, formerly the property of these good fathers, and fitted up for their scientific instruction (botanic, even astronomic) as well as for peripatetic philosophy in agreeable surroundings next to the Jesuit College (now a state lycée) she had understood English romanticism: lake, rocks with picturesque fake ruin, a little Chinese bridge and numerous miniature temples. Much drawing had been done here too. As she got more mobile she explored others; Duckshoot where the admiral had had a nice private heronry, Sharpsling where the archers used to practise, Mulberry where silkworms had formerly been cultivated: the public had of course never been allowed in any of these. Bit by bit dukes, private armies and holy nuns had been ejected from their large delectable possessions, and the city was now proud of its gardens. With some justice; the Garden Architect had landscaping talent and was actually fond of a tree, a thing unheard-of in France. 'We are very Tardy', said Castang sadly, 'in becoming civilised'.

This one was Mulberry: there were of course no mulberries but a lot of very nice maples, quite as good. A little stream, with justice called the Tordu, meandered through. The holy nuns had done their washing here: better said peasant girls of the more plain and pious sort did it for them. Vera dumped Lydia in the sandpit and sat.

The main problem with them all was that they were much too small for the overpopulated city. Castang had told her of the enormous English commons: she thought about these with envy. Nobody in France ever gave as much as a burnt match away to the people: they hung on to privilege until it was dragged away from them by force. Everything here has to be done by violence. The people – it is understandable – do not understand any notion of liberty at all. Too many people in gardens too small, with no notion that liberty means restraint, create friction; Vera preferred parks in the morning when there was hardly anybody there.

On a bench nearby sat a man snoozing and a woman contemplating her toes: the out-of-work. Further along were two very ill-behaved children racing about and two municipal gardeners leaning as usual upon rake and shovel and imitating statues: Rodin's Penseur and Michelangelo's Penseroso. She became aware that these had come to life and were uttering.

"Ey. Les gosses! Don't break off twigs, that's destructive." The ill-brought-up children paid no heed. The gardener let his rake fall and stumped up the path.

"Ey Missiz. Ces deux mômes-là, are those your kids? You gotta tell them not to break the branches; those young trees is fragile an' gottobe respected." The woman stared dully.

73

"They don't listen to nothing I say," she said as though that put an end to the matter.

"They gotta learn. We put in those trees, we don't just stand here to see them smashed. Ey Mister. Come on, it's your job to put a stop to it." The man woke up, very ready to be awkward.

"Public park innit? I can do as I bloody like there."

"As you like, hell. Look, I don't wanna have to go 'nget the park guard: 'fI have to, he'll slap you a hundred franc fine, I'm not warning ya I'm effing telling ya." As is frequent among the French when intimidated the man took refuge in legalism.

"I don't see no notice anywhere saying it's forbidden to break the trees!"

The gardener, open-mouthed, turned to his colleague who had come up in support of civic responsibility, and became rhetorical.

"Hear him. He wants a notice! Poor Jesus bleeding, we've millions of notices, all saying what's Forbidden. It's no use saying Please Don't, for people who're a bit thick and don't think: they won't believe that's serious enough; you gotto say ForBidden. Don't bicycle on the path, don't fish in the water, don't pick the flahs because there's billions and it Still ain't enough. No, he wants a notice saying don't Break TREES. You go break trees someplace else, you hear me!" The gardener was large, rubicund, robust. The man withdrew, muttering. Woman and children trailed apathetically after. The gardeners went on replacing the begonias with asters or something that would flower in autumn. Lydia grunted like a little piggy. A woman with a pram came and extracted an overheated child; dumped it in the sandpit where it bawled: the woman gave it a lolly to keep it quiet – it sucked this, then stuck it in the sand. The woman said 'Silly' and washed the lolly in the stream, gave it back saying 'Keep it in your mouth'. 'Stupid cow' said Vera silently. The child, since the idea was plainly a success, put it back in the sand: the mother promptly smacked the child and took away the lolly. The child had now *two* good excuses to bawl.

You are observing (Castang would say, as rhetorical as the gardener) a sound training in criminality. Fill the park with policemen. All carrying notices. Fornication, pederasty, the flying of kites and the sucking of lollies is Interdicted. The French are not interested in prevention; they want repression. Hence their devout attachment to

74

the death penalty. Commit arson in state dockyards and we'll hang you by the neck. Commit larsonny or arsodonomy; it'll be just the same.

Vera opened yesterday's *Monde*. 'National solidarity, says the lady who is Minister for Agriculture, will be exercised with equity and clarity'.

These two qualities being familiar, indeed a daily commonplace, to every farmer he will applaud wholehearted. Ey Missiz, are you out of your tiny wits or your knickers or what?

Lydia who had observed previous proceedings with interest came and stood and said "Lolly."

"No," said Vera.

Castang finished his 'legal opinion' and since there was no sign of either Liliane or Orthez, still out filtering, decided to go home for lunch, where there was a good smell of stew but no *Monde* so he had to read a book instead.

Divisional Inspector Jeanne-Marie Williez, always called Liliane because she came from Lille, was a woman Castang set much store by, relied much upon, respected much. Sturdy busty woman of around thirty-five with a big broad face and shoulders, no waistline to speak of, an unexpected small hard behind above the slim shapely legs: 'she improves as you go down' said the boys. She also improves, thought Castang, as you get deeper in: a taciturn and private person, not easy to know. Unmarried, lived by herself in a small flat that was in a narrow ugly building, that stood in turn in a harsh joyless street. Plenty of Polish blood there, so that there were always jokes about 'Jaroslavski says . . .' and on the surface a stubborn humourless brand of professionalism that was misleading, for she was sensitive and kind, as well as intelligent. She was nice to work with, being gay and sunny, and almost never complaining: she was also a tremendous worker, highly efficient and virtually never ill.

Typically, she had taken possession of the Administrative Director's office (Mr. Steinmetz would be back the beginning of next week and then we'd see the place buzzing) and gone through the theatre personnel like a dose of salts.

"They're hard at work right now – place like that of course has the programme set a year in advance. Irregular hours and it's hard to know when they're there and not there. Lot of this bohemian arty tommyrot." One of Liliane's favourite words. "Through the winter it'll be overtime the whole way so now they take days off when they can get them." Rather like the police. "You get a bit of everything, singers working away with a pianist in one corner, carpenter and electrician in another and dancers trying out a pattern in between but it all meshes pretty well together when you start to take it apart. Well good, I've a fairish witness and two gentlemen I'm not very happy with and I'll be interested what you make of them."

The fairish witness was an American girl called Barbara Witherspoon which Castang found a funny name. 'I do it with a knife and fork myself'. She was however no Barbie doll: a dry wit and a lot of character. No prima ballerina; a principal-supporting-rôle girl around twenty-eight, who had been 'something approaching friends' with Lonny.

"Independent sort of girl. Made her own mind up and stuck to it; I liked that." Lonny had kept to herself a good deal, but was friendly, open, a good enough mixer if she thought it worth the trouble: didn't waste herself on trivial people. Didn't shun boys, but had no known regular boyfriend.

"Preferred girls?"

"Mister, don't give me this tendentious shit, all right? I've been to bed with boys and girls both in my time, and liked it, but I'm only going to talk about what I know and so I told your Mrs. Villitz." Been in France five years, good fluent French. Two years with this company; knew it pretty well. "Pretty good company, good atmosphere. Lonny worked hard, had talent. They'd have offered her a contract, likely enough, in another year, with some real money. She didn't talk much about her family – I know they existed. Didn't talk about anything much. Nice to be with. Restful, quiet. Generous – I hate sewing and last spring one time when I was tired as hell she did a whole lot for me, without being asked and you can believe me."

The factual meat of the matter was that Barbara saw Lonny that evening.

"I know she took a couple of days off so she wasn't in to work and I didn't speak to her. Waved, like. I'd been working and was sweaty and wasn't going to catch a chill hanging about in that passage. She was being chatted up by this Indian bloke: Ram or Jam or whatever: well-named both ways I'd say. I'm not making any suggestions whatsoever and that's all she wrote. They were just talking like: nothing intimate or confidential."

"Ram or Jam? Indian?" Castang asked Liliane. "Some kind of Hindu?"

"Well, it's something long and unpronounceable and there's Jam in it somewhere. No, Mohammedan. Didn't like being interrogated by a woman. High horse. Evasive. So apart from not being very keen on him, I was interested enough to think him worth a go from you, so I told him I'd like to see him here early tomorrow morning."

"I see, and the other?"

"Another long Russian name and even I find it unpronounceable. Not from a Polish part of the world: somewhere down in the Caucasus. So I just call him Sammy. Not Russian now – second-generation Israeli – difficult boy. Got about ten shoulders and all with chips on. Good dancer, says Barbara, technically very accomplished but 'full of neuroses'. She's not antisemitic at all, but doesn't like him. 'Bloody rude', and 'smells awful when hot' and 'always indignant about something', 'a smoulderer'. Took a shine to Lonny, according to Barbara, but she didn't want to know. Barbara wants to buzz, incidentally; do you still want her?"

"If we want her tomorrow we'll send her a message. So tell her to keep herself available, please, in the afternoon. Now where's Orthez?"

Orthez had done his homework: all his odd items of information had been thoroughly matched against Liliane's work; held 'up against the light'. This recoupage, to use the technical term, had produced 'a funny man' to go with Liliane's two, and this one had also been asked to pop round to the PJ office 'in the morning' so that Castang could work him over . . . hadn't wanted to come; kicked up about the waste of time: his business, he said. Now, said Orthez, you want to be a good citizen, don't you? You want to cooperate. And since you're a stranger you want even more to be a good citizen. Like you're enjoying the hospitality of France, right? so you'll be much keener than the French would be to help the police, okay? His arm once twisted he had seen the light. But a sly hypocrite, said Orthez.

"Another bloody foreigner! I hate a lot of foreigners," said Castang xenophobically. "Lawyers and consuls and whatall."

"They're a rum crowd," agreed Orthez, "Sammy, Jammy and Yammy."

"That one yours?"

"Yes, he's Japanese with a long funny name. Been here a few years – came to learn French cooking he says, with some idea of a French restaurant in Yakasaki or wherever, but that's a racket quite a few had got into so he stayed on here himself. Would like to open a Japanese restaurant but meantime he's doing quite well with this healthfood place; seaweed and three-year tea and all. Lonny liked that stuff, all those dotty theatre people are peanut-butter maniacs, so she was in and out quite a bit and he admits she was there that evening. There's quite a lot of more-than-meets-the-eye if you ask me, but there's plenty meets the eye too. He goes out and does Japanese meals for parties; he knows that special butchery, he has a whole heap of fancy cooks' knives as decoration in the shop. Lives behind the shop. All this is totally circumstantial. I thought you'd enjoy wiggling his back teeth for him from close up."

Richard dropped in just before Castang could get off.

"Quite an interesting reaction you made to those files."

"I'm certainly not concentrated now and I'm not at all sure I was concentrated then: I can't even recall what my reaction was. Look, sorry, I've got a plateful here, I've three weirdos scheduled tomorrow morning and their names are Yammy, Sammy and either Rammy or Jammy, I'm still not quite clear which."

"The United Nations," said Richard, but any witticism was aborted by the telephone ringing.

"I have to tell you," said the bank manager's voice of the Kommissar in Apeldoorn "that the parents are flying to Paris and taking the train on." A disagreeable reminder about the overdraft.

"Very good." It was very bad.

Jam was first; standing in fact fuming on the doorstep at opening time as though this were an English pub; coinciding with an abrupt shower of rain, a squally gusty west wind telling all and sundry that holidays were now over, a sharp fall in the temperature. Jam yesterday, thought Castang. Quite possibly Jam tomorrow. And this early in the morning sticking to my fingers . . .

"You can hang your umbrella there if you like, and make yourself comfortable. As with the dentist; the less tension you feel the less painful the process."

"I went over all this already with a subordinate."

"Let me make one thing as clear as I possibly can," pleasantly, in his tenor voice. "You were asked a few questions. Prepare yourself to be asked as many more as Inspector Williez may deem necessary to ask."

"These are threats? Intimidations? Browbeatings?"

"Have you bad teeth? Have you neglected them? Are you afraid of pain? You have nothing to fear here but your own imagination."

"I shall take every step necessary to protect myself."

"To protect yourself from what?" A small cigar, thought Castang, will settle my stomach better than a cigarette.

"Officialdom. Bureaucracy."

"I see from this note that you are a trader, in your own words a purchasing agent. You are fifty years of age, of Iranian nationality. You have lived in this country for some fifteen years – that is all correct? You are thus a man of experience, a man of standing. In business matters, your word, your promise, your cheque, are good, and to be relied upon; isn't that so?"

"Evidently."

"The briefest query shows you to have no criminal record. Some further simple enquiries," pointing a negligent finger at the telephone "to the Customs service, or the fraud inspectorate, the tax authorities – these would show no little irregularities under the Description of Goods or Merchandising Marks, say?"

"Certainly not. Very idea . . .!"

"Equally, if I were to say good morning to my colleague over at D.S.T. – the political branch – they would not have tales to tell concerning suspicious affiliations or undesirable activities such as might throw a strain upon the goodwill of the French Republic?"

"Listen, there's never been a breath – not in the Shah's time nor since – "

"I'm sure of it. What have you to fear?"

"Oh absolutely. To be sure. It's just that . . ."

"Yes. A homicide investigation is an important matter, a serious thing. You find yourself tangentially involved: this alarms you. Have you reason for alarm?"

"Of course not. It's the waste of time – "

"Hereabouts, sir, we don't think of a homicide as a waste of time. So a little word of advice. Behave, towards Inspector Williez, as you would to any state official with important responsibilities. Open. Lacking concealment. Eager to help. Exactly as you would with the duty payable on some little consignment of carpets. N'est ce pas?

"That settled . . . let me enlighten you on little matters of procedure. Inspector Williez asks you factual questions, and wishes you to be very precise in detail. The answers are taken down. You are not under oath but it is very much in your interest that you should be totally candid. It's impossible as you tell me that you could be incriminated. N'est-ce pas?"

Nod. Tight lip.

"It could be conceivable – we have these little human weaknesses – that questioning would touch upon a matter you would prefer remained unknown. Not anything criminal. Something private. I'll make two points here, if you'll allow me – please do not interrupt. The first is that a homicide investigation allows nothing to remain private that the enquiring officer considers germane. Clear? It is within his – or her – discretion. And the second point is that we know, here, how to be discreet.

"Taking those two points into consideration, thinking it over, you would perhaps prefer questions to be put to you by a man?" Staring in that bleak rude police way straight into the man's eyes. "Because we're dentists here, as the little joke goes, and upon occasion we're gynaecologists. We ask intimate questions, without embarrassment. Let me give you an example," choosing a cigarette this time "You find yourself attracted towards young girls?" Short and flat.

"I don't see the relevance of this question."

"You see, you're hedging already. I'll remind you – candour. Here, sir, we are conducting an enquiry into a sadistic sex murder. The question is to the highest degree relevant: kindly give me the answer."

"Every young and pretty girl is bound to hold attraction to a normally constituted man."

"How young?"

"I suppose that would be a question of physical development."

"Sixteen? Fourteen? Twelve?"

"I repeat, I – "

"Have you ever heard of the American concept of statutory rape?"

"I don't understand."

"Are you aware that if you invite, accept or seek to procure sexual intercourse with a girl under a certain age you commit a criminal offence even if you offer no violence?"

"Uh, I – "

"Do you like boys?"

"With respect I must protest."

"Why do you protest? In Islamic countries no particular shame attaches or am I misinformed?"

"You have yourself pointed out that we are in a Western country."

"One can bring attitudes of mind across a frontier, wouldn't you agree? To take an evident example, leading frequently to misunderstanding, in a country such as Iran, Western girls who wear no chador and have uninhibited social manners are often thought of as shameless and even sinful by those of a strict Islamic persuasion. Correct?"

"I am not myself of such strict religious observance."

"But it is so. Not to put a fine point on it Western girls are often thought of as whores. Offering themselves. Ready for bed with no preliminaries. Do you share that viewpoint?"

"I have lived in France for a number of years and am free I should think of either puritan or provincial attitudes."

"How young do you like them?"

"You are bullying me."

"Perhaps I am. It is because you are not yet being perfectly candid with me. You met that girl in the theatre. You have seen her there before. You had business there concerning a detail of Oriental design. She spoke to you about Persian miniatures. This is what you told Inspector Williez yesterday. Do you wish to alter or deny that story to me, today?"

"It is the simple explanation of a trivial fact."

"I accept that. Trivial facts lead often to situations that are less trivial. So we take this one a step further. It crossed your mind that her interest could be an occasion for enticement? 'I have some miniatures I can show you – a book that would interest you'."

"You are imagining things."

"Certainly. It's such a classic old gag isn't it – come up and see my etchings. And remarkable how often it works. Today, perhaps, it's

81

often the girl who asks 'Haven't you any etchings?' You have had no such experience?"

"No."

"Sir, do you ever visit call girls? Or drive along at night, slowly, close to the pavement, in your car?"

". . . ."

"Would you have objections if I were to ask for your little pocket notebook? And checked the phone numbers I found in it?"

"I have done nothing – nothing – to render me subject to searches and suspicions."

"Then be candid. You live alone. You have a wife, or wives, in Iran. That is none of my concern. But here, in this city, everything is very much my concern. It's a flat fact of life. Middle-aged gentlemen normally constituted like to see and touch girls – that's another. So tell me who, how, in what circumstances, with what frequency, following what patterns."

"I beg you to believe that nothing with this girl took place. It is as I described and no further."

"I ask nothing better than to believe you, sir, and your full detailed answer to my question will aid this belief substantially."

"You put improper pressures upon me."

Yes yes, thought Castang. We're a gang of sadistic bastards. You wait until you've had an afternoon with Liliane, and find that she is a lot more clinical and direct than I am. To a gentleman of however enlightened Islamic upbringing, it might come as a salutary experience.

"If you think that, already, you must indeed have much in your life you wish to shield. What is it you feel ashamed of?" Castang kept him an hour longer. Yammy was downstairs, fair bouncing with his feet off the walls, he was told. Let the bugger stew a bit.

Is not cookery among the foremost of our arts? – the very idea, catching himself up short, of calling cookery an art! Perfect nonsense anyhow, Vera would have said cooking demands that you take trouble and the French won't. We will though, thought Castang issuing a secret instruction to keep the jam on a slow boil and to stir frequently to prevent its sticking.

A bourgeois softy, who has spent years making a comfortable bed and intends to go on lying on it. In the Shah's time all done by bribery and this would still presumably be the case, though he might get tremors at nightmarish visions of a mad-eyed ayatollah with a sabre wanting to know what he was doing for the Islamic revolution. Please Your Grace I export the revolution to the French.

Castang stopped his imagination and wondered whether there was a killer in the jampot. Not a 'psychological pattern for a murderer'? He knew very well no such thing existed. However, this middle-aged sybarite was highly vulnerable, and whatever he did to girls would show up in the cooking.

Unless he was much mistaken the Yam would prove made of sterner stuff and so it proved. This fellow you could spread over the outside of a rocket, and use him as a thermal shield when re-entering the atmosphere. A finger got pointed at Castang, finger much like a copper-jacketed bullet, and a voice of the same texture and similar muzzle-velocity.

"You paying me compensation for loss of business, isn't it."

"You paying me compensation," while laughing heartily and patting himself to make sure his steel-fronted underpants were in position "for wasting valuable police time."

"What is so funny?"

"You thinking yourself funny, isn't it, trying to take criminal brigade for pack of imbeciles, or what?"

"Why you talking that way?"

"Because if you go on like something out of a sampan flogging jade elephants to tourists, I can do it too. Me emptying shitbucket overboard on head, got it?"

"You calling me here to listening crap like this? My permit straight and my business straight; you knowing that bloody good. You narcotics bureau coming ten times after heroin getting flea in the ear. I making COMPLAINT," banging on the table.

"You bang that table once more," said Castang in a whisper "and I show you what the narcotics dogs do when they're kept short of sukiyaki for a week."

"Theatre," contemptuously. "I writing denouncing. Saying to *Canard Enchaîné*, saying to Gaston Defferre, saying to Monsieur François Mitterrand crooked cop with racial prejudice."

"I'll give you a choice," slowly. "You can behave violent or non-violent. Violence you can get, three francs worth a penny round here. You want to, you can spend the next twenty four hours handcuffed naked to the radiator down in the basement, and we'll start talking after that. I'm a non-violent man, but this is my office and nobody shouts at me in here. You behave with dignity and you'll be treated according."

"You respecting my human rights," sulkily.

"You'll find I will, and that cuts both ways. Either we're both men, or I'm the stinking crooked cop and you're the crummy seaweed peddler. The whole way, or no way." The shrewd eyes looked at him carefully.

"What exactly are you trying to get at?" The pidgin patter had vanished as though it never was. "I hear from your inspector, that pocket-size weight-lifting one," – Castang cherished this description of Orthez – "a big sensational thing about a naked girl chopped up and in a paper bag, and it's natural to think you're trying to fix something on me. She was a customer. So what? I put the noodles in paper bags, not the customers."

"There's a little old lady at the theatre who came in for a tin of octopus for supper – "

"Sharing it with the cat."

"Let me finish my sentence, all right? That evening. The girl was in the shop, alone, you were out in front, chatting her up."

"Yagh, I chat up all the girls. Good business," unperturbed.

"Get much crumpet, that way?"

"A fair bit, but not this one. She like the chat-up – laughed. Anything else not on," succinct.

"How do you know?"

"How do you know, you? You're not an imbecile. Can't always tell will they, but know straight off won't they. Straight girl," thoughtfully. "Should be more like that. Better world. But mustn't complain."

"In fact I agree. I never saw her, but that's the way I see her. However, the suggestion could be made that you could have invited her for a cup of tea and jumped her to see whether that might be fun."

"Stupid suggestion," said the Japanese borrowing Castang's lighter "from stupid person. Police thinking. He does things like that? No, all right, we agreed to be polite. Without impoliteness, still stupid suggestion."

"Very likely. Unhappily we've known an awful lot of very stupid and very unlikely suggestions turn out facts. Why? Because people do suddenly behave in ways that are both stupid and unlikely. So these suggestions get made and have to be followed up."

"Poison cat with poisoned octopus, but can't hang cat on circumstance. You make suggestion. You can't prove it. I can't disprove it. Where we go next?"

"Where we go is this. I leave facts to my inspector. He asks questions, you answer. Yes it is; no it isn't. He collects a few facts, and you're quite right, we're left staring at them: we don't want to interfere with anybody's liberty on that. Too often we find ourselves in that sort of hole. So I'm trying for a bit of unfactual stuff. Getting an idea of the man you are. We're very materialist here in France; we're not very human and we don't like people. Much the same gets said about Japan, where I've never been, and what I read I don't much trust. Too slick, too facile, you get me?"

"I get you. Japan is likewise a very different kind of place, and that you don't see, and what cops don't see they don't grasp. Anyhow you try. Fair enough. Just understanding," – backsliding for only a fraction of second – "business is business. Person is person. We keep that separate. Cops better do the same, otherwise trouble. Right?"

"So much right that I don't blame you for not letting the person show. But now there is a personal factor. The girl got killed, which is a pretty personal thing to have happen to one. I feel it personally. Not emotional; that would do me no good and blind my judgment. But in a duality, both as cop and person. I get to know her, I get to know you; just a bit. 'm'I making any sense?"

"At least you're still trying," with a movement of the fingers, a little like a pianist suppling the hand before touching the keyboard.

"You have this Buddhist stuff in the shop."

"Sure. She bought some. With that I am coming to know her, a very little bit."

"You have it just for trade, for noodles, or is it personal at all?"

"I don't want it, for trade, but customers expect it. It's a little personal. Here, – how to say, in this context – I don't like to talk about this."

"It interested me that you should say – about her – that 'there should be more like that', and 'it would make a better world'."

"Slipped a bit, didn't I," tartly.

"Explain to me, a little."

85

"No I don't explain. You read the little book – I sell it you."

"Try again. My understanding is that Zen is non-violent."

"Not Zen. Zen is not right. It is a . . ."

"Heresy? Schism?"

"What are these words? – they are stupid."

"A crock of shit," suggested Castang helpfully.

"It is a sect," with a prim mouth. "The followers of Nichiren have not this foolishness. Glamorous in the eye of the ignorant."

"The principle of respect for life in every shape, of rejection of violence – this however you share."

"You not approaching this subject with purity," in the old querulous manner. "Trying only habitual police trick, making fellow contradict self. Materialist European likes facts – okay, stay within facts. Got no facts, then wise man shutting mouth." No Zen master could have put it more succinctly. "Police not got an understanding of non-material world." Thus snubbed Castang said sweetly, "Then we'll both have to acquire more patience. Patience," with pedantic emphasis "we learn here."

Pay out line, he told himself.

He opened a door a crack.

"Be as clinical as you like," he heard Liliane say cheerfully. "It doesn't worry me at all – I'm Oriana Fallaci." Popes and ayatollahs could put on a show with men. Faced with the dreadful Impurity of women they got into a stew. There'd be a smell of burning jam there shortly.

The infernal Sammy succeeded effortlessly in being more tiresome than the other two combined. Wouldn't even get out of bed: morning began at midday.

A dancer. Splendidly muscled without any show of it; the light pliant balance of a birchtree. No; harder, denser. What was the stuff of which bows were made? Fibreglass, said Orthez. No no, don't be ridiculous. That stuff with the dark curly shiny foliage. Berries too that make children sick. Yew, said Orthez. Right. Got these Assyrian looks: hair all over like an Astrakhan coat – do I mean goat? – and great huge liquid black eyes that will hardly need any make-up. And pull the bow how you will, no crack shows. Nothing RiceKrispy about

Master Sammy. Even cooked he didn't go soft, and would make a most indigestible breakfast.

Violence everywhere, smouldering under the skin that was dark too and somehow greenish like an olive that was not quite ripe. But these corny black panther similes failed to apply: not feline. A goat, said Orthez, who was quite as cross and frustrated as Castang by mid-afternoon; agile, tough, randy old goat: all that's missing is the smell. The smell was that of a clean dark person in hard physical condition (the phrase 'making him sweat' didn't apply at all) lavishly helped out with Guerlain – to the cops who'd finally dragged him out of bed he'd said he was taking a shower first and they could just wait. A landscape metaphor will have to do, thought Castang. The violence of harsh highly coloured rocks and sparse soil and sparse scratchy trees. He had never been in Israel but palms and orange groves did not convey the idea he wanted at all. Beduin sitting on a rock eating a raw onion. We haven't heat enough in the kitchen to disconcert him in the slightest.

Jews there are of all sorts; as many kinds as Buddhist sects. We aren't experts on Jews; we haven't any in the department. Police forces, bar presumably their own in Israel, do not attract Jews as a career. A handicap. Poles, Czechs, the hardest-hearted Breton or the most chicanery-bent Corsican we could handle standing on our head. Arabs – we really are a stinking racialist crowd! Imagine Arabs in a French police unit (nothing impossible about it; plenty of French Arabs, excellent, reliable and most patriotic citizens). Must suggest this to Our Minister! We can certainly say that if we don't know how to handle Arabs they sure as hell know how to handle us . . . Right under his hand he had Liliane the Ch'timi, Orthez l'Occitan, Lucciani a Provençal orange-flower (came from Grasse) and himself – been a Parisien, once upon a time. No Jews!

You had the East European ones, the Ashkenazis: surprising how many there are too despite the earnest efforts of Herr Aitch. Sephardic weirdos from the Moorish lands of southern Spain and Portugal and throughout North Africa. What were the Yemeni ones who by all repute are the toughest nuts (which is saying a good deal)? But they were all Jews: they had that in common. Tcha, you could see they made good soldiers, boxers, gangsters – rape-murderers? There was nothing that gave, anywhere along the line. The police are mostly

87

fairly smart at finding a soft spot . . .

"Right, you're a dancer. Homosexual, it's to be presumed."

"That would reassure you? Encourage you? You'd pin on a pink triangle and then you'd know all about it?" Castang sniffed at the perfume-laden air. "You should be grateful: that way you can't smell yourself, as long as your mouth isn't open."

"Hostile to cops," said Castang indifferently, politely. "Put it that it doesn't worry me. Homosexuals are like everyone else. But I like to know, because it needs a little extra effort. Language difficulty."

"Ask Spoon River Barbara."

"Says she's both, herself. Likes it all ways."

"Like the Emperor Alexander. Or leave it alone. Gives us a wider range, from peachy little boys to rich old widows."

"You been in the army?"

"Everybody in Israel's in the army."

"What about the ones who nod, with sidelocks and funny hats?"

"You try pushing them about and see what happens to your head."

"Yes, to the onlooker you seem a violent lot."

"Wait till they've exterminated a few million of you, and try it again then."

"Yes. Knock, get knocked, knock again – vicious circle no? all the way down since old Abraham trekked over from Ur."

"Tell it to the Cheyenne."

"Did the Jews ever steal any Cheyenne territory? – I'd be interested to learn. Bit of gold, bit of uranium?"

"I don't bother with antisemites in Washington: I got enough right here."

"Boy, you're sui generis; your own antisemitism is fabricated rich and ready behind your eyebrows. I don't need to provide any. You're up against a plain possibility of raping and killing a girl. It could turn into an imputation and you yawp about anti-semitism. I'm not trying to force any confessions out of you. About your relations with her – make me an offer."

"Very Christian of you. The only offer I'll make you is to go sit on a scorpion."

One could see easily enough that the boy wanted to provoke him into violence and then get righteous about it. Since his own tactic had been roughly the same it was clever. Bad tactic; get rid of it.

Other tactics did no better. All the way; the big blank O. Time to withdraw, to previously prepared strategic positions.

"You are free to go."

"Free now?" The voice, Castang recognised, of a person who is properly suspicious of 'Greeks bearing gifts'. Of a person who knows that things coming free very rarely are free. Of the person too who has some experience of the police. Beware above all of the police at the moment when they appear considerate and even kind. His narrow smile tightened further.

"Not quite altogether now. Your declarations have to be compared with others made to us. Waiting-room down at the end. You'll be able to get a little sack time in."

"So I know your definition of 'now'; and what about 'free'?"

"Free means home or the theatre. The little daily round. At the present no further, until we see a little deeper into this. The judge of instruction – it's unlikely but possible – might ask for your passport to be surrendered."

"I see. Gestapo freedom, with strings attached. Rights! – I notice you stinking cops talk a lot about rights, and ethics, and morals. We happen to know that there are no rights, except by conquest."

"Correct," said Castang gathering his papers together. "We do well to realise that," smiling with his teeth, "in all the talk about justice and law. La loi du plus fort est toujours la meilleure" in the singsong of a child reciting La Fontaine. "Nous allons le prouver tout à l'heure. "

The troika was summoned to discuss findings. Liliane, Orthez and Castang had some desultory talk lasting about five minutes. Opinion? – of what use is opinion?

"They all three had opportunity. Motive? It's a psychological thing, right? whenever it's not as crude as money. Any shrink could fit any one of them up with a motive. All right, I'll take it in to Richard."

The Divisional Commissaire listened carefully. A little coldly, with his air of indifference.

"So as I understand you're more blocked than ever."

"Three possibles. None more a probable than the other two. An equal possibility that it's none of the three. There's a psychological fact buried: any of the three – or four – could have killed her. But which of them would have eaten her?"

"The judge, on what you now have, is not going to order psychiatric examinations for three or even any one of the three."

"You confirm my impression."

"So being blocked," said Richard, resting his jaw on his palm as though through sheer weariness it might be about to fall, "you hope for the Red Sea to part by supernatural agency?"

"I thought of something. Pretty tenuous. But a possibility. Of direct physical evidence. Which as I need not emphasise. We so badly need."

"Which is?"

Castang explained. Richard picked up the internal phone and pressed the button for Identité Judiciaire.

"We'll need a lab man," he said, glancing at his watch, "to stand by after hours. I don't just want a victim designated; I want the best there is at a microscope job, for slides and photographs that may have to stand up in court for a homicide case. I want him readied now, to accompany Castang for taking samples, so buckle on the gun belt. All right?"

"And if it's inconclusive? – a common blood-group, shared by one or more of them?" to Castang.

"Then we'd be shot. But she was rhesus negative. And even with a lot of washing . . ."

"It's worth trying. And if the lab technician gets anything have it rechecked. By Professor Deutz. Because in court . . ."

"Yes."

Castang marched heavily back to the waiting-room. Sam true to form was stretched out on a bench loose as a piece of string. Yam sat as immoveable as an imperial soldier defending an unsinkable carrier from American barbarians, jaw twitching in an odd way which might have been chewing gum or moving through passages from the Lotus Sutra. Jam was chain-smoking, and the usual inadequate ashtray was overflowing.

"The following proposal applies to you all equally. You are all free, upon a condition that I can enforce, to wit a perquisition in your living quarters which can be carried out quickly and without trouble, and shouldn't take more than a quarter of an hour each. No mess or disorder will be caused."

Sam went on sleeping, Yam went on masticating his cud of material or spiritual refreshment: it had to be that imbecile Jam that jumped about and hollered.

"It is intolerable. I am kept here the whole entire day I am subjected to mental torments and anxieties I am the target of sadistic humiliations and pressures I am – "

"Whole entire like the rest of your complaint is a pleonasm," cut in Castang to shut the tap off "and anyhow the day isn't either yet. These other two gentlemen are on exactly the same footing as you and don't complain – what for d'ye keep going on and on about?" Neither was this a strictly grammatical proposition but one got fed up with the silly git.

Orthez drove one car with Castang and the IJ technician with his big scientific magic box. Lucciani drove the see, hear, and speak no evil trio. One by one they were deposited and Castang enquired for the bathroom.

"You want a piss," said Sam, who was first, nastily "you can go out and do it in the gutter."

"The dead woman," said Castang who had been saving this up till he got them again one by one "was cut up, Sammy, like a rabbit for a stew. A human being has a lot of blood in him her or it. Is big and awkward and heavy. How would you go about that job? Lot less simple than it sounds. Common sense tells me there's also a lot of washing up to do. So we're going to do a bit of laboratory work. Blood cells will show up in unlikely places."

The technician, with little instruments like a miniature manicure set, scraped dirt from crevices between tiles, along the bath surround – Sam had only a shower built in a curtained alcove: Yam had one of these slipper-bath effects that are too small for a bath and too awkward for a comfortable shower: Jam who lived in a flat with 'standing', had a gorgeous bathroom with a bath and two showers – and paid particular attention to the areas where the chromed taps and conduits come through holes in the tiling. A sort of ring or disc screws down over the plumbing joint: the outside and inside rims of these never are quite clean. The black grease of dirt and the grey sand of household cleansers accumulated on glass slides, mingled with Sam's sophisticated toiletries, Japanese austerity – Yam seemed to use nothing but Marseille soap – and some plummy pink stuff Jam was given to washing with.

There was the further squalid job of unscrewing the waste pipes. Sam's shower had no siphon, but a copper trap under the grid for the hair, fluff and fabric fibres that collect in such horrid quantities. The faces that watched these operations showed apathy and bemusement, and nothing else that Castang could see. You can learn a lot from the study of faces, but not whether they belong to murderers.

Let them sleep on it. One of them – he was pretty sure of it – had to sleep with the realisation that here in this flat . . . he was pretty sure of that, too. How would they sleep?

For there is a class of person, with which Castang was unhappily familiar, known vaguely to the literature as the sociopathic personality, who just doesn't care. To him (frequently to her) the 'other person' is not really a person at all but an object. The object is tiresome, annoying, an encumbrance? Get rid of it. Suppress it.

This was not the state of affairs here, and of that he felt quite sure. One did not eat pieces of a girl unless she were important. There were cases like this too in the literature, quite well-known and well-described. He had not looked them up. He wanted to come to it fresh, and . . . there would be time to read it all up later. He told himself this, knowing it would not be so. The judge of instruction and the 'experts' who would be committed to give an opinion upon states of mind in psychiatric terms – let them read it all up. By then in any event it would be another disposal problem, very similar to that the murderer himself had faced – there was an irony in that. He had begun by chopping her head off. This would no longer be done with that legal solemnity, at once so odious and so foolish, to which the Republic had for too long been attached. They'd have a live person on their hands, and the difficult responsibility of trying to find a slot to fit him into. They'd treat him as an object, a parcel, a tiresome, annoying encumbrance, which they'd like to suppress; and they didn't know how. Give them a chopping board, and a few butchers' knives!

The Israeli boy had once worked in the kitchen of a restaurant. Had he learned anything there about the jointing of a carcass – a calf or sheep? In Iran, Castang thought, pretty nearly anyone in a country district at least would make no bones about slaughtering and cutting up an animal, if what he knew about Morocco and Algeria was anything to go by. As for the Japanese, wasn't he the most obviously equipped for the job?

92

But which of them would have eaten her? Wynken, Blynken, or Nod? No point in speculation: he would not get the lab results till latish tomorrow morning anyhow. Tomorrow is another day and today isn't over yet. Much as he wanted to go home and forget it all he had responsibilities.

The parents had arrived on the midday plane: a bite-to-eat in Schiphol or Orly; a taxi through Paris and a few hours in the train. Castang who had been busy with Wynken (the Japanese had developed a nervous tic about the eyes; Richard – the author of these idiotic appellations – had come in for a moment out of 'vulgar curiosity' and been impressed with the difficulty of getting dancers out of bed of a morning) had not wanted to let these poor people mingle with the squalid interrogations, had come down to the door and diffidently suggested a 'teahouse'. This went down well, the Dutch appetite for coffee and pastry being as wholesale as the Jewish. Castang was a little surprised at the hearty attack and put it down to the bite-at-the-airport, no doubt revolting. Nor did they seem 'poor people' in any sense of the word . . .

You can tell as little from clothes as from faces. There is virtually no 'working class' – judged by externals – left in Holland. These were of course the prosperous, professional business class he had assumed from the letters and the girl's background. People of education and sensibility, who spoke good English and made a shot at politenesses in French. But reserved and controlled: a highly polished surface that he skated about on, and was afraid to scratch. They made courteous small talk, about the city.

It might be only a veneer; but a classy one. The man was silver haired, slim, suntanned. The woman too, bronzed by summer holidays; fair hair brushed with grey and cut by a good coiffeur. The clothes of both were simple, elegant and of exceptionally good quality; fine silk and wool and linen in shades of cream and beige and café au lait that would show the dirt terribly but that was both spotless and uncrumpled despite planes, trains, taxis. Much but plain and unobtrusive gold jewellery. Wealth; poise; sophistication. They were not alarmed, nor impressed, nor confused by the French bureaucracy. They had simply come, to carry out a sad chore with dignity and responsibility. It was Castang that was impressed; and relieved.

"Have you already booked an hotel? Oh yes, that's quite good; they should look after you. Well, it's a foregone conclusion alas, there must be this formal identification. I think you'd rather be alone but I'll send one of my inspectors to drive you. The papers are ready and await only the judge's signature. I am afraid that I am much taken up with the enquiry, which is at a crucial stage; I'd better not bother you with it now but will give you all I can – all there is to know – later if you so wish. Would you rather see no more of me, or would you prefer that I came, say at the end of the day, something after six, to the hotel and placed myself at your disposal?'' The man studied him, said nothing, turned a little to the wife. She spoke, decisively.

"You are kind, Monsieur Castang, and helpful. Yes, we would like it very much if – since as you say alas, there can be no doubt – you could come. And tell us whatever you can.''

He found them now sitting in the lobby, changed – ashgrey mohair suit; a good frock, chocolate brown with little white and yellow marguerites – changed by an experience too, though it did not show on the smooth fine skin that was not much lined, barely crumpled. Both sets of eyes were red. It had been a bad afternoon. But the control was there. The veneer might be a scrap dulled, but was unscratched. Again, it was the woman who took the lead.

"We must thank you again for being generous with your time, and patient. You must please allow us – Frank, will you do the necessary – to return a little, your hospitality. Your inspector was very nice about our daughter's things. Those pathetic remnants . . .''

"Whisky all right?'' asked Frank.

It was the right medicine. Two strong brown throats vibrated with a powerful swallow of good twelve-year-old, and his own in grateful unison.

"You're throwing flowers at me I scarcely deserve.'' Frank threw him a shrewd look. Hard but human.

"I've some considerable experience of this country, in business terms you understand. You mustn't take it amiss if I say I find you untypical.''

She put it in sidelong. "We expected – I must apologise – a senior police functionary to behave in a highly depersonalised fashion which is unhappily characteristic.''

"I'm afraid I agree. We try here to keep in front of us – uh – it sounds so pompous. It's thought that good police work has to be depersonalised. I believe that the truth is the opposite . . .''

"Yes, the criminals too."

"I'm afraid there's not a great deal to say about the enquiry which is not yet quite finished, but judicially, one of the fellows we have is going to turn out the right one, and then it will be a rather prolonged affair of trying to fix a degree of responsibility." The woman drank some more whisky and said "Frank, find me a cigarette."

Castang leaned over to offer her a light. She drew on it from the centre of her lips with the slight awkwardness of a woman who smokes only as a social convenience. Or in an effort at concentration – that more than an aid (Castang relit his cigar which had gone out) in mastering an emotion.

"The blow was awful. But we are not going to make it worse."

Placid people. It was the cliché one used of the Dutch and it isn't good enough. Clean, proper, disciplined and dull. Not good enough either.

"To feel revengeful, to feel hate, to talk of an eye for an eye and a tooth for a tooth . . . oh, it comes in the Bible but I can't believe God ever uttered such a primitive sentiment." Would I be able to say this, wondered he, if my daughter – suppress that.

"The spectacle of suffering – he must have suffered horribly to be forced to do such horrible things – can't console me. Won't. Us. It won't alleviate my suffering to think of him living in fear, not knowing when your hand will be stretched out to take him by the collar. That long-drawn-out horrible process of justice, arguing to and fro in that cold-blooded buying and selling of emotional pleas. His head loose on his neck – no, his head is no longer in jeopardy, is it? But years and years – ten, twelve – or to be declared insane with a lawyer proud, as though he'd got you off. A state clinic for the criminally insane. We talk about it as though it were merciful, as though we were being progressive and civilised. I think I would prefer the executioner." Castang who had often thought the same said nothing. Are these Richard's people, those who live beyond the north wind? "We've talked about it; we agree that there is nothing more we wish to know . . .

"People die in dreadful ways. You must have seen many like that. Crushed and mangled in road accidents. A gas explosion, a plane crash – that tanker that exploded at the camping site in Spain. And I have been thinking of that terrorist, who walked up to some imam and simply held a grenade against the man's stomach knowing that he would himself be blown in pieces. I'm talking too much. Frank give me some more whisky. My greatest dread is of a press photographer and one of those gloating horrible pictures with a caption like 'The agony of the bereaved parents.' "

"I can't guarantee you immunity, I'm afraid, though I'll do my best."

"No, we don't want to add to your burdens. I'm afraid it must go much against your grain to hear me say so, but I could wish that killers should go unpunished and even undiscovered, as long as the best we can do is only to add the destruction of a second human being to the first." Castang nodded.

"But you know why we can't accept that."

"To be sure. You're a servant of the State, and the State . . ."

"It isn't only that. You could be right and are, at least nine times in ten and probably more. In the present instance I don't know and am not about to guess. But I am obliged to say that in my experience there are greedy, brutal and heartless people who make nothing of a human life in furtherance of their desires. Those ones would begin again. As for imprisonment, I agree it's crueller and even harsher than a death penalty. But at least it's not irreversible: there's flexibility there."
How strange they were, this couple so polished, so neat; and so very foreign. He felt uncouth, awkward, a tongue too big for his mouth. Why did the man leave it all to the woman? He doesn't seem afraid of anybody thinking him a tame tabby. Do I think that? Well no, to be honest, I don't.

"There isn't a lot we can do," he said, getting up to avoid the false position of people who wish to be polite and have nothing left to say, "except love our children." She looked at him queerly then but said nothing. Go back to Holland, good people, taking your daughter with you intact. I hope no press photographer harries you. There are a few hanging about. He was himself Mary, with little lambs in attendance. Mostly they were professional enough to avoid the furious injunction to shove-off, the threatened charge of interference-with-officer in the execution-of-duty: there were unspoken agreements. Still, ghouls. But there you are, we're all ghouls, and there's a stink off the best of us.

Waiting on his desk was a lab report in the particularly grey prose of somebody who had been kept up late. If there is no redress, what is the use of nurturing a grievance? Ah, the fundamental injustice of all human affairs. Heinrich Himmler never forgot the birthdays of his humblest typists, and spent the day before Christmas tying up parcels of presents for the ill, the lonely, and the unhappy. For Richard Christmas was over, and the Reichsführer in a nasty frame of mind.

"Come on, Castang, let's see some action."

"I am applying to the magistrate for an arrest warrant." A pedantry which would, and did, irritate.

Number two. It is depersonalised. You are not about to say that you'd really rather it had been number one, or three. It is number two and as incontrovertible as science can make it. Scientists (Ah God love them the poor things) have greatly lightened the policeman's burden. Even after a few days, this is blood, human blood, of the right type with a rhesus-negative factor, and there is a great deal more known about it too, and even if not as wide as a door 'twould serve, 'twould serve: no use the fellow saying he had a private bacon factory in his bathroom.

No more Jam or Ham neither. This was a human being. Brought in, yes, between two cops by Orthez, but take those handcuffs off and we'll try to be human too. Get rid of the legalisms first.

"Sit down. You have today been arrested in virtue of the formal charge against you, on which I am holding you for the instructing judge and of which I now notify you."

"*What* charge?" Tenacious as ever.

"The judge will decide. For me, blows and wounds resulting in death suffices. He may lay a premeditation charge against you, meaning assassination. He may decide to leave the rape out of it, and the barbarism might even get viewed as a sort of legal encumbrance. You have the right to silence, the right to assistance by counsel of your choosing; to consult, confer, construct a system of defence. There's not much to say really, and you don't have to say a word."

"On what ground any charges?" unyielding.

"Wash and wash, rinse and rinse but it's like Lady Macbeth, you don't get rid of it however hard you try. Your bathroom drain was full of blood. Her blood. You must have known last night. You stayed still, you chose to risk it. Perhaps you thought flight would imply guilt, or you thought nothing, it doesn't matter, this is formal factual expert evidence and it's staring you in the face. Before it goes out of my hands

97

it might help you, and I'm willing if you are, to talk a little. On a purely human level. I'm not allowed to hold out any inducement, and wouldn't if I could, but I could find myself testifying in front of the Assize Court, and it could be on your behalf."

The fellow was sitting too far away. Castang got up and walked round to the front of his table, leaned his bottom against it.

"To come to terms with it is what I'm trying to talk about" in the voice of sweet reason. "You've got to live with it from now on. I'm not trying to force a confession from you; I neither need it nor God knows do I want it. But accept – confess to yourself and you can live with yourself." Silence . . .

"Whether it's a rape, or an ambush, or just a fight in the pub and somebody pulls a knife, it's violence, call the cops. They're here to protect us, yell the good people. Stop the violence, isolate it, get it into a corner, bottle it up. Same as blood; the flow's got to be stopped. Does that put an end to it? – of course not, because the pressure has built up high and stop it at one point it breaks out at another. So I try to take the pressure off. With me so far?" Silence, and blackish glassy eyes staring at him.

"You stopped her life, her anima, the circulation of her blood. She'd been struggling, yelling? – you had to keep her quiet? The gears mesh, the transmission drives the wheels, the brakes have failed. It's a commonplace – I mean we see it as such. You see the marks on her throat, think that's bad, that points to me, I must somehow mask that. Saw her head off and rough up the edges like; sorry to speak brutally but isn't that the size of it? Gave you perhaps the further idea that cutting up into parcel-size pieces wasn't all that difficult, would make the smuggling of a body out of the building much easier, might avoid discovery altogether, make identification quite likely impossible . . . All quite – I'm tempted to say normal, so far. But then . . . what was this, a sacrifice I see it, maybe I'm wrong, you felt you must offer? You a Buddhist, I couldn't believe it was you, I was betting on the two others: stupid thing to do, but life to you I thought would be that much more important.

"Would it propitiate her spirit somehow? Would her nonviolence be passed into you? That she would ask pardon for your violence, efface it? Give you the peace that had been hers? I'm not making much sense, I realise; help me out a bit."

It came suddenly, very nearly too suddenly for Castang to offer any defence at all. One second he was standing relaxed leaning against the table watching the world go by, like a man out of work waiting for the pub to open; the next he was on the floor with every thought rattled out past his teeth, bar fail-safe. The 'coup de boule', the sudden head-down butt jabbed into someone's face, is a highly effective way of putting a stop to his yack. If the fellow is standing up there delivering a sermon, and you're sitting down, better still because you aim it like a shell straight into his stomach. With a charge. All rather different to the massive and chivalrous tournament tradition of slogging John Wayne in the jaw, with the twin immoveable conventions that he just stood there despite seeing it coming a quarter of an hour off, and that it didn't hurt your hand a bit in spite of sending him twenty metres and through several tables (the window glass in principle kept for Buggins'-turn-next-when he slogs you.)

Castang was helped by two things. The charge is mortal – will likely paralyse the nervous centres in your midriff – but you do have an instant to see it coming. And his being a professional. He had half-turned and dropped a shoulder so that the head went into his ribs sideways; lucky for the ribs, lucky too for the head as it happened because lucky lastly for the table.

He was in fair physical shape. Smallish, close-knit, and had once been a gymnast. Not of course that he jogged (a habit he found as farcical as it was fashionable). Nor – perish the thought – allow himself to be entrapped in the hideous boredom of Being Fit, nowadays made more humourless yet by 'Hah! Huh' and attitudes with that great big hairy forearm. Put it rather that like Mr. Polly's Uncle Jim he was strong on fighting with bottles, dead eels, tablecloths, cellar flaps and Night Surprises in general as well as guns, knives and heavy ashtrays.

None of these things was handy right now. He was on the floor in the clutches of this little Japanese bugger who like all such would doubtless be very hot on yuki and ouzo and pulling one's shirt out of one's trousers. This was nasty and he had to get all his own latent basic nastiness to the surface, and better get a ripple on.

You have to get in close, because of protecting that idiotic bullspizzle and adjunct swingers, so uneconomic as well as unaesthetic in design. Likewise face, uncomfortably full of eyes, lips, nose and ears, all intensely vulnerable. A great deal of togetherness helps you from getting hurt and makes it as hard to hurt or otherwise neutralise the fellow participant. Time for Hare Krishna, for wishing you had not quite as many knees and elbows to bang, for recalling that Ray Chandler decided that really his favourite weapon was a wet towel. Keep moving and don't get pinned down. In the end you're too breathless to keep moving, but so you hope is he. Things even out – Castang had taken his jacket off which helped mobility, but he got a fierce bite on the already-sore shoulder through a thin cotton shirt. Several buttons popped too, which would displease Vera. He got caught in a scissors and broke it with a twist that would have dislocated any but a Japanese foot but only made a shoe come off: he got an elbow into a navel and was rewarded by another gasp. Running out of steam but so was he.

Eyes full of water because of his nose that had been polishing the floor for some moments with more energy than he cared for, he found at last the sciatic nerve he had been searching for and dug with both thumbs: there was a yawp and a limpness, allowing him to get a knee round and rattle teeth with it, consequent to which bump that hard head against the floor till the floor was found harder; twist the arm up into small-of-back and hold it there while wondering whether there were any handcuffs anywhere.

Knee again and in the sciatic nerve again; the 'béquille' that sends the leg dead, so the chap sat down heavily. Castang profited to cuff him to the central heating and go for a long sploshy wash under the cold tap. In the interrogation office opposite Davignon, clerkly in horn-rims, was talking to a fat bod.

He could have yelled: Davignon, a lot tougher than he looked, would have answered. Why hadn't he yelled? Not bothered about being found dishevelled on the deck and being rescued by one of his inspectors: that could happen to anyone. A weird notion of keeping things private, just between the two of us?

"You can stay there for a bit," caressing his nose, still red hot despite cold water. Attached to it still, in all senses of the word. He shouldn't smoke so much, so had a cigar to celebrate. Have a glass of water, meaning another glass of water. Less vengeful now he brought a glass of water for his friend, undid the handcuffs and said "Enough is enough, eh? Then sit quiet or you'll get a gunbutt over the ear. I'm calling the dutydoc because I wish for no lawyers claiming I roughed you up." One torn sweaty shirt as evidence, one nose twice the proper size, one shoulder bruised and bit, both elbows smartly sandpapered. Enough is enough. Interlude for evidence to be taken.

"Couldn't hear myself think," said Davignon meeting him in the passage. "All that bumping and scuffling; you been raping somebody?"

"Been getting raped," gloomily.

"Was that fun?"

"No. Didn't do me much good either. What are you looking so busy about?"

"That fellow on the autoroute with a lorry-load of automatic pistols. Don't you read the papers on your desk?"

"No." Decidedly, north wind country was a long way off.

"Well, that's finished with," said Castang letting himself fall down in the chair he knew by experience to be the most comfortable in Richard's office.

"Well done," with irritating lukewarmness.

"Not at all well done. I was having a shot at undoing a few of his weird knots and he jumped me out of the chair. Got a thrashing for my pains."

"It doesn't do to fiddle with knots. Too painful. Which one was it?"

"The Japanese."

"Ah. Least of all Oriental knots."

"Yes. Well. I wasn't going about psychoanalysing anyone. I was mildly curious how one goes about professing Buddhism and eating people."

"Usurping the functions of the judge – who is it anyhow?"

"Colette Delavigne. I said to Orthez tip her off; she'd need a gorilla sitting beside her before she asks any questions."

"It will do her good," pronounced Richard, "to learn about cannibal Buddhists. That's a nasty cold east wind blowing there."

"I suppose I thought I owed it to the girl's parents. Very nice sensible people."

"The Dutch . . . They want to be protected from Russian invasions, but they don't want any rockets on their territory. Difficult choice. Rather like ours. Good, good – business. You'll take up, now you've made a hearty meal of your cannibal, those two homicide dossiers I asked you to look at."

"Oh poop poop," said Castang. It was far from triumphal or like Mr. Toad. Had he but known – the Dutch could have told him that poop-poop is Dutch for Oh Shit.

"However," said Richard deftly alternating stick and carrot, "you may as well take the rest of the day off: your nose looks rather funny. And Castang . . ."

"Yes?" at the door, warily. Richard had a penchant for good exit lines.

"I was just wondering whether you intended to pass the evening horizontally with a sack of ice cubes over your face."

"It's nothing much. He bit my shoulder but I didn't let him make a meal of it. I had the doc go over me – and him too. Just to avoid any suggestion that I'd been hanging him up by the heels to extort a confession."

"I've a small suggestion in case it would seem agreeable to you. If you and Vera would like to come to dinner tonight."

"Certainly. Are we going to Maxims? You got an anniversary or something?"

"Er – no," sounding (if that were possible) embarrassed. "It's true that I've a matter to discuss with you that I'm keeping," going all machiavellian, "outside the office. But that was not really in my mind. I thought perhaps at home. And we'll get Judith to make a huge pot of something disgusting like paella and eat it with our fingers." Castang was doing his best to hide a monstrous astonishment. It was true that he and Richard had become in an obscure and probably Japanese fashion 'friends' but this . . .

"We shall be," with formality, "delighted."

In the outer office, where rubbish had been piling up for a month, Fausta sat anew enthroned. Back from holiday; was this why Richard was in a good mood? Beautifully tanned, the famous hair in a long plait, the lovely pink mouth a strange orange colour in harmony with a smart frock. All very festive.

"Where have you been?"

"Sicily. And you've been in the wars, I hear." Fausta always knew everything.

"Yes, I need a nurse." She had a first-aid box in her cupboard – what didn't she have in her cupboard! – but her second-aid was better still. At one time or another she had aroused the lubricity of the entire

102

regiment but was, she said firmly, no company inkwell for pens to be dipped into.

"My love to Lydia," grinning. The hint was enough: he went home. People getting conked in cars – he had forgotten the details – was definitely to be thought of tomorrow and then with the greatest reluctance.

"Fausta," on the intercom. Boss-Richard voice.

"Yes?" Was his Worship coming out of the brown study (as it seemed to be called, nobody knows why) he had been sitting in all morning?

"Am I lunching with someone?"

"You'd better be because I haven't had time yet to make up your commissariat. One moment, I'll look. Yes, a Monsieur de Biron, sounds rather grand. Do you want a table booked?"

"No, we only go to Maxims when he pays. Oh, apropos of Maxims get me my wife would you?" This was obscure but the convoluted reasonings of Worshipful frequently were.

"So you're going to the golf club? I mean, in case of emergency."

"That's right, just a bit of salad."

"I'm dialling for you . . . Madame, the Commissaire for you." She knew better than to listen in to that line. Nobody was more private about private life. No one had ever even seen Madame Richard. She was rumoured not even to speak any French – 'bribes de conversation' if accidentally overheard were conducted in Spanish. Fausta didn't know Spanish; found herself when leaving messages talking like Stendhal in a weird mixture of Italian and English. The monosyllabic enigma at the other end never said anything but 'Compris'.

"You aren't going to play golf are you? – it's pouring rain."

"No no, this is business. I'll be going straight home this afternoon. Oh I forgot, get me Commissaire Salviac on your line . . . Salviac? I noted last night a tendency to stretch a standing instruction of mine, amounting now to disregard . . . Oh if you want me to spell it out. I'm talking about uses of violence that leave no external trace . . . Yes the violence squad deals in violence: I was and am aware . . . Very well, particulars you shall have. A man of yours who shall be nameless was holding a suspect's ear up against a thin panel – nicely resonant – while some other clown gave a massive clonk with a hammer on the

103

other side . . . Just so. There'll be now no further discussion: this and similar practices will cease forthwith – that is clear? I appreciate your standing up for your men and these same men will kindly stand upon their own feet without recourse to barbaric behaviour: compris?"

Well, good for Worshipful. Fausta was well aware that saying it in front of her was an extreme step. Nobody makes it a written instruction since nobody ever admitted such barbarities existed: putting it in the outer office was tantamount to throwing it straight into the photocopier.

There was a fact that would have surprised and indeed disconcerted Fausta: that the Divisional Commissaire was not as pleased to see her back this fine rainy morning as he should have been. The thought did cross his mind occasionally that Miss Confidential Secretary was a bit too bossy. The advantages outweighed to be sure the slight irritations one felt from time to time: the safety net of certainty that she reminded him of his appointments, including those he wished to forget and would, deliberately, have forgotten was precious; and the feeling that Nanny, sitting knitting beside that nice lake (dim memory of the Round Pond in Kensington Gardens) was about to say 'Don't go too far, dear' was a small price to pay. And a tendency in Mother Hen to fuss about his digestion; equally, a burden that rarely became irksome: he hated having to go out to lunch. The truth was simple, and had nothing to do with Monsieur the Divisional Commissaire in command of the SRPJ: he loved her, and she loved him. Love doesn't need going-to-bed together. He did not enquire, but if Fausta felt a need for someone to go to bed with she would certainly not run short of offers.

It was just as well though that she had been away; and it was to be hoped she hadn't come back prematurely. Because for a few days Commissaire Richard had been living a secret life.

There had been altogether too much that was over-smooth about Mr. Aldo de Biron. His bedside manner was too perfect. He was like a surgeon specialising in rich women, so paternal, so reassuring. 'Och, there's this tiny little nodule. Hardly worth bothering about. Simply for our own peace of mind we'll whip it out, shall we?' And you woke up to find your breast gone.

104

You didn't drive all that distance for a day's golf, even if the course was a pleasant one, in pretty up-and-down landscaping. You didn't buttonhole someone you didn't know with quite so enveloping a charm. You didn't instantly get seized with such affection for the new acquaintance as to call at his house upon a pretext too slight for the trouble taken. Mr. de Biron had wanted a good look at his private circumstances and family set-up. There had been no real invasion of privacy. Richard would have preferred it if there had been: he felt it would have been a lot more natural.

None of this meant anything. No. And he didn't have a high opinion of Intuitions. Good things to have in their time and place. Some cops of course got them. Even good ones. Castang was liable to them. It went with having a little too much imagination, with being a bit too brilliant. The judgement on police officers is very much the same as that upon the staff of a university faculty: in the superior ranks of the hierarchy is a sturdy ineradicable notion that being brilliant and being 'sound' is somehow mutually exclusive. Richard was a good craftsman and liked a wide choice of tools well-tried, well-worn, well broken-in to his hand. There were tools for being sound with, and others for being brilliant with, and he knew how to use both.

He would have liked to use Castang on this particular problem – problem no; more a nagging disquiet, a slight grating in the gearbox and the feeling that the synchroniser is not all it should be. Those intuitions – like most people in authority Richard regarded them as an intermittent fever; something malarial. He was a believer in old-fashioned remedies like a daily dose of quinine to discourage people like Castang. At present it was the tool called for. But there came in this infernal suitcase-homicide. Couldn't take the head of the serious-crimes brigade off that: it would look bad and be interpreted all round as a failure of confidence. And come to think – a suitcase-homicide is a good proving-ground for the intuitive type of cop. They were very quick or very slow in the solving. Leave Castang alone and you stood an excellent chance of having it quick, and since it is gaudy, and appeals to the Press, we're all for having it very quick. A good mark for the department, and bloody good luck to that: it would put a stopper for several weeks upon any eager new broom in Paris anxious to show his attachment to the new régime: all policemen will now henceforward please be Good Socialists. I am a good socialist and I don't want any telling how to become one.

105

Monsieur Richard's secret life had begun thus with a syllogism.

Major premise: Castang would be fine as a metaphoric dose of castor-oil upon Mr. Aldo de Biron, but I can't in conscience take him off this homicide.

Minor premise: there isn't anybody else in this department who is to be trusted with anything this slippery.

Conclusion; unwelcome: I'll have to do it myself.

He found small enthusiasm for the enterprise. He had made absence of zeal for barking himself (what did one keep dogs for?) a principle, for some years now. And he didn't feel very happy about it either.

There were a good few things he didn't feel happy about nowadays, and the feeling dated from that odd moment of personal crisis in England. What had possessed him then, and what was possessing him now? Internal disturbances: probably a good dose of Alka-Seltzer was what he himself needed.

In straightforward police terms the problem was quite simple. To find out some more about Biron's thinking one kept track of his movements. Especially as concerned this area. If he came over here to play golf, and be pally with senior government functionaries there were (it seemed likely) other notions in his noddle. And movements led to affiliations; meaning if you wish to know the chap know his friends.

What would a (close, interested) observer make of Biron's recent, sudden, enthusiastic chumminess with Richard himself? What went on behind that hitting of little white balls?

The official jargon term for the police technique implied is a filature. A tagging by one, two, three people, varying in intensity and length of time. To avoid getting rumbled it has to be pretty sophisticated. Richard was only one person and didn't feel sophisticated at all.

With all my will, but much against my heart, we two will now improve our acquaintance without you realising.

Sullenly, Richard went to pay a call upon an old lady of his acquaintance, known as the Westmore Sister because she had once worked for the Studios supplying glycerine tears to busty females in California. The old girl was seventy odd now but very spry, with a fine fund of comic stories. She'd known Harry Cohn and Louis Mayer; lots of Greats who'd stepped in wet cement outside Graumans

106

Chinese Theatre and not gone deep enough.

She did a job for him from time to time. Could only be used with caution. Castang last year had been got up as a banker, looking and behaving like the short-sighted Mister Magoo; flirting with catastrophe. Richard had deep misgivings.

"Need to look like, uh, not even Monsieur Tout-le-Monde. Mister nothing at all; Mister Doesn't-Even-Exist."

"Must be very simple? – to switch in seconds? And from not too close up? A wig then; rather flat and greasy. No glasses. Hm, I can do you a mask; there are wonderful ones now, thin and supple. Good for a couple of hours without discomfort."

"Like having a condom over your head."

"No, it's elastic but you can breathe. No adhesive or tricky adjustment. Or the back of your head – this will change your neck and ears. Perfect in a car. Oh, lovely that: no knowing whether it's Rossignol Skis or Baccarat glass you're travelling for." Give her half a chance and she'd turn him into the Avon lady.

"No masks," said Richard firmly.

A car was no great problem: his own car pool . . . He got one with stickers saying 'Hands off Citizens Band', windscreen dollies and a virulent hand-embroidered cushion for the back parcel-shelf: which could all disappear like the registration number, making way for 'I listen to Europe No. 1' and the football team's Fan Club.

Monsieur de Biron was careful, certainly experienced, possibly watchful. Richard got himself a radio telltale, a magnetic sort that clips on a car's undercarriage, emits beeps telling you how close you are. Because it wouldn't do to get too close.

It is a job needing a lot of patience, and he came also equipped with crossword puzzles, and that sort of best-selling fiction seven hundred pages long that can be opened, even read awhile, at any of them. Because hanging about outside people's houses . . . There was plenty of warning. A high gate much like his own; another one who liked his privacy. A little homework had been done, enough to know the wife was in Paris but Monsieur de Biron was in residence in the province; generally for a few weeks at a time.

Nothing happened the first day. Biron appeared, but on foot (good for the health) and pottered about the little town, upon apparently innocent pursuits.

But the second day the car was brought out – and turned towards

107

the city. Hereabouts he had an anxious time keeping it in view: it parked eventually on a meter in the centre. Richard did the same, stopped to tie a shoelace, foot propped on the bumper; slipped the telltale in along the exhaust pipe. Wouldn't be too hot for it there? – he had forgotten to ask. Battery ought to be good for a week.

He sloped after his fox, who was strolling up the street and turned ... ho. Into a courtyard. Richard skipped past taking an interest in window displays opposite. Urban police headquarters! Now people don't enter the Hôtel de Police in search of a room for the night.

He hesitated between a small picture gallery and a travel agency. Fussing about next year's holiday went better with the character than looking at pictures (plainly a chancy investment). He went in, and became absorbed in high-coloured stuff about the Seychelles.

Biron had a high sense of his weight and importance; wouldn't fuss with underlings. His likeliest target – presumably – was Commissaire Fabre, Richard's own opposite number, the 'Central' of the Police Urbaine: fat jovial person with a smell about him that Richard had never yet been able to identify. Peppermint? – not quite peppermint though.

Knowing by heart the 'organigramme' he ran the others over in his mind. Maltaverne, Principal Commissaire, in charge of Security; adjunct to the DDPU: Perregaux, Principal commanding the city sectors: Lamennie, Agents in Uniform. Old Riquois fronting the Sureté Urbaine, and his unpleasant Maisonneuve of the criminal brigade – it wouldn't be him. Nor Verdurin, a dim soul at the head of Means (vehicles and so on.) Hm.

It was getting on in the morning; maybe a lunch was planned. He'd have to stay here. The Seychelles exhausted, he went on to Bangkok. Worrying a little about cholera in the drinking water.

Ho. The uniformed cop at the entrance of the courtyard had straightened up, showing he was disciplined. And there they came ... and yes, by gum, he would have bet on it. Maltaverne the highflyer. In his early forties, which was youngish for a Principal. And bucking hard (Richard knew) for further promotion. An eager type. Roland-le-Rapide, they called him in the fast-intervention group, the SOS. (No soul-saving there: Service Operationnel Spécialisé, which is unpronounceable).

What was it about Maltaverne that caught the eye? And – which interested Richard more – did not catch the eye at all? For a start his camouflage was good; involving a bluff of several folds or dimensions. Double? Triple? More?

A bulky, round French face that did not look French, because of a sporty haircut with a fringe over that forehead which might be high and intellectual or just low and apey. The eyebrows were straight, but sloped in a V to the centre, where a nose at once sharp and fleshy stuck out between sharp shiny little eyes.

This hawkish, military look, like a Norman knight in a helmet, of the upper half of the face was in contrast to the mouth and jaw, which were heavy and brutal, and his ability to keep those restless little eyes dull and stupid-seeming while he was actually looking at you – which he seldom did. That face was under good command. You looked once and it was as blank and stodgy as bad sculpture: you glanced again and it was a gun pointed at you.

The head sat upon a thick neck: the neck sat upon a thick short body: a lumpiness that looked slow. When you discovered the contrary it was always too late. Richard was fortunate in having seen the personal dossier, which had some very good marks in it. Among miscellaneous, seemingly irrelevant information was an approving note that when younger, as a young inspector with good examination results, Maltaverne had been a good club rugby-player. If he had concentrated more might have made B-international level, in the trainer's opinion. What place on the field? A tactical-kicker out half? Wrong guess. Wing threequarter. Roland-le-Rapide was also very very fast on the heavy lumpy legs.

Perhaps, thought Richard, he should be feeling flattered, to be thought a suitable harness-partner for this the coming man (very much so in his own estimation, and it would seem in the eyes of Charlemagne) . . . Of course, Biron had prepared him, during the golfing sessions.

'We need long heads, Experience, pragmatism. You and I, we are not dazzled by ideologies. A Committee of Public Safety, yes, but without bombast . . . old-fashioned rhetoric . . .

'Younger men. Who will wait for their rewards, who will not snatch . . .

'Public recognition will not come our way, Richard, but it is the nobler path. At my initial observation of yourself – there, I thought, is a man above vulgar material prerogatives'.

Biron would be giving Maltaverne a good lunch (the thought made

Richard hungry) while establishing the doctrine of how not to snatch. But at the end of the rainbow would be a massive pot of gold.

'Opus Dei' he had said gently, with a breath of query in the words. A fly laid delicately on the water.

'Yes,' said Biron, reflecting. 'Oh blow, I'm in the sand again. They aren't to be left out of reckoning. Not the same here of course as in Spain. Always a difficult decision' addressing the ball, 'to balance the advantage of existing structures' – whack: still in the sand – 'and the disadvantages of being lumbered with the débris, one almost said the debré, of bygone days'. Whack. 'Wouldn't want to hitch SAC to our wagon!' Both men laughed. Not the Strategic Air Command, but a disreputable private army left over from the Algerian war.

The anniversary had just occurred, recollected Richard, of their climax in 1961, the Nuit des Noyades when some scores of dark-skinned folk had been tipped into the Seine. Coinciding with the anniversary of the Battle of Yorktown. Why can't we dress up a few hundred out-of-work film extras as cops'n'robbers, and re-enact the Saving of Paris from the Nigger Horde? He sniggered, swallowed a crumb the wrong way, coughed his eyes full of tears. They were taking their time, the pigs, swigging claret in La Maison Bordelaise while he was sidling round pavements with a hamburger.

'The Vatican is a spent force' after five goes at getting out of the sand trap.

'And how do we stand, regarding the Americans?' He had been the professor at golf but the eager neophyte in geo-politics.

'A good question: with the utmost caution, I should think. How long did *their* thousand-year-reich last? – thirty ... their incapacity to understand, the mediocrity of their public figures ... they're necessary, of course. Remark upon the present economic dominance however of the Japanese and ask yourself; how long will they last? We'll have barely time to plan, and put the structures in place. Alliances yes, but whose? This talk of our lack of strategic raw materials; much exaggerated. Our most precious capital is in grey matter'. Tapping his head with a putter. 'Getting as far as the green is all right, even quite pleasurable. Once on the green – madly frustrating.

'But recall – the name Charlemagne. He came so near. And Frederick of Hohenstaufen ... France, Germany, Italy: we belong together. And Spain we must have. These little countries, Richard,

110

England or Holland, we may leave to dream about the past . . .'

There they were at last, Maltaverne nuzzling a cigar; a slow straddling walk as though he had just got off a horse. Which, thought Richard, he has . . . They parted on the pavement with gestures of mutual esteem and affection. Monsieur de Biron strolled back towards his car. Was recruiting duty over for the day? How many of these trips has he made? Are there other interlocking pieces, arranged for mutual surveillance?

There was a clown parked up against his front bumper: Richard, unaccustomed to this vile car, spent a minute wondering where the reverse gear was, got stuck on a red light, lost his man, and drove round one-way streets for a tiresome ten minutes with the tell-tale making indeterminate noises. Like the reverse gear; he was unused to its little ways. He ran the quarry to earth in the underground dungeon belonging to the Hôtel de Ville. The car was empty.

Moot point. The municipal administration? The Bank of France? One of a dozen wealthy and self-satisfied corporations with a front on this pompous square over his head?

Perhaps he had been lucky enough for one day. Maltaverne! And would Biron mention these fine new friends, at their next meeting? He had no wish suddenly to find himself face to face with the bright fellow now. He got back into his box and drove it to the office. Where it did no harm to put in an appearance: now and again . . .

The office, thought Richard, could be left to its own devices. There was the entire criminal brigade, Castang in the lead, racing after that unhappy girl. Academic business. She'd been killed first or she'd been raped first and it would be insanity pleas all along the line: he'd eaten her and it was legal pathology as well as medical.

Salviac's bandits: causing him some concern, but he didn't want to think about that now.

Mister Biron, you're a pest. Cattle of your sort should be left to the political branch. Maltaverne made this different. The office was not a good place to think about this. Nothing here anyway but a lot of Economic Crime. Fausta was back and high time too – and with her the people who enjoyed economic crime. And whose job it was. He was going home.

And while driving home (in his own car, smelling just a little less

111

awful than that pool-wagon) he got an idea. How to get a grip on Maltaverne. It happened occasionally that the PJ was called upon to investigate a bent cop. And recently one of Fabre's inspectors who had uncovered a house-agency fiddle and left the dossier stewing for a month until the house-agent came to the boil, sidled into his office (a mistake, for Richard had the place bugged) and heard a nice clean little deal proposed to him: for fifty thousand in cash, liquid and immediate, the whole file would get put in the shredder. A deal snapped up instantly. Greed. Snatch . . .

Maltaverne was no ordinary bent cop, but something could be worked out. He'd go and have a chat with Fabre. But not today.

Judith was sitting reading, in a characteristic position, propped forward on a wooden chair, long bony thighs wide apart and elbows resting upon them; hands holding the book forward of her knees, glasses down at the end of her nose. Gardening gloves, gumboots, and secateurs lay about as usual in picturesque profusion. He tidied these automatically. Nothing said, nothing even thought. Too much had been said, and thought, too long ago. They had been married a long time.

One day she will die; this girl of mine, whom I love. I hope – but I feel fairly certain – that it will be quite quietly, keeling over off the kneeling mat on to the moist earth. The last bush cleanly pruned. Selfishly, I always hope that I will have gone before.

One didn't – as a rule – see her indoors a great deal, between April Fools Day and All Saints, unless driven under shelter by heavy and prolonged rain, but there, rules are made to be broken. Indeed Judith had no routines, which for years and years had been a source of heated friction. Policemen have far too many. This ghastly Spanish habit of not even thinking about supper before sundown; a trial, at times a breaking-strain. He was used to it now.

Whatever the book was it was work: full of slips of paper covered with her tall spidery handwriting. (Richard himself was one of those terrible people who massacre books; dog-earing, scribbling in margins – a cannibal not even above tearing bits out, of paperbacks.) She was a person too with the habit of having four or five books 'on tap', which hung about offensively, being otherwise unfindable. They were unfindable anyhow. Most unfindable of all were her glasses, and an agitated ghost would flap about wailing until the Detective was called in, when long practice would suggest 'kitchen drawer next to the potato-peeler' but the house was large and full of corners. Yesterday it had been the china mug in the bathroom where normal people put toothbrushes.

Nobody said anything: couples long married know, each, for the most part what is passing in the other's mind. A sniff or a sigh speaks three pages of prose. Why does one talk? To communicate? – too frequently the method is self-defeating. The insensitive need to talk, blunting receptivity with a blare of egoism, noise, vain behaviour. They indulge in this incapacity to receive, and transmit through the wasteful bombast of their own voice. Which they enjoy listening to.

Animals do not speak for they have no need of so crude a medium. The French talk far too much, said Judith.

'But you talk to plants'.

'Yes, but I don't have to do so out loud'.

However, people get ideas. Few of these are any good, but they need expression. The voice comes into its own, acquires value when not used for complaining, bullying, or a threadbare repetition of futile platitudes passing for thought. We are fortunate in these skills; speaking, and laughing. But the first is consistently misused. As are virtually all our clever tricks.

Judith's big bony hands (which sounds awful; their shape was beautiful) were expressive. They turned pages, twisted locks of her hair, arranged her long and invincibly shapeless skirt.

There was plenty of daylight left in a perfect September evening. With all three French windows to the terrace open Judith's house was full of outdoors, the woodwork of the living-room soaked in sunlight like a barrel filled with sherry. There are not many days like this in northern Europe. The frontier between north and south is generally taken to be the Loire in France, the Danube a little further east. Arbitrary: here was south of the Loire but distinctly still septentrional. It was her character, more than sun or soil, that made Judith's garden meridional. The ubiquitous rose is common to both. She understood roses (like the Empress Josephine, that nice woman from Martinique, who made such a good garden in the grey luminosities of the Ile de France).

She was thinking about Vera, whose garden was still non-existent but – northern woman – dreamed about the highly-coloured, violently

113

scented cottage flowers of northern gardens. Delphiniums and hollyhocks, wallflowers and sweet-williams, 'great masses of nasturtiums'. Things Judith had never thought of or condemned (wrongly, wrongly) as 'vulgar flowers'.

The book fell on the floor: she did not bother picking it up.

"Phlox," she said out loud, tasting the word, experimenting with it.

"Sherry," said Richard. He was in a rattan armchair, tilted upon its back legs by his own, which were on the terrace rail. Thus too he sat often in the office, pulling out different drawers of his desk to prop his foot on. Use of the top drawer, suspending him as it were above earthly cares, anchored (by hideous gravity) to only one precarious point of the earth's surface, teeter-tottering, was as subordinates had learned a metaphysical sign and a bad one. It was at these moments that he asked the rudest and most direct questions while staring at the ceiling.

Logically, or so one would imagine, he was thinking about Spain. Instead he was thinking of England. Along the way hither, about the French.

"The French!" he said with self-hatred, perhaps self-contempt.

"What have they done now?" Judith loathed the French! Xenophobe, protectionist – no, chauvinist – madly pleased with themselves. It had been a bond to find Vera did too, though her sense of justice added 'And so is everybody else!'

"No, it isn't the insularity. Why, the whole country is pickled in whisky. But they don't drink sherry. Why?" The English drank sherry in large quantities. True, those barbarians oscillated between drinking it warm and putting iceblocks in it.

"What are you shuddering for?" asked Judith.

"England – is it really a northern country?" She was used to these oblique approaches towards whatever was on his mind. She did not know much about the subject, but she was not a totally uninformed woman. Apart from gardening books, so expensive now and so difficult to find (those foul antiquarian booksellers cut them up, to sell the pretty coloured prints separately, thereby vastly increasing their already obscene profits) she was a student of history. Professor Braudel, Le Roy Ladurie, Georges Duby – the book that had fallen on the floor was Volume One of *Urbanism* . . .

"Danes all over the north and east. Saxons – I'm never quite sure

114

what are Saxons. But it's the being an island, isn't it?"

"You have to go back further. Britons – no, that's just Bretons, pot-headed Celts. Further."

"Windmill folk; Beaker folk. Nobody knows, I think, really." A deep grunt expressive of deep dissatisfaction came from the terrace.

"Vera says the climate changed. Fifteen hundred is it, B.C., or two thousand five? The Orkneys were temperate then, like the Scillies now."

"DOES she?" with great interest. A pause. "Where are the Scillies?"

"You don't catch me. I looked them up in the atlas. Daffodils, earlier than anyone else's."

"Kent – part of Brabant; no, Flanders. Probably isn't a person there in a hundred knows where Brabant is. The thing about islands is that they're insular."

"Majorca," agreed Judith. "Terrible place."

"Haven't been invaded for too long. People need invading now and again or they fall asleep."

"Like here. Hasn't been invaded properly since Visigoths. Incest. Needs new blood."

"At least they're Protestant. The English, I mean. Not, of course, like anybody else. But at least they flung the Pope out."

"If for the worst possible reasons."

"I'm thinking about corruption," said Richard, and Judith realised that this, now, was where his mind had been aiming all the time. Gassing about sherry!

"Do you want some sherry?"

"Yes, badly, and I'm too lazy to go and get it."

"I'll get you some," said his devoted wife.

"Tired?" bringing back the drink. Vera would have said (not catty really) that one must always allow men to explain it at some length. Women do not get tired: it is not expected of them. Life would be so boring if they did.

"No-o-o. Nor even worried really. Preoccupied perhaps a little; that yes." He remembered that she had laid eyes, that day, upon Biron. "Man who came to the house one day – you recall? Very grand and odiously polite?"

"Vividly. A bad man."

"Now what makes you say that?" interested: Judith's moments of extreme shrewdness were disconcerting but enlightened.

"A bad smile internally."

"I see. It's quite true." A wound that does not show, bleeding inside, is a bad business. A laugh of a similar nature is likewise an evil sign – to other people.

"And he was very rich," added Judith.

"True, I believe, but how do you know? – it isn't ostentatious."

"I don't quite know – there's a sort of insensitivity that comes from having too much money." Richard nodded two or three times slowly while tasting his drink, but Vera would have been on it quicker because Charles Dickens put it in a vivid metaphor. 'Gold conjures up a mist about a man, more destructive of his senses than the fumes of charcoal'.

"You help me," said Richard simply. "He's been attempting to corrupt me. Oh, not with a large bribe," laughing at her big alarmed eyes. "We've always had a mania for secret societies. I simply do not believe that in the north there's fertile soil for these never-ending intrigues. It's a Catholic thing isn't it – an Inquisition thing? We aren't talking about bent cops; they'll have plenty of them: a commonplace everywhere. . .

"Backstairs conspiracies. A trapdoor world is one of our Latin specialities. Nineteen hundred years of secrets whispered in confessionals. We're never happy without a Mafia of some sort, preferably with a cardinal on the committee." A gross over-simplification no doubt, but what's the use of complicating things (another French mania . . .)? Look at Northern Ireland; you could argue all night without getting anywhere, and wasn't it just snake and monkey in the same sack? The sherry had made him hungry.

"I could nibble on a biscuit," he announced. "What about supper?"

Judith was a good cook, once her concentration had been properly brought to bear upon the matter in hand, and her hand was light. Two 'elderly frugal people' (said Richard) had yesterday eaten half a duck. The other half of the duck now appeared as a lentil salad. Everybody knows of the revolting Spanish habit of putting in too much oil – if the toxicity doesn't kill you the taste will. Fewer appreciate a Spanish economy of means. Judith used real olive oil in the most grudging teaspoonfuls: it's a perfume, like saffron. The salad was quite lovely and Richard ended the evening in high content. She could sometimes be persuaded to play – a guitar competently – and to sing; quite well. A violin, a pianoforte; these are wonderful technical ingenuities, to the credit of our (on the whole pretty feeble) Christian civilisation, but a guitar is the gift of a people's heart, to its soul. We have been guilty, said Judith, of monstrous unmentionable barbarisms: we must now be very careful to put the tiniest stone or grain of sand back undisturbed as we find it.

'I'm too ignorant,' she added, 'properly to appreciate symphony orchestras. There's so much of everything'. She could have added – including toxic oil. 'But I do understand a song by Schubert'.

If there is nothing you can put in writing, and you find that telephones, like garden slugs, leave a shiny trail behind them, how do you get in touch with people? It is the obverse of the classic Don't-ring-us-we'll-ring-you. You had better believe in telepathy. Richard next morning said a little incantation, and instantly the phone rang. Castang – too much imagination there – would have made a sign against the evil eye: Richard simply picked the thing up.

"Biron. How long is this splendid weather going to last? To suggest some golf – would that be Ajax defying the lightning? It might be my last chance for a few weeks. I don't like Paris when it sizzles – isn't that Cole Porter? How it does date me."

"If I suggest tomorrow, will it then instantly rain? Lunchtime."

"Splendid then; see you."

Richard contemplated the telephone, gloating: was interrupted by Castang with his idiotic tales about Ham and Jam. They didn't sound comestible, but the tomato-ketchup advertisement says Pour it over Anything. Including Biron; it's known as blinding a suspect with bullshit.

It's just a Mafia, like any other. Political rather than financial but experience shows the two to be the same. Power, says the Mafia exactly like a bank, comes in the wake of a great deal of money. Acquire the power, reason politicians, and all the money you could wish for arrives in its train; a natural corollary.

You are invited to join the Mafia. Ride along as a true believer, gather a detailed dossier, turn it over to your superiors. Don't fall out

117

of character, meaning show no enthusiasm, and wait for Biron to get a bit confidential. There've been nothing but generalisations so far: We've got to keep hold of France. Clean up the Niggers; rubbish like that. Can't put this in a little pink memo to the Minister. He knows it already.

There is a formidable barrier to cross. It does not suffice merely to profess True Belief. Throughout your career you've made a principle of having no opinions. You are being probed, to find out your true opinions. Beware of playing the provocator.

He had reached a conclusion while cleaning his glasses. Get a bit of help; you'll need it. When it comes to shadowing people, and suchlike imbecile activities, you need a Detective. There's a very good case for keeping this to yourself and well away from the Police Judiciaire. The argument that someone's needed for legwork, and I don't mean playing golf, is likewise cogent.

There's nobody in this outfit, senior enough, experienced enough, I'd trust on this save maybe Castang. He has a talent for complicating things, and putting his feet in the dogshit; he's good though.

What about Maltaverne? No amount of make-up on faces or cars would stop that bugger from smelling a footstep-dogger within five minutes.

You could, though, put him to work following his own sweet self.

Richard didn't like any of this. It was tricky, and if he had got on in life it was through knowing when not to be tricky.

One would see. Invite Castang to dinner. That would be nice for Judith too. Nice for me as well: I'm fond of Vera. And Castang is a friend.

You are surrounded by four-letter men, Richard, and you've made few friends in your life. Forgetting about the conspiracies, and getting to work upon what happens behind the north wind, a friend is a good way to begin.

Wild horses, and even if it were a worn-out metaphor as Richard said he was still using it, wouldn't get Castang into a disguise. At the dinner last night, Richard had made him laugh considerably with a hilarious description of the Masked Avenger tracking down corruptible government functionaries: they'd both had a good deal to drink by then.

118

Judith and Vera hadn't been exactly behind-hand, either.

Maltaverne . . . with hindsight one wasn't a bit surprised. But with hindsight one rarely is. Interested was something else again altogether: he felt flattered at being taken into Richard's confidence this way, but not very happy at the prospect. If you asked him (not that anybody had) it sounded like a most unpleasant sticky business, and he'd have much preferred Richard keeping his mouth shut.

There'd be time to think about it, because this other job looked like the kind that would try the patience of Job: ah, these phrases with unconscious puns in them . . . The dinner had gone on till three in the morning, but next day was a working day for all that, and Richard this morning had been again very much the Divisional Commissaire and nothing was said about friendship.

"Right, you get your Japanese ferried off, and that's lovely, you've time on your hands."

"The mountain of paperwork doesn't count?"

"Tcha Castang, stop pretending to be bleary-eyed and wool-gathering – odd phrase that – you've people to do paperwork, I should hope." And the groaning Orthez had been clapped to the typewriter and screwed firm. "Now, Castang, what ideas have you on this subject?"

He had known he would get stuck sooner or later with those two infernal unsolved homicides: hadn't thought though they would arrive with such horrid speed. He made efforts not to be woolgathery.

"As far as I've had time to think about it at all . . . there seems to be only one firm starting point and that's the station."

"Yes?" encouragingly. He made a struggle against lethargy.

"Well, Maisonneuve's people sat about a lot waiting for someone to come hand them little packets of heroin, and I don't intend to start all that again."

"I should hope not indeed."

"Nor am I about to hang about Disguised."

"No . . . Well . . . Good, come to the point." Relishing the hit, which had undoubtedly been shrewd, Castang felt better, though not much.

"In the uh, cadre, of uh, a narcotics investigation, could we persuade the narcotics bureau to lend us one of those systems, you know, like banks? Closed-circuit television. There must be an office in

119

the building which we could borrow from the railway people and keep a beady eye on the doings."

Richard thought about this lengthily and then nodded.

"And we might even catch somebody with little paper packets. Not that we will, but they'll be hoping we might. Very well, where's our electronics expert? Fausta," picking up his internal phone "try to find Lucciani for me and send him in here . . . Where d'you propose to hide your cameras and things?"

"I don't know that one would need to, all that much – I'll try and explain . . ."

And here he was.

The big hallway of the station was (like the entire building) a riot of Victorian grandiosity, with Corinthian columns outside and caryatids representing Steam or Energy or whatever else fat ladies in a lot of classical drapery could be said to stand for. Inside there was a monstrous amount of stucco, refuge for a lot of insect life. Castang's point was that the Railway Board was busy with what they called modernisation, and was really the usual effort to cut the staff in half (known in France as Degreasing the Effective, which is jargon for slimming, and sounds better than sacking).

There was, and had been for a year, a hideous mess everywhere, excused by those perfunctory little notices saying We Regret any Inconvenience Caused to Passengers. There were piles of rubbish: there was also a great deal of scaffolding.

Now can we have some scaffolding in the hallway here, inconspicuous-like? And some tarpaulins? Better not say we're going to knock down that stucco – that might make people look up. Better say we're going to wash all those fat female faces. Better still – say nothing at all; why should we draw attention? Nobody ever does look upward in a railway station.

The narcotics bureau, delighted with this zeal, provided a great many tracking cameras, and were mum about the results of the experiment when it had been tried previously (slender, as Castang knew). However, the material was there.

"Lot of work," said Lucciani, grumbling as usual.

"Yes."

"Hardly worth it, is it? Meantosay, any fly boys pushing narcotics would have this lot rumbled inside twenty-four hours."

"Yes."

The tone was unforthcoming, and the subject better left unpursued.

Likewise grumbling as usual, the SNCF was persuaded to move loads of yellowed forms dating from 1910, great bales of computer-paper and suchlike rubbish, from an unused first floor office. There were notices on the wall printed in German, and exhortations to the populace from the Vichy government of 1940. Just shows you, said Lucciani; hereabouts they don't know yet about the Liberation. There was still a great deal of dust, but there was a big bank of television viewers along the wall now, covering the central Departures area and the bays on each side where one bought tickets, asked for Information, changed money, and so on. It would cost too much and take too long to have the cameras on rails, but this was good modern material, said Lucciani happily demonstrating for him: look, they're very flexible, and wide angle – here you can go right from the sweety-shop down the passage of the left-luggage lockers, and the other side back again to the bookstall. And with this control here – don't be dim, press the button – you can zoom in on any camera you choose. Look; Fat lady, scratching. Grandpa, wishing he hadn't put on his new shoes. Mum – can't find her ticket. But you can't get into the lavatories: not, said Lucciani, that I'd want to.

"No, no," said Castang. "So far it's a public place, but snooping in the shithouse is unconstitutional."

"But it's there if anywhere . . ." Yes yes, we know. A million francs, to catch two prostitutes and a pickpocket. Modern methods: wherever you see the word 'technology' you know that money's getting wasted. A lot he cared: the narcotics bureau was lavishly funded by the Americans anyhow.

He left Lucciani on guard through the afternoon, while he went home for a kip. There wouldn't be any action before nine at night: he'd be back after supper, ready for the evening trains in from Paris and Lyon and Marseille.

The dinner had been an enormous success. 'It's only paella' Judith kept saying (strangely elegant in those shapeless floating garments). 'Only': it was a very grand one, with a lobster as well as a chicken. "And clams," said Vera 'exclaiming'. And sausage.

"The fact is," said Richard enjoying her exclaiming, "you can put

121

in the dog's dinner and it makes no difference, just as long as the saffron's fresh." Castang could not get over his being a totally different person: it was as though the 'office-Richard' did not exist. Nor was it only the externals – 'Richard-without-a-tie', a thing scarcely imaginable and now here he was in a cashmere pullover; piratical. The face was completely different. And the manner.

"Mr. Wemmick," said Vera much later, getting ready for bed.

"He's a lawyer's clerk," went on the Dickens-reader "very tight and cautious and forever talking about portable property. And at home he lives in a little castle he has built himself, and even has a tiny cannon he fires every evening."

"I see perfectly." One would buy a tiny cannon for Richard.

There wasn't even any whisky. Richard, or so he said, had not needed to go to England to view drinking whisky before dinner as a French bourgeois barbarism. Champagne and a flinty white wine as Spanish as the sausage – very unpatriotic, said Castang happily.

"I've seen what being patriotic leads to."

But the real surprise came from the women who had decided to revolutionise police thinking.

Castang leaned forward: he was beginning to build up 'a collection of faces'. Lucciani before leaving had added further sophisticated toys to the collection. The first was the dingus that would put any sequence he fancied on videotape, to be played over afterwards for study if so desired. The other dingus froze the frame and made for you – if you pushed the right button – a still photograph. The Sony Corporation will shortly abolish policemen altogether, thought Castang. Wonderful. Roll on this splendid dawn.

The National Railways, having modernised Departures, were now making Arrivals disagreeable, and the incoming passenger found himself led by roundabout mazes, through a horrible tunnel, and popped out exhausted at a point a hundred metres away from any taxi: apparently with the ambition of making a comfortable journey by train resemble a beastly journey by plane.

The relevance of all this was that if he had wished to keep the whole area under surveillance he would have needed eight men, hanging around picking their noses, probably catching colds, and easy marks for any villains in the area. Anything better than that needed the kind

122

of elaborate stake-out everybody hated, being most uncomfortable and of a usefulness at best dubious. Whereas now, all by himself with the Japanese magicians (they would neither answer back nor suddenly hit him excruciatingly in the belly) he was like King Louis XIV with the whole of Versailles under personal control. All done by Lucciani with two technicians running up and down scaffolding which was there anyhow.

The one drawback to 'all this' was that if it produced no result he might get sent a gigantic bill from those frightful narcotics people for the use of their equipment, and the Controller would do his nut.

This did not send shudders up the spine the way it should. It had happened once before with a helicopter loaned from the army. Richard had sent them back an equally enormous bill for Labour (including Value-Added-Tax) and that had stopped their gallop. What would the hourly rate be for a commissaire? – on night duty too. Hey – there she was again. He was too slow, damn it, to tape her. She looked very young. Probably another Christiane F., thirteen-years-old-drugged-and-prostituted (sounded, and was, the title to a sermon such as made all cops groan like wounded cows). Pretty girl though, with a striking full face of the sort journalists would call sensual. A big fall of long dark hair. If she was waiting for someone off the Paris train why was she dodging about restlessly like that? Why not stand still like the others? Now she looked older – fifteen, sixteen? One couldn't tell, with girls of that age. Like all the others; jeans, a man's pullover much too large – the uniform that year, for teenagers. Nicely-formed bottom though. All right, I only remarked it passing by.

Dexterous as an eel among the people stolidly standing in good prominent positions, waiting to give the three classic formal kisses to Aunt Marguerite, who would put her suitcase down in everyone's way while returning them, leaving her umbrella sticking out. Here they all came, the ones in a hurry out to the waiting car, the ones with luggage wondering where the hell all the taxis had got to, the usual bearded Viking stopping to heave a monstrous aluminium-framed backpack on to the camel's shaggy shoulders; the belated ones trailing with the look of being absolutely certain they left something behind in the carriage.

Tcha, he'd taken his eyes off for a second, and she seemed to be gone. Foreigners, changing money – he watched that closely a moment. While they stood puzzling over it – one always somehow got

123

so much less than expected from the rate printed in the paper – was a notoriously vulnerable moment, in which the skilful robber collected passports, American Express cards, travel-cheque folders. A girl? Why not a girl? Who noticed a teenage girl in jeans, standing up close enough that no casual bystander detected the razorblade going effortlessly through the shoulderstrap of handbag or camera? But she was nowhere to be seen.

Oh well, she'd seen Pa or Ma or even boy friend, and undemonstrative as the young were had simply said Hallo. The car's over the far side. And led the way. No need or wish for all that hugging and What-a-heavy-bag-Dear.

He went back to the routine. Hundreds of people rushed for a quick pee or a hot dog, dozens more drooped or slept over half cups of cold coffee or beer gone flat; people gazed in anguish at the indicators because the southbound expresses stopped for barely two minutes, and that was hardly enough time for all the inadequately corded cardboard boxes, immense rolls of linoleum; skis – he could understand fishing-rods, mountain boots, great sausages of tent and sleeping-bag, but what could they be doing with skis in the month of September? Where were all these people going, and why did they have such incredible quantities of luggage? No old man now at the barrier to punch your ticket, knowing it all by heart, automatically putting you right. 'Toulouse? Number Five, last three coaches; you've got ten minutes'. Now only that horrible yellow robot which you had to feed your permit to, rejecting it disdainfully if you got it upside down. No such thing as a porter or a nice black man (on the London Underground) shouting 'Mind the gap', not a soul on the platform; nothing but that odious loudspeaker girl gassing away like a television announcer. Modern. Three languages, not that you can tell the difference. Mountains of information, except what you wanted to know which was how to get out of here.

Nobody buttonholed people in any sinister fashion, and least of all did they slip anyone any little paper packets or banknotes, not even dirty ones. Animation at Departures subsided slightly. Saint Raphael, Cannes, Nice, and Ventimiglia – what a lot of places there were to go to. At Arrivals there was a gradual regain of activity; more stolid watchers took up position. From Sète, Nîmes and Avignon, due in five minutes. And there she was again. No no, if somebody expected

124

does not arrive on the Paris train you do not anticipate that they will appear like Father Christmas saying I just had to go down a chimney in Avignon. Something here is not quite right, said Castang. This time he resisted the beginner's temptation to get close up; held the camera back in long shot to try and follow the pattern of her movements. Or was there any more pattern than that of a bee gathering honey? As the passengers filtered out she was hanging back, close to the exits; the pickpocket notion lost ground. She seemed content to observe, and her observance grew intenser as the mill slackened, and the thrusters, the anxious and the hurried filled with self-importance passed. Simple surely; a juvenile prostitute looking for a mark, and if she saw a likely 'micheton' she would follow to try and make the pickup in the car park. Her mark would be the elderly – or at least middle-aged and sufficiently flabby to be attracted to the very young: the un-accompanied, unencumbered, who has been to cinema or café and isn't in any great hurry. A person in fact like – Castang got up abruptly and whipped along the passage, down the stairs and out to the car park – there was a delay. You stupid clot Castang, you're slower than an old cow on its way through a gate.

Hopeless. The station car park, like most such that over the years have sprawled over more and more surface ground, had been sent underground. There were several ways down, either by the moving staircase to the shops and the walkway to the far sides of the square, or by spiral staircase straight to the car level, or by the ramps, forbidden to pedestrians but the French paid no notice. Down there were more television cameras, out in the open to warn off car thieves, muggers, rapists, flashers – she wouldn't try anything down there. Why shouldn't she though? Who would pay heed to a schoolgirl? The surveillance was casual anyhow. The machines for giving change, cancelling tickets and raising the barrier were perpetually on the blink, and the supervisor was obliged to do it by hand half the time. Such a large proportion of the population is busy with some petty fiddle for saving sixpence that there is even a name for them in the language: les resquilleurs. Or the people who will put chewing gum in slots, though he rather sympathised with them – they waged war against the machine and he wasn't sure they weren't right.

She was gone, anyhow. She and her protector, some big rawboned yobbo for the badger-game. Pay up, mister, or I call the cops for attempted violence on a minor. He would have his car above ground, in a nearby street or close to the famous piece of ill-lit waste ground where she would have steered the mark, dazzled by lavish promises of joys to come.

All this was so damned obvious. Why hadn't he thought of it before? More to the point – why hadn't Maisonneuve thought of it? So go slow. Test it for snags. Red herrings come all shapes and sizes. Go for a cup of coffee. Leave the cameras to themselves for a bit.

One obvious snag: why kill anybody? The 'micheton' once lured into the back of the car for a quick blow or whatever was on the programme was much upset, not to say abruptly deflated, by the sudden appearance of the accomplice.

After all, this situation is a classic, and is so for an excellent reason; it works like a charm. The mark is too flustered, scared or plain humiliated to offer much resistance. And were he the type to go to the cops and complain he'd been had, the story of a fourteen-year-old girl that she'd been driven into the bushes and 'interfered with' would keep his mouth shut.

There might have been a complaint or two. One could find out. Never followed up – a man coming to the police post with this sort of tale would quite likely be told he'd better go home and forget it, unless he wanted to lumber himself with a lot of grief.

Second snag: it didn't explain the woman who had been killed. You could counter this by saying that those two homicides weren't connected and never had been. He could have instincts: Liliane could have instincts: they were both nuts.

All this speculation is a waste of time. Make a forecast: prove it by demonstration. Nothing else is valid.

The loudspeaker warned him of another arrival and he switched his attention back to the cameras. The girl did not reappear. Either she'd made her mark, or she'd given it up as a bad job for this evening (the cinemas would be emptying soon and she would have other lurking-places depending on the time of night) – or she was totally innocent and had been there for some reason nobody knew about. She had looked very innocent: as evidence, it was double-edged. Castang decided that until his relief appeared at midnight he'd better do some work for the Narcotics people.

They hadn't split up, last night, into those terrible cliques, the men talking shop and the women clothes. They'd all done the washing-up

126

together (Vera being firm) before drinking coffee in the kitchen; cosier that way. There'd been five minutes when Vera had gone to powder-the-nose and Judith had disappeared mysterious, saying – Richard claimed – goodnight to her lemon trees. He had grimaced, sitting down.

"Ribs sore?" asked Richard sympathetically. "Japanese ... Are they more violent than we are? Is that just folklore? Buddhism upside down, as it were?"

"This Buddhist was upside-down all right."

"I don't know any Japanese," regretfully.

"I'll let you have this one free and welcome."

"I've known people who'd been in Japanese prison-camps." It was true – Richard belonged to that dim far-off crowd of oldies who had lengthy terribly boring war reminiscences. He looked so young – one easily forgot that he was past sixty. Could have retired – bloody near had, the year before, rather more suddenly than he would have planned. Hung by a thread for a few months: probably it had been new administration that decided to have him stay on. There'd been too many senior commissaires, prefects, heads of administrations through-out the shop that had asked for their pensions ahead of their time, feeling a bit over-tarred with the giscardian tar-babies. "Endless tales of maniac violence," he went on. "No I'm not about to reminisce. Tales about the moon. Anything in that?"

"I've no idea. We can look back, see if there was a full moon the night she was killed. Make a nice piece of psy for a defence lawyer."

"I'm just thinking. Violence all around us all day and night. We're saturated in it. We've acquired a very high level of tolerance towards it. But this Japanese is something extra. Comes as a shock. Killing her. Eating her. Leaves a mark."

"Left a mark on me," grumbled Castang. "Be green and yellow in stripes for a fortnight. Bit a lump out of my shoulder, too."

"Think yourself lucky it wasn't a carotid artery," finding it all much funnier than Castang had. "Here's the girl back."

"Do nothing," said Vera, "without girls." It was her perpetual theme; King Charles's Head, as she admitted herself when not being over-subjective. She had found an unexpected ally in Judith-the-Obscure (one of Richard's coarse English jokes that had to be explained) and a frontal attack was made upon Men. No, attack was the wrong word. Gritty and aggressive as she had been often during the last couple of years, tonight she was more her old self.

"It's terribly simple really. Every woman knows this: it isn't just me or Judith. But so few have it worked out or do anything about it. It's this; a man and a woman are inseparable. We can't have a man's world any longer. One has only to look at history to see how ruinous it has been."

"One has only to look around one now, and never mind history."

"But on the very rare occasions when the women had a say in what went on it was worse still." Helpful examples and suggestions were arriving from all over the room. The Empress Catherine of Russia being compared to Mrs. Thatcher, to the advantage of neither. 'The-Gandhi-woman' and the Pharaoh Hatshepsut. But Maria-Theresa surely . . . "Women imitating men," went on Vera unperturbed. "Not a good idea. Female characteristics – clearness of thought, power of decision and concentration, force of character – get perverted."

"Was it always like that?"

"Can't tell, can one? Nearly all the documents of antiquity are lost. Everything that survives is written by men. Highly prejudiced propagandists like Saint Augustine."

"The Romans in England," said Richard, "had a lot of trouble with a lady called Boadicea who fomented an insurrection. She's represented as a fearful bloodthirsty harridan whooping about in a chariot urging on the savages to massacre innocent Romans. The historical truth might be the total opposite. We know nothing whatever about Pre-Christian Europe except what Roman propaganda chose to dish up, and they were the greatest crooks going. Compare the filthy stories the Tudors spread about Richard the Third: the mud stuck for five hundred years. Tacitus mentions a lady named Veleda doing the same thing in Germany, meaning Lorraine perhaps. He was an honest chap but he had only Roman sources to go by. It's like trial evidence; sounds bad if you've nothing but the police case before forming a judgment."

"The whole point is that you've got to have a man and a woman working in harmony together," said Vera, "and is that possible at all when the one or the other is forever getting on top? I feel gloomy about the prospect when I look at the frightful old fascist ruling my household." Which turned the laugh on Castang.

Past midnight, he expected to find Vera asleep. But she was very much awake when he got home, sitting up in bed and terrifying – a modern Veleda. Was it the unliberated females who were so aggressive? But her smile was gentle.

"Would you like some milk?"

"I'm not really tired," taking off his shoes. "Nothing to do really but sit and stare at television sets. Yes, that's tiring; one can always turn them off though."

"I was thinking: about inviting them back; I mean here – do you think that possible?"

"Why not?"

"I've become good friends with Judith, but I'm still frightened of him. I was thinking chiefly about you though, and your relations in the office."

"He switches it off. He understands your Wemmick theory – at home he's a different person. I admired him, rather: it can't have been easy."

"Never had any friends, you mean?"

"Very solitary person, and secret by nature as well as profession. She hasn't always been a help to him."

"Like us, you mean."

"Comparisons," said Castang primly, "are always dangerous and I find here no real parallel."

"Mm . . . So it wouldn't be wrong, or humiliating? Tactless? You're always telling me how tactless I am."

"Oh yah," said Castang, getting into bed with a flop. "You have these fantasies."

"Make love to me then," said Vera, snuggling.

Despite the kip yesterday afternoon, Castang was yawning rather in the office; feeling slack. The reaction from the concentrated effort upon the cannibalised girl. Poor Lonny. Was she going to be no more than a 'classic case', a 'legal nicety'? The Proc, it reported, was not satisfied with Blows-and-wounds voluntarily causing death. Assassination. He would definitely go for a life-imprisonment requisition. As for the barbarism, he was prepared to admit that cutting up a dead body and eating bits did not fall under torture. But the rape was while she was alive; Professor Deutz was definite on the subject. Aggravated, all of it, in the worst possible sense. He wasn't prepared to listen to any insanity pleas and would take them to the cleaners, but definitely. And life imprisonment was going to mean life where he was concerned: if the court handed down anything else he was prepared to envision an appeal a minima from the sentence.

"Come come," said Castang "there's no appeal from the Assize Court; even a schoolboy knows that."

"Just showing that he's rather agitato."

"Talking already about the sentence of the court, and the instruction isn't even started."

"Pity the judge of instruction," said that personage, with feeling. Quite! A criminal instruction is 'à charge' meaning that it seeks to establish guilt, and 'à décharge'; must search for every element that could absolve. When the police evidence is technically sufficient to make guilt certain; mm, this blood in the drains, mm, I suppose we can call it conclusive . . . we're driven back upon this infernal stuff about Buddhism and moon madness, and the Proc will be whipping everyone up with tales about the commandants of prison camps, decapitating folk with ceremonial sabres: I don't like this at all, Castang.

However, He (the Procureur de la République is quite often, nowadays, a woman but this was definitely a He) has thrown some flowers in your direction. Compliments would be paid in court to the rapidity and efficiency of the police judicial enquiry.

"I don't want any compliments. He can say right now how sorry he is for my sore shoulder, and give me a medal, a promotion, and another month's holiday this very minute."

"Yes," laughing, "but you did nicely with the press too."

True: in its usual style of overblown emphasis the local press had been highly flowery. 'Abominable crime . . . odious violence . . . unmentionable barbarities . . . all the energies and resources of the Police Judiciaire . . . total determination of Commissaire Castang, Head of the Criminal Brigade . . . said with teeth gritted to our reporter . . . shall not go unrequited . . . Satan in our midst'.

Teeth gritted yet! Still, since he'd had a slight turn-up with this imbecile on the subject of Lonny's parents, they hadn't tried to be nasty. Anyhow, that pack of old fascists (the local paper, six months after the event, had still failed to come to terms with a Socialist

Majority) was in duty bound to thump their Law and Order drum.

He even had a paragraph of sober approval ('an affair rapidly elucidated') on the Judicial Affairs page of *Monde*. As Richard had piously hoped, a good mark for the department, and not before it's due.

Orthez was extremely gleeful.

"Maisonneuve is furious. Wiped his eye for him. Just because it happened to take place outside city limits, he says, we get all the credit for a job that was a piece of cake anyhow, and it's all a personal grievance." Orthez had some sort of informer over there; a drinking companion in fact, some earnest young inspector bucking for a transfer to the PJ, but careful not to say so too loud. Castang contemplated a 'quiet word over a pot' with old Riquois, but the 'confidences' Richard had given him – so far very summary, and there was plainly more to come – gave him pause. He took his heavy feet over to Fausta. Richard was fond of saying that the door was always open, but it wasn't necessarily so. However, there were sunny smiles, on both sides of the door.

"White water ahead," letting himself fall down in the chair.

"Breakers. Submerged coral reef. If it were just ruffled feathers needing soothing . . . but you're, you've got this private thing."

"Beat in the bush and not around it – what's inside it?" said Richard.

"Maisonneuve, making barbed comments about our Japanese deal. What's really up his nose, no doubt, is that I've reopened the file on that railway affair. He's heard or smelt out that we set up cameras in the station, he isn't duped by the narcotics bullshit, he thinks I've got something, or am up to something clever. I'm the cold spoon in his soufflé." Richard uncrossed his legs, crossed them the other way, did not look cross but was.

"Are you up to something?"

"No, least of all the wish to dip Maisonneuve in boiling oil. Pleasant thought but life's too short."

"Get anything?"

"A notion just barely within bounds of a possibility, no better."

"Mm, it's Riquois plainly, not averse to shoving a broken stick up Thingummy's behind; if by so doing he can also irritate us, why so much the more enjoyment."

131

"Right, and if I go conciliate he'll wonder what's behind it, Fabre will hear, and ask himself what's going on, which isn't going to help you."

"No, you did quite right to come and tell me. What are you doing?"

"Judges and stuff, Japanese trade agreement. Then sit some more behind my candid camera." Hoping in fact to do a little better, but keeping that in reserve.

"Leave it to me. Makes an approach towards Fabre that will serve as a convincing pretext."

"All right."

Commissaire Fabre, the head of the Urban Police, was a large man. Fat he wasn't; there was nothing soft or jouncy about his massive frame. Stout, or perhaps portly? – not quite right either: he had slow impressive movements and a pompous voice for the Prefect or the Mayor or any political commissars from Paris, and of course for journalists. Richard knew him better for, like himself, Fabre had been in this city and this job for a longish time, and they had enough in common to get on well together for the most part. He could be soft moving and rapid – there are fat men with light quick feet. And he could be a bear: when he seemed to be praying for mercy he was most dangerous. He didn't like being pushed into corners or harried. Not perhaps terribly bright but quite bright enough. About fifty-five, and unlike Richard still promotable. Not perhaps Paris but quite possibly Lyon. Centrist in his politics; a chap who knew how to reconcile his left and right wings – he'd do well in Lyon . . . But for now he was still here.

His office at headquarters was large and comfortable, in the old building, with high beautiful windows and a marquetry floor, and pictures on the walls borrowed from the museum's reserve; Italian masters a long way after Caravaggio, third-rate to an expert but impressive to the visitor, in highly ornate frames. Well-nourished Sienese or Bolognese women with fat babies. Fabre's family. He had a wife whose infidelities were known to him. His own were better concealed. Domestic harmony reigned. He had highly poisonous breath, and Richard wondered how it was that women did not seem to notice. He had a pipe, thank God, which helped. Richard's own cigars, Brazilian and also of a venomous nature, completed the necessary process of disinfection.

"Well, well, Hallo there," getting up – Fabre knew the value of politeness – coming out from behind the Louis XV map-table that served as desk (a fake, but an expensive and well-made fake) and holding out a solid palebrown hand of soft suède leather, dappled with leopard spots of a brown very slightly darker. "How are you my dear chap?" Cigars lived in a leather box got up to look like a book: drinks too lived in a cupboard pretending to be a bookcase. These delights were offered, in the knowledge that they would be refused; but it was more politeness.

"What I have to say is in real, absolute confidence."

"Shall we go somewhere else?"

"By no means." Tape recorders and lord-knew-what lived behind those false leather fronts that gave a warm cosy feel, and helped Fabre be a warm friendly person. Erudite chap he must be too, to have read so many books.

"Fact is, Paris is on at me, that tiresome way they have." Nods. "Wanting a confidential report."

"Been something of a clean-out in high quarters." Sympathetic.

"Had a scare thrown into them by all the nonsense in Marseille. So are there any S.A.C. men left over from the old private-bodyguard days? And this great wash of dirty linen surrounding those infernal princes." Allusion to a monstrous scandal of a few years before which the previous government had done its best to sit upon, without quite enough success. Creases appeared upon the face and the pipe nodded up and down. "It's not a job that has any appeal for me.

"While nothing would be easier, on the face of it, than to write a whitewash, it might not go over at all well and could be two-edged. I wouldn't welcome R.G., full of zeal, in our midst taking notes. And I don't at all like the idea of a witch-hunt, with barbed insinuations about the right-wing sympathies of so and so. In my service as in yours ... If there's somebody who we both feel would be happier with a posting to uh, the Pas de Calais, we'd like the suggestion to be ours, right? And not an expression of popular opinion in the Ministry.

"As a safeguard, it might be nice to have a co-signatory of a thing like this. Scylla and Charybdis – tcha, getting literary is a bad sign. On the one hand an imputation of collusion: on the other any smell of inter-departmental hints; a holier-than-thou attitude. You agree? – well of course, but do you have a suggestion? On the whole – since the

133

initiative is left to me – the right choice is all-important, and I'd be glad to know what you thought of Maltaverne."

Monsieur Fabre smoked and looked out of his big clean windows. When it became apparent that he'd have to say something he knocked his pipe a bit and said, "How well d'you know him?"

"Not well at all, which is why I ask you. Level-headed fellow, who'd understand the discretion needed? It's more how it would strike Paris than how it strikes me. It's no secret to you that my marks with the preceding reign were rather lacking in enthusiasm, which is why, we must presume, I've been thought of now. I've no intention whatsoever of being thought a pliant instrument. I'm quite clear;" said Richard with perfect truth, "any time they want to give me my pension I'll be delighted."

"Which is why" said Fabre "they pick on you now, if I may say so without causing offence."

"Causing offence!" laughing heartily "you know me better. They'll certainly feel that at best I'm a lukewarm kettle of fish: that doesn't sound quite right but you get the point. Zeal is notably absent. So that if anything I write is stiffened by somebody strong, who could legitimately expect advancement, my view of the matter is that a good balance would be struck in the opinion drafted. Do you like my choice?"

"Much more than if you'd asked me."

"That might have a bit of a smell, I was thinking, and that's why I didn't. It's what they'll expect, and taking them off balance a bit . . . We've managed over the years to fit in fairly well together; a fact noted over the years by successive Prefects, and that's one file which will have survived when others went into the incinerator at the change-over."

"I'll have a little word with Maltaverne," said Fabre, "and to avoid any notion he might get of a cook-up I'll suggest he pops over to see you. Open. Frank."

"I'm delighted," said Richard, "that the same idea occurred to you."

"He's young enough to feel flattered. Don't on that account flatter him any further."

"Need to flatter myself," laughing, "and haven't any to spare for others. Incidentally, and talking of flattery, you may remember that

134

file about the man in the car, near the station somewhere, that the examining magistrate made a fuss about?"

"Vaguely. Riquois after all is another specialist in absence of zeal. And his pension is safe. Man after your own heart!"

"Absolutely. Which is why no hard feelings. But Proc sent the file on to Castang, and he has to make a show of working on it. Like to feel that this wasn't too untactful. Meaning that Riquois doesn't have hard feelings about anything bar somebody pissing in the Muscadet, but Castang doesn't want to tread on Maisonneuve's corns, nor show more zeal than the Proc will think proper."

"I'll take care of that for you – and in return don't give Maisonneuve a bad mark, huh? Until I get rid of Riquois . . . Otherwise I'd never get any criminal-brigade work done at all." Fabre cast around for a suitable phrase of adieu. 'Remember me to your wife' didn't do with Richard: she was never displayed in public. His own wife, a regular at the Prefect's bridge table, caused on the whole more anxieties. "What about a drink some time?"

"That would be very nice. Shall we say," pressing the point of his nose with a pensive forefinger, "when I've had a chat with Maltaverne? Get my girl to ring you, shall I? Remember me to your wife."

"Of course." At least he's never been to bed with her, thought Monsieur Fabre, sighing at the lengthy row of those who had. We've got a little list: one not for the edification of the Ministry in Paris.

He has problems with his wife, Richard was thinking, wending his way back to the factory with no more zeal than was needed to shift gears with; and I have problems with mine – they aren't quite the same problems! But it makes for a bit of unspoken sympathy between us, that is real. All these hypocrisies . . . and all those infernal office politics . . . he sighed deeply. It would be nice to be honest for a change.

The light went green in front of him, and behind him a hurried man in an eager great six-cylinder hard-charger tooted impatiently: come on, Grandpa, wakey-wakey.

Fabre is basically a decent kind of bastard. One mustn't look at that terrible phony office, any more than one must get too close to his breath. He has kept to the elementary rules for cops, meaning don't-suck-up-to-the-Prefect, and keep your administration straight, and don't ever imagine yourself the Great Detective. Good at shutting either eye. Perhaps a bit too good at shutting both upon occasion. Well well, thought Richard, driving in the middle of the road to annoy the hard-charger, maybe he's less of a hypocrite than I am. Let a north wind come, and we'll both be swept away, and which of us will deserve it more?

Since coming back from England, I haven't been quite my old self, have I? Perhaps it is not too late to remember that I have a marriage too.

Castang was running videotapes of his fancy camera-work.

"All the same," Lucciani was saying dubiously, "a fifteen-year-old girl . . . seems pretty far-fetched."

"My dear boy," answered Liliane, "within the last week a man in Lyon was killed by a fifteen-year-old girl, and that one made the broadcasts only because television announcers, who are so up to date with what they call news, are always five years behind in their ideas."

"I'm not to know what happens in Lyon," uncrushed.

"No because you never read printouts which you're supposed to; or you'd know there've been a score like this all over."

"Anyhow, is she fifteen?" asked Davignon. "Looks more to me."

"It's this fanny-by-gaslight artwork. And is it important?"

"It will only be important to a judge, if we're right."

"Exactly," said Castang. "All that's important is that she should look fifteen to the mark. If there is a mark."

"Right," said Liliane, "suspension of disbelief."

"What Liliane's telling you," Davignon liked explaining things in a prim, scholarly way, "is that a television announcer treats the public as though it were halfwitted, and the public doesn't grasp it yet or really believe in it. 'That young!' they say. Shocked."

"So they ought to be shocked," said Liliane curtly.

"Who did the girl in Lyon kill?" asked Castang, who never read printouts either: there were far too many of them.

"Some business-man. Claimed he tried to rape her."

"I don't see that we've anything at all here much. I mean to build on," Davignon thinking aloud.

"It's very little," agreed Castang, "and very poor quality technically because I was so clumsy with the camera. What struck me was a sort of skill. The way she worked the crowd over; it had that practised look that gives them away. I thought straight off – a decoy for somebody or something. Pickpocket? – but there was nobody I could see catching her eye or steering her. Then I wondered whether she might pin a tag for somebody outside. Couldn't see anything, but I was too late anyhow."

"I don't see why there should be anyone outside. Direct pick-up," offered Liliane.

"Come off it, Lil, who wants to pick up a scrawny thing like that?"

"You're too young. No, I'm serious. You aren't looking for girls in the street. If you were you'd see plenty, semi-pro or pro, some of them looking very good indeed; take your choice. You're not interested in any teenage child."

"No indeed." Lucciani sounding heartfelt. "Knowing what they're doing and able to look after themselves."

"But men as they get older – sorry but I know what I'm talking about – have a thing for very young girls. Experience; a pro is going to give as little as she can for as much as she can get. Ten minutes, and about as much fun as a cup of coffee. Mistrust – is it clean, is it reliable, will it create trouble? Anything over twenty starts to look pretty shopworn to their eyes. And the vanity angle: they're getting old, fat and bald. If a young girl shows she still finds them attractive it seems irresistible."

"She's quite right," said Castang.

"You getting old, Dad?"

"Textbook: the older the schnook, the younger he likes the flesh. Being fatherly with a youngster: the psychological rôle is easier to play. Being gallant with a nineteen-year-old – they're frightened of the snub, that she'd laugh and say 'You're old, and fat, and ugly – and greedy': brings them to face themselves and that hurts."

"A very young one might still listen to Dad's war reminiscences without yawning."

"All right, you're convincing: then what?"

"Provide her with a mark," said Liliane.

"Who do we have that's over fifty, fat and bald?"

"Castang." Sniggers.

"I don't much like it: it's too obvious, and we all look too much like cops."

"You can wear a disguise."

"No."

"Richard then. At least he's got war memories he can tell her."

"You going to go and suggest it to him?"

"No."

"That's that then."

"Go and do some work," said Castang. "Liliane, you stay."

"Favouritism," said Lucciani. Castang waited until the door shut and said, "Do you think, seriously, there's something in it?"

"Yes, I do."

"Predicting?"

"I think I very nearly am."

"Tell me why." Simply – humanly – he was fond of her. There was no one in the department to whom he felt closer. It was not only respect for her hard level head or esteem for her never complaining. The heavy plain face and the sharp grey eyes in peculiar diamond-shape orbits showed qualities of intelligence and character. It took work to go deeper, but you found an extremely kind and plain-good human being.

"It fits so damned well. I've always believed those two cases were connected, as you know. I don't think that she tries a pickup, necessarily. If she hooks a man, and it works out that way, well and good. I think it more convincing that she behaves pathetic and down-trodden. Some tale of a brutal father or a family that threw her out. Beg a lift to some girl-friend's house. Who knows, there might even be a girl-friend. Why should we be certain of a man as accomplice?

"The psychology of it doesn't worry me at all. People say how can it be possible that a young girl could act inhumanly. I'd answer that humanity is a thing you learn, the hard way too, through experience. Children are inhuman, hard because they haven't learned love and sacrifice because they've never seen any, how can one expect them to present these qualities spontaneously?"

"If the enticement technique is the right one – and I don't see any other – who do you think would make a good mark?" asked Castang.

"Me," said Liliane. "And I don't see why we shouldn't have two to make the chances better. Maryvonne. Looks less like a cop than any of you." Castang thought about it. The young, redhaired junior in the department looked kind, too. And a lot more vulnerable than Liliane.

138

"Where is Maryvonne?"

"She's off. But I can get her in for this evening."

"Wouldn't it mean splitting up too much? We'll need everybody we can get."

"I don't see any weakening. We need two cars anyhow. If I'm right then the girl picks one or the other, and makes her pitch to get into the car. The other just follows on; no further act to be kept up."

"I'm going to be guided by your judgment in this, and I'll take the responsibility."

"I'm not certain at all. But I'm predicting."

"'Prediction'" pedantically "is the only sound basis for discovery."

A man that is born falls into a dream. Castang awaking from reverie with this phrase upon his tongue; it seemed to be part of a quotation but . . .; found Liliane still sitting on the other side of his desk looking at him, her face placid, showing no inclination to fidget. Reverie, dream; no, it had been a little better than that. An imaginative projection? A bit of crystal-gazing?

"I don't feel very happy, Lil, about this. Accept that it works at all, the odds against are heavy but we can say that is a familiar position to be in; it's putting you – and Maryvonne – at a considerable risk and I'm not convinced we can cover you adequately."

"That's only theoretically so. Forewarned is forearmed, and we'll be both."

"Very well. Dress rehearsal at six this evening; tell the others and do the planning."

Yes, it was a quotation from one of Vera's writers and the other half was 'one must oneself in the destructive element immerse' which sounded vaguely Germanic and romantic. He was too much so, or not enough. A good cop would not have immersed himself in the destructive element so far as to be frightened at what he was planning to do . . . or had he got the whole thing all wrong?

"It's Conrad," said Vera. "Stein in *Lord Jim*. Comment upon the young man who jumped off the boat because his imagination pictured a disaster so vividly that he forgot his courage. Won't happen to you – you're too French."

"Bit too romantic though," preparing to have a siesta.

"You've got to go out again, tonight?"

"Yes."

"I see," said Vera bleakly.

He wished he had said nothing about his own cowardice. It was not pleasant being a cop's wife at night, alone.

Vera had learned though how to immerse oneself in this destructive element. Castang is a good cop, Richard had told her out of his hearing, because strongly brigaded on the domestic side. He was a bit too romantic? Well, she was not so at all. Stolid pig of a Czech, she told herself.

Castang assembled his troops.

"Cars," he said. The PJ had a motley collection. The latest acquisition was a very grand BMW. The pride-and-joy in this was much diminished by the youth of France deciding that these things were disgusting bourgeois status symbols: there'd been a strong tendency lately to steal them and then set them symbolically on fire. Preventing these twin calamities had been taking up much too much of Orthez' time recently. He'd got altogether too possessive about it. However . . . There was an elderly but respectable and well-polished Mercedes. This seemed to fit Liliane's stage personality fairly well.

Maryvonne was a girl who spent nothing on clothes, never bought any, was happy that way (this was a different problem) but had a rather nice car of her own, a dashing Opel coupé – secondhand but smart – which was quite an object of envy.

"If you agree," said Castang. "Anything happens it'll come under barrackroom damages." But she had to be dressed to fit the car, and 'catch the eye a little'. She was peeled, protesting, out of those awful jeans and stood ruthlessly in her underclothes while the female wardrobe available was ransacked. A dressy sister-in-law of the right size was found and she was outfitted while Lucciani, who sniggered, was sent out to do a radio link: both cars set on continuous transmission to be received in the police cars, which would have the usual send-and-receive between themselves in addition to eaves-dropping.

Inside the station the cameras, with Davignon sitting behind them, gave a good visual control. The forecourt outside, obscured by cars, taxis, buses and all that folk eddying about, was much more dodgy.

140

Orthez and Rabouin (stolid soul, but conscientious) would have their cars ready to roll and see that the exits were not clogged. A couple of plain-clothes agents on the pavement. Castang himself would tag Liliane, and Lucciani Maryvonne. A code was worked out for the breast-pocket beepers they carried.

If Maryvonne refused to wear clothes, Liliane's problem, thought Castang privately, was that she had no dress sense.

"The most respectable and reassuring bourgeois exterior – remember the car. Nothing gaudy. Good quality but well worn." A large ugly handbag, genuine crocodile, was substituted. "That's better. The suitcase is good too. An umbrella – you can get rid of it in the car. And your heels look too high – can you run, in those?"

"Like a deer."

"Good, mustn't lose mobility. I'd like something a bit eye-catching on your lapel, diamond clip or whatnot. To have you a bit more wealthy, to make you a good target for a ripoff. Maryvonne, on the other hand – a bit too whory, dear: the velvet trousers are fine. Rings and a bracelet – is the pendant overdoing it? – all right, I'll take your word for it; just the hair a bit less extravagant." Satisfied?

"You're all well aware that this is perfectly ridiculous. Remains for us not to look more ridiculous than we can help so okay, we'll do the contingencies.

"The girl doesn't appear at all. Davignon gives us a negative beep and we try again.

"She's there but she doesn't go for any of the bait; has some nutty game with herself we haven't grasped. Nothing for that but to shrug and go home.

"She goes for bait but not ours. We're flexible enough I should hope to keep her tagged and see what it is she does play at, intervening if we see occasion. The girls, who are nicely dressed up, may find a rôle to play.

"Assuming I'm mistaken and she's just a crude pick-up, there's a chance she'll go for me. I've the spare key of the Mercedes, I change places with Liliane and she tags me. If I get taken off in the bushes how lovely, but don't let me catch cold out there.

"She thinks up something none of us have thought of – that's what the back-up car is for. Whoever's in the second car hold well back, and look for any boy-friends in the parking lot, possibly in a car of their

141

own. Our own cars will be recognisable from in front because of the defective headlights.

"Assuming a mark, be it one of us or anybody else, for whatever purpose, our tactic stays the same and is consistent. Be it nothing better than prostitution, and the criminal brigade sitting there, we hold back, for the chance of extortion, a staged rape, any of these teen-age tricks, because we get a beginning of execution for a legal proof or we've all wasted our time: we can't run anyone in on enticement alone.

"The girl herself may be innocent, or acting in fear, with an enforcer somewhere: we've seen nothing that wouldn't be consistent with either, remember. All right, who still needs synchronising? Comments, Liliane?"

"It's either a comic operetta, or it's likely to be dangerous for whoever," said Liliane. "If that turns out to be me I'm quite clear about it and I take myself in hand. Speaking for you too, Maryvonne?"

"Of course. And – well, we rely upon one another. And isn't that a very good thing to do?"

If two possible marks were better than one, then three is the choice on the menu, and Castang was 'rigged up' to look slightly less hayseedy, and a little more ponderous with financial cares. Nothing (said Liliane taking charge of this transformation in no spirit of reprisal) could make him a True Believer in Marketing, but a production-line look had been achieved, with a flash suit of Davignon's (nearest to his size), a silky highnecked pullover from the bandit-brigade, and a new hairdo accomplished with giggling from the girls. Nobody had a brief-case, but in the office of the chief inspector who dealt with Economic Crime a kind of Gladstone bag was found of pale polished calf: very suitable, as he remarked himself, for the smuggling of gold bricks to Switzerland.

He stood now in an inconspicuous corner of Number Three Platform, with the girls further along, mingling with the ragged group of oddities preparing to board the southbound train: earnest ones who rush to the extreme front, thinking that will get them there quicker, and crafty habitués who know which carriage stops closest the exit: belated and flustered souls with angular parcels, and the usual fat woman in a fur coat who will have to be bunted up the steps from behind. A fur coat – in the month of September . . . twilight was

142

turning to darkness and the soft drizzle, not enough to wear a raincoat for, was making a pretty, fuzzy halo for the harsh sodium lighting up at the end where the Steam Age glass marquee on its elegant cast iron pillars came to an end.

The loudspeaker-girl was droning through her fulsome patter about buffet cars and Ambulant Service, wound up to her terminal flourish 'Attention s'il vous plaît, ce train entre en gare', there was the serpentine ripple of expectancy, the big diesel slid majestic and oh-so-slow down upon them in its whale-like gliding gait, and there was the soft gong-chime of an Arrival: High–Low: High–Low.

There went Maryvonne as arranged among the first, gaudy silk scarf of cerise and navy blue, black shiny hatbox, earnest and competent. Liliane in the middle of the ruck, defended from jostling by that massive impressive handbag and overnight case to match; solid indestructible prewar stuff (inherited from her mother!). His turn, timed after the ruck but before the stragglers who had been asleep or were pessimistically struggling into anoraks. It was all routine. Nothing would happen.

Yes it would. Eep, eep, eep, went Davignon's signal just north of where his heart began at once to thump. He swallowed, gripped himself, changed hands upon the bag which suddenly felt heavy though there was nothing in it. As though he were the Doctor, come to bring a baby for Mummy. The phrase 'in the bag' acquired a meaning. In fact several. He stalked pompously along the tunnel through the smell of wet umbrellas and catpiss. Nothing to be seen; he accelerated past the greeters and through the swing doors. Blessed fresh air. He peered anxiously, crossed the roadway where nervous cars were accelerating brutally to catch the green light at the end; crossed the brief queue where a man was already tapping his foot in irritation at taxis not coming quick enough; crossed the bus corridor. At the ramp of the car-park a man with a magazine dropped it and picked it up, straightening with a jerky gesture of the shiny cover towards the surface park. There were only a couple of score slots on the surface, and their transport had been arranged at the end of the rush hour, as gaps appeared. Something had happened, but he did not yet know what.

He stopped short of the BMW and began to search leisurely for the keys in his trouser pocket, because Orthez was out at the other side, breathing on chrome and rubbing with a paper handkerchief, fussy at an imaginary dint in his good new lovely wagon. Castang stopped to unhook a paper tucked under the windscreen wiper, saying All Stocks Must be Liquidated – Giveaway Prices!!!!

Liliane was unlocking the boot of the Mercedes, stowing the overnight bag with housewifely neatness, and yes . . . The peacock feathers had caught a cold careful eye. Castang had never been fishing in his life, but remembered suddenly a twilight evening years ago when he and Orthez made an interesting find in a shallow reach at the bend of a little country river, and Orthez nearly caught his fingers in a murderous triple-hooked, triple-barbed pike-spinner whose tackle had broken off, and left the horrid thing there trailing in an eddy. A bright steely glint that would tempt the greedy toothy jaw to gape and snatch.

But it wasn't surely . . . Standing next to Liliane as she slammed the boot shut was a girl, certainly but – podgy thing, pasty-faced in the street-lighting, stringy fair hair; shapeless pullover of a vile emerald green. Huh?

Then he saw her, flitting round the bonnet with that neat agile walk – unmistakeable, as Liliane (stupid but natural) tried to open the driving door with the key upside down. The girl's face split in a beaming smile. 'Ever so kind of you' she was plainly saying.

"Neat," said Orthez softly as he got under the wheel and the ready motor caught and idled. "Hurry up." Castang flung the ghastly bag on the back seat. There wasn't any hurry. Liliane was smoothing her skirt, not wanting to get it creased. The girl – seen again in the flesh not pretty but gay, engaging, reassuring – got in beside her, tossed the long brown hair. Green fatty got in at the back. "Neat," said Orthez again.

"What?"

"Peppermint syrup there – it's perfect. There's always a plain one with a pretty one. The accomplice, but it adds to reassurance." As Liliane slammed the door her microphone came alive. A slight puffing as she heaved the safety belt and buckled it on her sturdy body. She's being a bit too leisurely, thought Castang with impatience. We're in position: move, or you'll make us look stupid. But Orthez' imitation of a fusspot driver was perfect; clicking the light-switch through all its different positions to make sure everything functioned, even the foglamps. Bourgeois trog, self-important. He let a couple of cars go by as he drifted into the traffic. Liliane was a good, careful driver and her nervousness evaporated with something to do.

"Are you sure it's not taking you too much out of your way?" A light high voice. Childish, but one could not trust the distortions of the metallic loudspeaker. It would be softer, gentler in reality. Polite and 'nicely-spoken'.

"Not much," said Liliane "and I'm glad to see you home safe." Maternal.

"It was ever so silly but my mate and I spent our last penny in the pictures and then she'd lost the little folder, you know, with the bus tickets. Thought we'd have to walk, but it's ever so far. So we plucked up courage to ask. Hoped you wouldn't mind."

"You were quite right. Saint Just's too far to walk." Sensible; letting them know the direction.

"It's just a bit beyond, ackshally – that won't matter?"

"What's a minute more or less?" comfortable.

"I think it's horrid – ten minutes to walk to that ol' bus terminus, and it always pulls out just before you get there. And it's always raining," selfpityingly. But it was good.

"Not much to do, out there, of an evening."

"Bugger all but the stinking telly. Oo, can I turn on the radio?"

"I'd rather you didn't," came Liliane's voice, calm, "but I don't think it works anyhow."

"Nice car," as though to console: no radio, poor her.

"It's a bit old but it's solid. Like me. D'you have far to go, to school?"

"Oh school . . . don't talk about that, it's a bore. Or sorry – you perhaps a teacher?"

"I am in fact, but how did you guess?"

"You asking. But you have that look, if I'm not being rude."

"Not at all," (a bit too pleased with the disguise). "Do I go left here? – I don't know the quarter all that well."

"The bus does, but straight on is quicker and left at the next lights."

"You lived out here long?"

"No-o; not all that long." Prudently, Liliane did not press it.

"You all right there in the back?" Peppermint bullseye had not uttered. There was a masticating sound as of teeth getting unstuck from gum.

145

"Yes thanks." Castang picked up the hand mike.

"You all right, there in the back?"

"Sure," came Rabouin's placid tone. "Following handy directions, about four cars behind you."

"Nothing in between?"

"Pretty sure not."

"We'll turn off then, just in case. Been little lamb far enough and you can move up. Maryvonne?"

"Shit," said Lucciani's voice, "she won't hear you: her post's set to transmit."

"Can't be helped. She's probably keeping radio silence so as not to confuse us."

"Saw her behind us a little way back – she isn't lost."

The Mercedes was cruising through the long, untidy suburb.

"Know this part of town?" interjected Castang.

"Approximately," said Orthez.

"Don't get us lost."

"Comes out on that long stretch by the north fire station," Lucciani, whose mind was stuffed with useless information.

"I know it," grunted Orthez, slowing for an abrupt left turn.

"Helpful for once," said Lucciani sarcastically.

"Don't want to get too close," came Rabouin's voice. There was no traffic on the road but themselves.

"I don't know this road," said Liliane, sensing embarrassment.

"We're almost there." The girl's voice had an odd high note as though gleeful. "Crossroad there ahead will bring you straight back – that's the main road, see? This was shorter. Left here and this is it."

"Attention," snapped Castang. Orthez who was on the crossing shot the red light and accelerated in the turn.

"Where do you live?" asked Liliane politely.

"Don't bother – here," in a voice suddenly loud and sharp.

"I'll just turn the car around," unable to stop herself sounding breathless and nervous. The gearbox gave a loud squawk and the motor revved noisily.

"There!" said Castang but Orthez had already seen the police car at the corner. The doors were open and Rabouin and Lucciani both running. Their own car skidded roughly on the right angle and mounted the sidewalk. Liliane's hoarse scream of alarm and pain

146

came tearing distorted from the speaker as Castang stumbled and half fell on the kerbstone. Orthez had had to stop abruptly: the Mercedes was broadside across the narrow street.

'Avec des si on construit Paris', say the French: with Ifs one can do wonders.

Perhaps if Liliane had not acted the conscientious driver quite so thoroughly, and left her safety-belt undone. Or, in a well-meant effort to gain time, had not tried to turn the car too hastily, showing the girl her sudden awareness of danger.

If Rabouin had driven the car a little further than the corner – by leaving it where he did he narrowed the right-angle bend too far for Orthez to take it swiftly. If the damned municipality had not decided to smarten up the street with a sidewalk, a ridiculously high curb and horrid little flowering prunus trees. If Maryvonne had not been deprived of a radio receiver, and had consequently arrived a few seconds earlier. If Rabouin, grabbing the fair-haired girl and pinning her by both elbows had not spun her round, timing it exactly for her to lash out with her feet and catch Lucciani in the crutch. If there hadn't been a footpath between the houses at the bottom of the one-way street. If that damned girl had not been able to run like a deer. If Lucciani, the only one of them who knew the district in detail, had not been the one staggering about holding his crutch. If Castang had not ricked his ankle putting his stupid foot in that goddam gutter. If the subsequent confusion had not been greatly increased by nervous householders in the street thinking that a latenight television serial was in progress, turning on lights, running about in pyjamas, yelling a good deal, enjoying themselves greatly, phoning goddammit for Police Secours – which arrived in a station-wagon with horrid speed . . .

The balance-sheet was a defeat for the police judiciaire.

True, they had a prisoner. True, they had avoided loss of life and any grave injury: Liliane's broken collarbone was the sort of thing you got, said Orthez comfortingly, falling off a horse. True they had a solution – of sorts, to a homicide enquiry and perhaps two. But the girl had got away and they'd lost Maryvonne's car – doubling back in those crooked little streets she'd come across it, standing handy there with the key in the lock, and caught up this bonus in passing. Nobody said or thought it was Maryvonne's fault, but she was a bit shaken, crying rather and first-aiding the unlucky Liliane, who was cursing her own clumsiness in a dry hard little voice between clenched teeth.

Orthez, finally the only one of four men and two women unhandicapped by one nonsense or another, might perhaps have caught her, being quite speedy, if he had concentrated on pursuit, but he had been held up for a fatal second by being on the wrong side of the Mercedes; distracted by seeing Liliane slumped half out of the driving seat, stunned by the blow that had not, mercifully, hit her on the head, but he had thought her badly injured and – he admitted ruefully – like a cretin had dropped on one knee and drawn his gun instead of sprinting. To the flitting shadow between those 'farting little trees' he had shouted stop-or-I-fire without producing the slightest effect. He'd been sensible enough not to fire, but not sensible enough to chase, without all that bullshit of giving a fugitive proper-warning. When he did go racing down the unlit footpath where the locals walked their far too numerous dogs, all he succeeded in doing was to tread in a lot of dogshit and take the wrong way at a fork.

"All rather a sorry business," said Richard. "I would have been very tempted to bellow at those two goofballs, but for being such a clothhead myself."

"We were all that tiny bit over-anxious, because this girl doesn't leave witnesses alive to tell tales afterwards," said Castang.

"You've got, though, a witness."

"Not only that but we'll have this other – child I suppose I must call her – by nightfall."

"How are all the invalids?" asked Richard dryly.

"Liliane's okay; a clean break: we had her vetted of course and strapped up first thing at the clinic in Saint Just. Pretty sore for a few days and she'll be unserviceable for three weeks. Lucciani is going on about his balls which were exposed to the derision of out-patient nurses. She didn't catch him square on – forty-eight hours off and he'll be right as rain. If the kind enquiry includes me, then the ankle's a bit swollen but it's nothing. Vera wound it in a bandage soaked in Synthol and I just look stupid going about in one shoe and one slipper. Be all right in a day and I look stupid anyhow: I've little margin for self-pity."

"Get Maryvonne's car?"

"Patrol picked it up this morning in the centre of the town. There are fingerprints – not that we need them; it's watertight. No damage – she threw the key away just to be spiteful but hadn't even stopped to rip the seat cushions. Remarkably cool customer but it gave her a panicky moment to realise the cops were on to her."

"Exactly what happened to Liliane?"

"To give us time to close in she'd thought of a manoeuvre – to make a three-point turn and keep the car rolling, as soon as she saw she'd been led into an unlit street and this was it all right. She was ready for the girl behind, but whatever it was – something heavy, flexible, we'll find it, must have chucked it in the bushes there around – it was passed to the girl in front, who couldn't get a good swing at her luckily, with the car turning and being a bit off balance, and Lil took it on the shoulder. Girl jumped out on the right-hand side, wrong side of course for Orthez, and ran like smoke. Knew the street perfectly; they must have picked it for the caper. Hardly lit at all and people there go to bed early."

"You think she lives out that way?"

"No I don't. No problem; all they need to do is go a ways along the main road and pinch a car. In the other cow's carrier bag we found a tyre-iron."

"Have you thought of the implications of all this?"

"Except that we plainly were lucky – we could have been watching the station or anywhere else for weeks. I think it likely that we'll end by tying in two or three oddities that got classed as accidents. There was a fellow a month or two back whose car fell in the canal."

"I've been thinking along these lines; and I don't like what my thoughts have been telling me. All right Castang, go – limpingly – upon your ways. And be grateful it was no worse."

Without his invalids he was short-handed, adding to his self-pity: here's poor me with my poor kaput foot: he was touched when his door opened and Liliane appeared with her arm in a big white sling, a beaten-dog expression in the eyes and rings under them, but much determination in the jaw.

"You ought to be at home at rest."

"Maybe I can't jump about, but I'm blowed if I admit I need cuddling when this was my fault, so whatever I can do I'm going to do, even if it's only answer the phone."

Castang not going to admit, but much comforted.

149

"You can think for me, since I'm so bad at it. You properly doped?" She grinned at that.

"The fuss they make. Ask for a pain-killer and they give you something with a bit of codeine and a trace of phenacetin as though it were morphia, and practically make you sign the poison book. Asked solemnly if I had kidney trouble!" Castang, who had been persuaded by his wife to swallow two aspirins (he had furiously resisted lime-flower tea and had three cups of coffee instead) felt cheered: it was going to be a good day after all. "Stuff," finished Liliane crossly, "that's on free sale in all the other countries of Europe."

"Ban instant coffee, fluoride toothpaste, and white bread."

"Yes, if I buy a packet of biscuits they've Additive A 357 in them and what's that?"

"You're exactly the person I need," happily. "Davignon didn't waste all his time last night. With his little candid camera he found some clown pushing, ho ho. That's to say money changed hands. Sensibly he did nothing but followed the fellow to a pub and lo, there's a flourishing little traffic."

"Heroin or hash?"

"Neither, it's pills. I'd like you to find out. Even if it's trivial we can build it up – there's all that expensive equipment borrowed from the narcotics bureau and if we can justify it with a pompous report and maybe break a network . . . ."

"I see, but it's Davignon's thing, no?"

"I've other uses for him. Here – a lot of literature on the subject."

Rabouin appeared, penitent – another one who hadn't been very bright and was now being zealous to compensate.

"Made a find. Had to crawl about in a lot of bushes, but had the feeling she might have ditched it around there."

"Did you get very wet?" asked Castang happily. It was pouring rain outside: there was something to be said for having a sprained ankle.

"Yes." Laconic.

"Conviction piece, very nice," pushing it about on the desk, "What's inside, shot?"

"My children made something like this at school," Rabouin had two little girls. "Cut out two bits of material in the shape of a dolly, stitch them together, fill it loosely with raw rice. Flops about but it sits up; got weight and balance."

"This feels heavier than rice," hefting it.

"Ball bearings or something. Pretty carefully made." A piece of soft leather from the upper part of a boot had been wrapped and stitched on a cobbler's sewing-machine after being filled with steel pellets. A 'pacifier' of the most dangerous sort.

"No wonder it broke Liliane's collar-bone," said Rabouin.

"You'd kill somebody with that, very easily. So easily, probably they killed the first one by accident. And found out how simple it was. Like trapping a mouse. Tock, its neck is broken. Just don't hit your own fingers," thoughtfully. "Bring it to the lab, Rabouin, and then to Professor Deutz at the Pathology Institute. Show him the photos of that man and woman and ask if it's consistent." It would be, Castang knew in his heart. There is no mistake. It was watertight last night, but it has to be inexorable, for a tribunal. A tribunal for minors . . . he sighed.

Orthez entered, sulky.

"Well, have you interrogated your suspect?"

"Just sits there like pudding. Won't utter. Can't do anything about that. Minor! Knows it, profits by it. 'You can't touch me, I'm a child'. Have to ask the Proc for permission to dispose of it – much too hot to handle. Refused to let the doctor look at it; what the hell am I to do? – I gave it breakfast and it threw it at me, and then said it was hungry."

"Give it another breakfast. We've got to find its parents."

"If it has any."

"Good, first you ask the commissariats whether any missing children are reported."

"I already have. Nowt."

"Then we do it the hard way. Photograph, and with the description Lil will give you, you and Davignon and Maryvonne go round all the schools."

"We've the stills off the television."

"Right, I'd forgotten. A schoolteacher somewhere will recognise those two; they're both under sixteen."

And the other one is loose, somewhere in the city, and knowing the police are after it. Good, we see Richard.

Monsieur Richard had finished the local paper, which had a dinky little paragraph about dangerous malefactor arrested after high-speed pursuit: a second evades capture. He was now deep in the Paris paper and *Libération* lay ready to hand.

"Well?" without looking up.

"Routine is set afoot. What's the hot news?"

"The hot news," said Richard, laying *Monde* aside, "is that the former principal commissaire of the town of Carcassonne was caught with a hundred bottles of whisky in his car on the border of Andorra." Castang burst out laughing.

"A perquisition," went on Richard, reading "disclosed over a thousand bottles of whisky in his cellar. He's been doing it twice a week for months." Castang holding his sides. "Further implicated – and jugged – is the departmental president of the lemonade syndicate who also happens to be president of the local rugby club. In Carcassonne this ranks as the sensation-of-the-year. What are you laughing at?"

"The Head Lemonader" – it is the French word for anyone in the bistro business – "and the Former Commissaire" wiping his eyes.

"Yes, it's the perfect piece of Midi folklore," said Richard, not laughing. "He jumped a customs' barricade, and somebody described as a crack shot knocked the tyres off his car: it's 'Gangbusters'. Where's Dutch Schultz? Hilarious and why? Because we say a thousand – five thousand – bottles of whisky, even made in Andorra and probably deadly poison, is a small-fry fiddle and therefore laughable."

"Not that small-fry. Two hundred a week, let's see, that's ten thousand a year. Give him a profit of twenty-five francs a kick – that's a quarter of a million francs. Typical that he was caught for being greedy. Get someone else to make the run for him, for fifty per cent, he'd have been safe. He just couldn't bear to let go of that lovely gravy."

"That's the way you'd play it?" with a nasty sarcasm.

"That's the way we've been taught."

"That's a fair comment. Hm, the 'former' commissaire: he was fifty-eight: we conclude that he'd been caught out previously and asked to retire ahead of time in exchange for not being prosecuted – you see how one thing leads to another? All right; what d'you want?"

"This girl – she's on the loose."

"Out of doubtless misguided sympathy for yourself, no comment."

"She may hitch-hike out of this and try to hole up in Paris or somewhere – when I get a proper photo I put her on the telex. Or she may sit tight here: I can't judge of her mentality. I'd like it if the bandits could help pick her up; I'm lamentably shorthanded. Assuming something better is needed than a sweep through the amusement arcades, can Salviac help me on this?" Richard grunted, nodded, and went back to sociology.

At lunch-time, his foot hurting less, he got a shoe on, limping about gingerly and making faces, but walking, he thought to entertain Vera with the Commissaire-from-Carcassonne. A future for Castang. Not anything idiotic like smuggling whisky from Andorra. Something legal; he couldn't quite think what for the moment but would come to it. But Vera didn't laugh, any more than Richard had.

"Come; have you no sense of humour this morning?" Humourless? The accusation was unfair. A helplessness, yes. But to take refuge in, these acrid sarcasms that were the cop's protection against his own sense of a hopeless, senseless task – that was not her notion of humour. One could do better. One should, at least, do better. Why else had she been enrolled? Her contribution must surely be something more than to laugh at their sour sidelights upon their own condition. Why else had Richard taken the step, and no exaggeration to call it an extraordinary step, of inviting her to his house? It hadn't been an ordinary social occasion.

She had always been frightened of Monsieur Richard. She had only met him once or twice, and only 'tête à tête' upon one occasion, when she had been in childbed with Lydia, and he had appeared (sudden, disconcerting at a moment when she had felt too drained and sleepy for anything much but to lie there and grin feebly at his jokes) – but she had been much more touched than she could express. She had not seen the hard and secret man who was the Divisional Commissaire and her husband's direct superior, on whom so largely the job and the career depended; but a kind and gentle person who had come to see her for no crooked ulterior motive, with none of that dreadful maziness about him (how could they ever be honest when their thinking and reasoning ran in such subtle bypaths?). He had told her with perfect simplicity, albeit sidelong, between two jokes, that her man was a person he respected and valued, and that he understood the rôle she played in making him so.

But she was still frightened of him: this was the same man – the next

153

time she saw him – who had kidnapped and held prisoner and tortured that unhappy woman Alberthe de Rubempré; a man reckless and ferocious and unpredictable as a wolf.

She too had been kidnapped – on the face of things as a kind of exchange pawn for Alberthe: it had been more complex than that and she had not really understood much. Not unnaturally, for though not physically maltreated she had been brutally seized. Orthez, good man lying there on her living-room floor, struck down trying to protect her, dead for all she knew, and she anaesthetised and put on a stretcher and carried away in a phony ambulance. Kept in a cellar knowing nothing, understanding nothing. She had seen Alberthe kill a man before her eyes. She had seen Alberthe try to kill Richard, before her eyes and everyone else's. It had left a trauma. Richard had not come well out of the matter, even when Henri had tried to explain. How could she feel anything but fear for that man? At the least a cruel, vicious man. That he had other and better qualities was certain, or Judith, that sensitive woman, would not have gone on living with him. It was all too complex, and better left alone, for fear of injuring Henri. She had not dared make any approach until this sudden impulse had led her to go and seek Judith out.

And then the ogre had invited her – specifically, not just Henri – to his house. For dinner; a business of best frock and party behaviour. Why? Henri had no idea. Said simply that Monsieur Richard was at all times a complicated and unexpected character; that one would obey; that there was no evil or crooked design.

It had helped, to have been in the house before, to feel allied (no, not secretly) to the woman who lived there (how ridiculous ever to have thought Judith bizarre, or neurotic; 'weird' – the foolish things people said . . .) But she had been horribly in awe of the house's master. She told herself in vain that she was an intelligent and balanced woman, of at least some education, experience and what Henri called bottom (character, judgment, resource). She knew herself to have simplicity, an absence of vanity that could avoid the traps of sophistication; the French mania for over-complicating everything, thinking themselves cleverer than anyone else (yes, they were cleverer: what good did that do them?). The man was not evil. Very few people are truly evil – she had not been for two years a prison visitor, until sacked on the grounds of over-sympathising, for nothing. The appalling background and heredity of some has asphyxiated the humanity in them; good has been overcome by evil. But it is relatively rare. Nearly always the wickedness is a perversion, a drugged dependence upon selfishness, greed, lust or envy, and vanity most of all. Don't talk to me, said Vera, about drugs and vices. They are all small affairs. Vanity is the big one.

Fear lasted only until Richard himself appeared, ebullient. She held her hand out; he kissed it and said, "I'm more pleased to see you than I can say. Come and have some champagne." That excellent chemotherapy against pride, self-righteousness, priggish puritanism and dogmatic justifications (diseases that Vera felt she suffered from).

"I have been frightened," she confessed.

"Of me?"

"Of the wolf."

"Ah. The wolf. They do not, you know, attack women or children – or only when they feel trapped."

"And poor Alberthe?"

"Ah. Poor Alberthe. She's all right. A couple of months in the bin. Not the sin bin, the shrink one. And then sympathetic shrinks declared her cured."

"Wouldn't she be tried, then?"

"Come, Vera – and, by the way, in this house you call me Adrien – you know your code better. Once you've been section-sixty-foured, declared unfit to plead, you won't be retried for the same offence. *Non bis in idem*. Not that any proc would have wanted to push it on her: everyone wished to forget and to bury as soon as may be."

"And is she cured?"

"Vaccinated, let's say. She had sort of tetanic convulsions there. She's had a couple of shots of anti-tetanus vaccine, and that should keep her feet on the ground a few years. I hear little of her . . . There's worse about . . . I didn't bring you here to talk shop. To make, put it, a confession. While in England, how can I put it so that it won't sound absurd? – impossible probably – I had a vision."

"A vision!" Castang was not trying to be sarcastic, but taken aback he was. "Monsieur le Divisionnaire!"

"Adrien, my boy – in this house. That's going to be one of the hard parts, for us both. That's why I hesitated, long. Out of the office . . . But back in the office . . ." Vera explained happily about Wemmick, Mr. Jaggers' clerk in *Great Expectations*, who ceased to be the same

155

person at his house in Walworth.

"Except that I haven't an Aged Parent, but a dotty wife," looking at Judith with love unmasked, " – that's it exactly."

"Very well; explain about the vision."

"I was on Eggardon Down, which is really a most peculiar place and rather frightening. Even to me. Intensely violent. But the violence was brought by human beings. And I thought well, what is a cop for? To ensure the traffic runs smoothly. Because transportation is civilisation? Or to do a little better – if one could. I see that I am talking shop. Have some more champagne."

"You couldn't do better, just on your own."

"No. Nor resign from the job. Or go preaching to birds."

"Or doing," said Judith, "without the women. This is for you, Vera."

"I think," said Richard, "you've hit the nail with the hammer there. Can you describe the vision, Vera?"

"I don't even know whether I can describe my own. There's been a world, all these hundreds of thousands of years, run by men, and women left out of account. Goes back to Adam and Eve, I suppose. Woman got the blame for wishing to know about good and evil and man never forgave her taking his illusions away. And ever since, she's been suppressed. Bad theology? Only from a man's view."

"And we haven't done too well?"

"You haven't done too well. Mechanistic. Material. Bad metaphysicians, leading to bad physicians."

"And what do women offer?"

"Precious little, so far. Wanting equality and jobs. Which is just wanting to be bad copies of men, seems to me. Judith and I were talking about it, the other day."

"No good appealing to me – I'm dotty."

"Very well – be serious."

"We do have some common ground – no more wars, no more bombs and rockets. Get rid of General Egg."

"Good and then the Russians come."

"Let them. We know perfectly how to deal with Russians," with the tranquillity of a Spanish woman who has dealt with many invasions. "It's ourselves we must combat." A sensible Spanish remark.

"In the long run," said Vera "the cancer is called money. Combat

156

that, and men can't, because it's their pet invention. But give women the chance. And in the short run, we count on you."

"To . . .?"

"You can't beat the fascists – just look at Spain – because they're the bourgeois and in the event they have all the cards. But do your best. You are cops and you're clever, and you have some organisation, and you know their cunning, crooked ways."

"This is something of what I saw," said Richard. "It was sunny, and bright, and big lovely clouds marching out of a south-west wind and throwing big shadows. And then the wind dropped, and it seemed to blow cold out of the north. I had a memory, strange as it may seem – am I being romantic? There was a legend, that beyond the north wind lived a people who understood happiness."

"It's true," interjected Vera soberly. "Champagne illuminates.

"Before Vikings, before absurd Hitlerian notions about Aryans – they had a clue but characteristically got it wrong – before the assiduously fostered notion that all civilisation came out of the Mediterranean basin, spread by the Romans like so much more bullshit, there was a people in the north that understood. They're quite well attested in antiquity: the early Greek historians knew of them. But they got drowned in idiot folklore about oh, Atlantis or Stonehenge or whatever, so one can hardly mention them without blushing. They were governed – in a metaphysic sense – by women. But the women were degenerated by propaganda into goddesses and priestesses and everything ridiculous, by the Romans, those efficient, material, modern destroyers. And of course what the Romans failed to efface, the Christians did, who scientifically obliterated any trace of previous belief so now," sadly, "it all only lives on in myth. Where did you ever meet a pope" with some bitterness, "who could bear even to admit the existence of women? I don't believe that Christ was really like that, but horrible phallocrats like Saint Paul made sure the lid was put good and proper on the girls – ." The two men looked at each other and began to laugh guiltily. "Laugh, you bastards."

"Speaking as a good Spanish Catholic, brought up on Teresa of Avila who understood something," said Judith, viciously for her, "Vera – "

"As a sound, Czech, Slav, Stalinist, ignorant slave," said the lady. "Has it right. You must listen to us, you know. You have, my poor

157

Adrien, never listened to me. Because you were a man, and a cop. And now this Eggardon, what a peculiar and ugly English name. A Road to Damascus sounds better. But even upon men the light must sometimes shine."

Richard emptied the bottle into his own glass. Castang helpfully untwisted the wire off another and eased the cork in a skilful male technical movement.

"We're going to eat," said Monsieur le Divisionnaire slowly. "Henri, I have a male technical material fascist conspiracy I propose to unfold to you. To the girls I say, let's first eat Judith's rather nice woman-cooked-spanish-made paella which is full god-be-thanked of French coastal shellfish from a long way from here – and then we'll talk a bit seriously, because light is needed. Now do you want to drink Spanish, or will you all stick to Monsieur Taittinger?" Everyone agreed. Northern, bourgeois, chalkland, magic champagne. They were all a bit pissed by then.

"Humourless," said Vera. "Yes I am, very." Serving him his dinner, one he enjoyed. Only a can of tuna, but she had made a cream sauce for it, flavoured with a little Dijon mustard. "Let the mutton and onion sauce appear" in an effort to cheer up, but unable to stop it sounding dreary. Lydia sat in a high chair with her mouth open, in which Vera pushed spoonfuls of dinner from time to time.

"No, though; why so downcast?"

"Because there's nothing one can do, really. Form a secret society, to combat all the others? How can a whole world that lives by violence be made non-violent?"

"It isn't a matter of a secret society," with his mouth full, grinning rather (there were so many already). He was in a good mood. "Of mentality." For whatever you did in the way of repression the others would go one better. Security forces were armed to the teeth and it simply encouraged whatever terrorist-group was in fashion (they were all terrorist-groups, and there were new ones every day) to acquire a few Sam missiles.

"It's true that in Norway or Holland there seem to be no private armies going about bombing everyone."

"And the cops are armed with some old seven-sixty-five pistol that is about as much use as a pea-shooter and probably rusted up anyhow.

158

Isn't that the proof? – mentality."

He got another proof, that afternoon.

Good, the situation in France was not quite as bad as the nonsense in America, where the-right-of-the-people-to-bear-arms shall not be infringed, meaning every loony has a gun, portable, concealable and exceedingly lethal. But pretty bad, because of the sacred hunting lobby. The .22 rifle is on free sale, and though a recent rule says it must be single-shot only that's sort of loosely interpreted. There is a very comfortable traffic in revolvers; it's no more than a question of price. That pacifist tradition in Scandinavia was what counted, surely, and you had to possess it for a few hundred years before people began to feel an active dislike and horror of firearms . . . Maryvonne and Orthez entered, looking virtuous.

"Thérèse Martin, aged fourteen years and seven months."

"The Little Flower of Lisieux," added Maryvonne.

"She's what's called out of parental control," went on Orthez.

"Parental is good."

"So's control."

Castang paid no attention to this by-play, stretched out the poor foot and wiggled it experimentally. Fairly satisfactory, the result.

"So we went to the parents," Maryvonne took up the tale "and they were highly uncooperative and said fuck-off or we'll call the cops." Nod; familiar version this of 'I'll tell the vicar': 'I Am the vicar'. "So we twisted their arm a bit: she'd been home and picked up some clothes, perfectly cool."

"Cleaning out any money lying about handy – how much they won't let on. Say they know nothing about it and stick to that – well aware we can't get anything on them much. Never done time – System D," said Orthez succinct. "Petty shoplifting, receiving and translating."

"And proud of their daughter – smart wench, good breadwinner. Habitual delinquent from school, and all the teachers have to say is she had strength of character, exerted much influence, all bad, so naturally they left her alone and she interpreted that as their being afraid of her."

"Tcha," said Castang, the judge preparing to sum up, "she seems to be a competent assassin. Almost certainly good head, skilful planner and good organiser. We wouldn't wonder when she was a lot smarter than us. And she's also a child."

Richard-like he went into a trance. The two inspectors waited dutifully for the oracle.

"So she has clothes, brains, at least some money, and much daring. She won't try the railway, having surely tumbled that we had it in the eye. I've left those cameras up, and Lucciani resting his balls watching them, but – " shrug, "she's almost certainly too smart to try hopping a long-distance truck because she knows we'd think of that. We know her to be expert in hitching private lifts but even as a double bluff – she knows the place swarms with cops and that we're feeling thoroughly aggrieved. She knows we'll get her identity quickly, through her sidekick she saw pinched, or the schools or whatever. Now what does she try to do?"

"She sure as hell doesn't hang around any amusement arcade."

"She probably has a stable of boy-friends who'd put her up for a few days lying low and wait for heat to diminish," suggested Maryvonne.

"I think she might not be that trustful," said Castang drily. "Alert to the thirty-pieces-of-silver syndrome."

"And where would they hide her?" grunted Orthez. "Privacy's the problem as much as trust."

"So she can hole up several hours in almost any café, get a meal, do her planning. Put yourself in her mind. The town is too hot and on the whole too small for her – Paris she'll think of; Lyon or Marseille if it works out that way. To get a lift on a main road is vulnerable and conspicuous; she wants a new identity and it takes time to pinch or acquire papers she could show if tapped. Bus, train or autoroute she's liable to be pinned down at the first barrier. She's got to win a little time."

"So she'll steal a car and take sideroads out of the town. Knows we can't block them all."

"Can she drive?"

"She pinched Maryvonne's car, remember. Any child can drive that's big enough to reach the pedals. Abandon it on the outskirts of Paris."

"You're over-estimating her," said Castang quietly. "Joy-riding a car a short distance on roads one knows well, I don't say no. Paris, where it's unlikely she's ever been, is another matter. I realise she's formidable, but she's a child, and will act like a child. She's alone for probably the first time, and however tough an act she puts on with the gang she'll be bewildered and frightened. And she's desperate. She knows how to kill and she may have a knife or some other toy such as she hit Lil with. We must get her before she becomes totally reckless, and she may be on some dope. A handful of uppers and she gets over-confident, which might help us. A girl, a child," lighting a cigarette and pointing it at Maryvonne.

"I think," she said, "she'd seek a protector, a male, even if very temporary. For the reassurance it would give."

The phone rang. Salviac. Not very thrilled with the word-from-Richard.

"You sending me up or what?" said the Bandit chief. "You need us to catch a fourteen-year-old girl?" coat-trailing. They'd rather shoot it out with Alain Delon; quite, but it was the moment to be tactful.

"By my estimate she's committed three murders, and we may collect more."

"Well," defensively, "the boss said it: I've to comply. What is it you want?"

"No more than the usual. I'm shortstaffed. I've a photograph, a description. The likeliest is she'll feel cornered and make for the big town. If she does what's expected of her." It was a child: who knew what a child would do? Ask three shrinks and you'd get three differing opinions. What cheese would fetch this mouse out into the open?

A disproportionate number of policemen hung about until two in the morning, when Castang, cross and sleepy, decided that mousetraps with no cheese in them were of small use and that rattling with a stick along the wainscots was the better tactic, but he had forebodings. Words like 'calculated risk' had no appeal for him.

"All right, give it to the press, we've just time, and then go get some sleep. A 'Have you seen this girl?' thing as though it were a fugue." He didn't much like it: increasing the pressure on her simply strengthened her impulse towards violence. But the emphasis on her physical appearance might increase her need to try and change it.

"Hairdressers?" he was asking Maryvonne – men were not much use at this – by eight in the morning. "People who sell wigs?" She was looking dubious. "No, I suppose a fourteen-year-old is not very likely to try a wig. I'd hope more for some childish extravagance like a blonde bleach. Or a fuzzy-wuzzy perm. Even if you just cut it short into a Joan-of-Arc you wouldn't try that at home, would you? Need professional cutting, or it would be the pudding basin and vanity wouldn't allow that." They were studying the photo in the local paper, which could be that of several hundred thousand girls in the country.

"Sitting still all that time? All those mirrors? People studying your face? She'd never take the risk, surely." Liliane entered.

"Hallo, Lil," said Castang pleasantly. "I'd forgotten your existence. How's the arm?"

"All right thanks," briefly. "I've got something; not very much but well padded out it might be enough to help us." Castang had allowed the pill trade to slip his mind, but tactfully did not say so.

"Come and give us your opinion on this."

"Yes I think she might well," upon consideration. "Shift all that hair out of her face and she has a false maturity which is what she's after if she's going to gain a living by prostitution. The risk is minimal. Who looks at those photos, or would recognise the subject if they did?"

"But would she take the gamble?"

"She likes a gamble," said Liliane. "What else is picking people up at night? Half the time there isn't even any money; the fun is in the risk."

"All right, Maryvonne, off you trot. A boring job, but we'll hope to walk in while she's under the dryer or whatever."

"Don't want to seem discouraging," said Liliane after the door shut "but she doesn't have to go to any shop. How many girls not much older than that are hairdressers' apprentices, and will do you a backstreet job at night? However, close all the doors we can think of. You want this now? Making it brief since I can't type?"

"Put it on my tape and the girl can do it – just give me the nugget if there is one."

"We've known it for some time – Methaqualone at thirty francs apiece. What's new is a phony clinic – you're an addict, right, on heroin: you pop in here asking to cure your habit, all quite legal; pay seven or eight hundred francs a consultation. They say they'll lift you off heroin and put you on a synthetic substitute, idea of decreasing your dependence gradually. Write you a prescription. All legal, the pharmacy is covered, everyone. You get your pills, pop back here, and at thirty francs a time – fifty any day now – you're showing a handsome profit."

"I don't want to know about any drug problem whatsoever, but it's perfect – you make a big pompous thing and we won't be billed for the television, you've these characters of Davignon's to send up to court and we all acquire a thin but glossy varnish of virtue. Bless your heart, girl; it's a weight off my mind."

He dragged his ass in to Richard, who agreed. Nothing to do but wait.

"Want light entertainment," slumping down in a chair. "We've all these television cameras, and a big transmitting aerial on the roof. We could make some money then. Instead of using the basement for beating up Turkish immigrants we could have pretty young housewives. Amateur striptease – prize of a packet of cigarettes for the best each night. Lucciani as talent-spotter." It did raise a snigger from Richard but immediately afterwards "Bugger off now, Castang, I've work to do." Lucciani was thrilled with the idea, but "You stay glued to those cameras; that does four men's work. And the eye well peeled for pill-poppers. Earn your living," tyrannically.

Nothing happened all day. It was cloudy, windless, and the autumn drizzle, so fine as to be almost imperceptible, went on and on. "Night must fall," said Castang fatalistically. No phone calls were received from hairdressers, people selling wigs or other sorts of costumiers. The Path lab rang up and said that injuries likely to be caused by Rabouin's pacifier were consistent with their autopsy reports but they weren't prepared to swear to anything much. Orthez, who had done a lot of work on boy-friends, found a couple to admit grudgingly to being acquainted with the Little Flower, but none capable of sheltering or concealing same. Davignon, who did a neighbourhood enquiry, had found evidence of a lot of juvenile delinquency, but nothing to interest the Police Judiciaire. The district had a bad name for shoplifting and so what? Now if you had found the four heavy machineguns and the hundred-and-fifty machine pistols artfully lifted from the army camp in Foix, said Castang, we'd have something to crow about. Packets of panty-hose from the five-and-ten, fornications in basements – these don't make headlines. At his desk he experimented with a few headlines for a sensation-press such as might earn promotion-credits for the Serious Crimes Brigade. 'The Martin Gang'. 'La Bande à

163

Thérèse'. 'The Little Black Flower.' Pooh. Night fell.

A watch had been kept all day by a complaining bandit-brigade, by gendarmerie, by cooks and dishwashers from wherever he had found them. On all the good pick-up points for hitch-hikers, on the tollgates of the autoroute, at filling stations or hamburger bars, on the whole national network for fugitives: they'd caught three Arabs interdits-de-séjour, two phony work-permits and two army deserters. The troops were getting bored, and grumbling was rife. It was all enough to make you wish you belonged to the Economic Crimes, who were getting juicy headlines practically daily from villains smuggling millions into Swiss bank accounts.

He had to make a gamble too. He chose the long-distance truck depot. He'd always rather fancied it.

A bleak spot for the stake-out. The usual windswept stretch of grease-stained concrete, old newspapers and Coca-Cola cans, garbage bins that never seemed to be emptied and the sickening smell of spilt diesel fuel. Rows of staggered slots with power hook-ups, the usual clean-up bay, spare-parts shop and service station. In the middle the usual motel for overnighters, restaurant full of quiet men playing cards, slot machines selling outer space and contraceptives; smells of frying and foreign cigarettes, disinfectant and deodorant and exotic aftershaves as sickly and pungent as ether.

In this world the outsider is not welcome, and least of all a cop. The men who haul the big TIR trucks from Malaga up to Sweden and the Black Sea back to Scotland regard cops as an unavoidable pestilent hazard, like black ice or mosquitoes. Castang knew it the way he knew there was nowhere on that parking lot to hide a PJ man, let alone a PJ car.

He'd had a lengthy talk on the phone with a suspicious and hostile manager. Much too much talk. Did these people ever keep their mouths shut? Would they ever? Had they ever, in the entire history of the human race? Castang thought, afterwards, that he had insisted much too much upon the point.

However, their arrival was smooth: the unobtrusively slipping in was well planned. No car on the main road, where the inconspicuously parked auto is exactly what attracts attention. The trucks take a side road that bends sharply back to the entrance of their domain, and meanders on through a dreary industrial quarter. It is a good place to arrest somebody, because there is no way out bar a flight of steep weed-grown steps up the embankment of the railway bridge, which the main road crosses at this point.

He had only Orthez with him, and a Breton boy called Le Goff, which is much like being called Davies in Wales; both chosen because they looked more like truck drivers than anybody else in the department. At the last moment Maryvonne asked, or rather volunteered, to come. He didn't much like this, suspecting that she wanted to efface her 'stupidity' of two evenings before. And the truck-driver's world is one of the few exclusive-male precincts left outside a Wasp Club – say the Petroleum Building in Houston. There are waitresses, their profession written all over them, and prostitutes – likewise – and that's it.

However, he had an idea regarding Maryvonne: she was sharp and alert as no man ever is, and he put her in a room on the top floor of the motel (where she would have a good view) with electronic snoop-binoculars. If, as seemed likely, the Little Flower was disguised, a woman would penetrate it quicker. What seemed a great deal more likely was that she was already a thousand kilometres off (laughing at policemen) with the complicity of some deluded taxi-driver – Castang was no longer feeling lucky.

The Breton boy fitted in well, with a round obstinate Celtic face that could have come from anywhere down the Danube valley, belonging to one of those trucks with Cyrillic lettering that are the reason why Poles have no ham, Roumanians no fruit, or why foie gras does not appear much upon the Hungarian table. Orthez was all right too – where he's concerned there's no odds between a truck and a Porsche prototype. It was himself that stood out like a cherry on top of the Crème Chantilly, the blushing bridegroom. Anywhere horsey, it had frequently been noticed, he passed muster, but here he had the uneasy feel he didn't know an air-filter from the main drain and had cop written all over his backside. He went to light a cigarette, that face-saving gesture like looking at your lipstick in a pocket mirror, and of course the lighter clicked seven times without working. He shook it crossly.

"If you please," said a driver with ironic courtesy – he stood up, the whore, to make it worse, with a box of matches. Being French matches three in a row went out as soon as lit: the driver thought this very funny.

"Did you know," said Castang "that the Seita is bringing out new matches that don't break?"

"Yes?" Polite.

"Thread of tungsten down the middle, nuclear warhead on top and a little rubber handgrip."

"Oh yes?" laughing heartily. Much too heartily. The whore.

"You want to eat?" asked the waitress.

"What I came for. What's good?"

"Plat du jour is choucroute."

"Suits me." When the sauerkraut came suspiciously fast – it was pale and watery, the sausage so bleached and the ham so blanched that he went the same colour. The truck-drivers got over this little difficulty by adding a halfbottle of ketchup, a tablespoon of mustard and a lengthy shake of Maggi Aroma, which got ostentatiously passed him by the driver-with-the-matches, who added "Anything I can do, just let me know." Sodom, though Castang, now I have to eat it, with the whole room sniggering. That bastard Orthez drinking beer and reading *Penthouse* without a care in the world. He pressed it down somehow and went for a pee: Orthez obediently did the same.

"Take it easy," said the inspector comfortably, turning on the hot air blower after washing his hands at length. "They'll be going."

True, a couple did go. It was like being in an airport restaurant looking out upon the brightly lit apron, watching the big Boeing taxi heavily out to the runway, all winking lights and bellow. Much better, thought Castang; the truck is the lesser evil.

A couple more pulled in. But that infernal pair sat on, talking peacefully across empty glasses, with all the time in the world. Perhaps they'd overdone the previous stage, and must wait for the clock to catch up in the black box. He borrowed *Penthouse* and time passed lost in a jungle of pubic hair. There was a good deal more gynaeco-art lying around in varying stages of disrepair. Truckers are mostly a well-balanced crowd. A few magazines had been decorated with Dali-moustaches, but only one had been mutilated: every sad vulva attacked with a burning match-head: violence, always violence and when the north wind blew here it carried a miserable débris in its wake, whirling and eddying on the stained greasy concrete under the tall yellow lights, under the stilled wheels of the beached blunt space-cruisers. The clicker in his breast pocket, under Maryvonne's thumb

166

three storeys up, sounded as loud as a telephone.

She showed a good eye – he remembered to tell as much. A walk is distinctive, but none of them had seen Thérèse walk. They'd seen her run.

Let her get well on in, and she's bottled. She'd really gone to town. Clothes, to a cop, do not change a person much; not even high boots under a lime-green miniskirt, a tight sweater and blonde hair done just the way Lil said: smart girl. That and the heels gave her ten centimetres more height and that would still deceive no professional. A cop or a cameraman looks to the modelling of forehead and throat, the setting of the head on the shoulders. A fringe, a highnecked sweater, plucked eyebrows. Would he have known her? If she had not made the mistake of the over-extravagant clothes that drew the eye, then . . .

Castang sat mum behind his magazine, telling himself she did not know him, could not know him. The entrance was prolonged by a screen of ribbed glass to keep draughts off, and Orthez was the wrong side of it. The Breton boy, who had been playing the electronic squashcourt on a television screen, was not quite sure what to do and began edging round the maze of tables, watching Castang who frowned – the movement was much too furtive. She stood in the doorway quite coolly. She had a large envelope handbag and no other visible luggage.

The drivers, accustomed to looking the whores over, and being choosy over a fleshpot (there had been two dilapidated examples earlier, drinking coffee at the counter, to whom nobody paid the slightest heed) were quick to notice her fresh prettiness that the appalling clothes could not mask, but they were too lordly to offer any encouragement. She stayed still and took the scene in, self-possessed and very wary indeed. Castang crossed his legs and Orthez, mistaking the signal, stood up. It was a mistake. There was light behind him; it threw a shadow on the glass screen larger and more ominous than Orthez was. At this moment she smelt Castang's tension. She shrank back, now thoroughly alarmed. The truckers were amused by the by-play. Not in the least averse to teasing the police a bit.

"Come on in, little lady."

"We'll look after you."

He could not let the false situation develop. He felt for his police 'medal', stood up abruptly and said "Don't interfere". The voice came out colder and curter than he had wanted. Thérèse had already her hand on the door-handle, but the voice of authority irritated the truckers: this was their terrain and they disliked interference, particularly when it had that officious sound.

Orthez started forward as though fired by a trigger and the one sitting at the outside of the table tripped him with a deft foot so that he went sprawling from his own impetus.

"Police Judiciaire," snapped Castang furious. Le Goff, knocking a table askew, bumped into the waitress who was cleaning it with a damp rag, and had been too dulled to notice anything, but was standing now with her mouth open. "Hey," she said catching him with a wrist as muscular as his own "Manners!"

"Fascist!" said the other trucker, neatly knocking Castang's hat over his eyes and ramming it down. They were all three entangled, imbrogliod. Thérèse had a clear run across the forecourt.

"Easy now," said the driver holding Castang loosely but very powerfully by the shoulders. "A bit too hostile, ain't you?"

"She's wanted," stupidly.

"Three of you, for one little girl?" It was the most fun they'd had all week. The other, now on his feet, tripped Orthez again as he was getting up and did a tango step in front of the now frenzied Le Goff, dodging his broad shoulders in time to the other's evasions. They had lost forty-five precious seconds.

"You looking to be pegged for obstruction?" asked Castang, singularly belated, his anger at missing an easy pinch blinding him with rage.

"You got some quarrel, then, with the little lady?" asked the trucker, astonished.

"She's wanted for homicide." An idiotic remark. How could a girl as fresh and as young as that be wanted at all? For hawking her mutton? Every duchess did as much.

The other two had lost a minute floundering about but Castang lost near a minute and a half. Explaining to the populace.

Maryvonne, luckily, had had the sense to stay where she was, but had had an unmerciful struggle opening the double windows that had never been budged since installed and were recalcitrant. She leaned out of the window and screamed "Over to the right." It had been true, but was true no longer. Le Goff, flustered, had his gun out. "Put it away, you fool," bawled Castang.

The trucks stood in a row as obstructive and sullen as a school of hippopotamus. Much worse, the orange street lamps cast the most confusing, foxing shadows ever known. Orthez was coasting along the line, dropping to a crouch every twenty paces, hoping to catch a glimpse of those twinkling sexy legs.

"Whatever you do don't shoot," panted Castang a long way back.

The answer froze them. As though on cue a bullet whanged, dramatic as a movie. It had hit the fatted engorged profile of a tanker that might be transporting something as innocently necessary to Western Economy as refined aviation spirit, and might as easily hold something that needed the fire-brigade, the Civil Defence, and the Nuclear Regulatory Commission to hold it down. Simultaneous with the John-Wayne-whang came a pop. Not a big gun, but it would kill you just as easy as a forty-four magnum: Orthez got behind a wheel and stayed there.

"Jesus," he groaned aggrieved "she's got a gun." Not very extraordinary. The Police Judiciaire has a normal human dislike for being shot at.

"Jesus," said the Breton boy. He'd rather a force-nine gale off Finisterre. That way, he knew where he stood.

Somewhat to his surprise, Castang's brain was still functioning. He didn't know or didn't care whether it was intelligence (in suspension), common sense (dubious) or experience (non-existent) that told him it was a .22 target pistol. While coping with the nasty feelings – a shot in the anklebone, like one in the hand, is a very horrid idea – he was wondering why a single-shot pistol is thought to be a harmless sort of thing really. It isn't. One shot is quite enough. Get rid too of the notion that reloading is a Brown-Bess affair of powderhorns and ramrods. To eject a cartridge and put in another takes just two seconds.

"Don't shoot," said Castang softly. Three of them – no, four. It should be a simple affair to outflank her. Sure, but there were large brightly-lit open spaces. She can only pick one target at a time but that one can be you.

"Making for the steps," screamed Maryvonne shrilly. Rewarded by another bullet and the crack of a pane of glass. Castang whisked round his truck and scuttled for the row on the far side, with a prayer he might be right about the target pistol, for the last report had sounded louder, more like a seven-sixty-five, and that meant an automatic. On the wide space of the parking lot, in the damp hanging atmosphere, a cartridge might sound smaller than it was. So evidently thought Orthez, advancing prudently and obviously wishing for a cannonade to cover the assault.

He reached cover, panting a scrap from the fifty-metre sprint, keeping moving because here they were under much brighter light (he had forgotten all about the sprained ankle in the apprehension of a shot ankle). Three big tough cops to assault one fourteen-year-old girl. But both he and Orthez were remembering what she had done already.

The Breton boy did not. He broke cover over there on the left in a high-kneed, long-paced gallop that was faster than it looked, and the other two went with him because they had to, ready now to go to ground and shoot. They didn't have a choice in the matter.

The bottom of the embankment was not well lit, and visibility the worse from the dazzle of street lamps at its top. Thérèse was scrambling up the flight of steps but slowing. They were steep, and she was already tired. They would get her on that street. There would be no people about. They would run her down.

She was at the top. But she did not run. She turned, and the pistol looked very big and Le Goff, coming up two at a time, was only six paces off. Orthez, down on one knee, had her silhouetted.

The two shots went together and both seemed to take effect because both figures crumpled together and stayed in a heaving, twitching lump that stilled. There were some forty steps, and it took Castang what felt like ten breathless minutes to climb them. Both bodies were heaving. Meaning breathing, though he could not hear it through the noise his own lungs were making. He dropped on his knees. Le Goff's face was buried under her hips, a position he might quite have enjoyed in other circumstances. His arms were pinning her waist fast and though she was wriggling like an eel – she wasn't hit anyhow – she could not free herself. Castang took her shoulders and forced them down on the ground. "Stay still! You all right, Rob?"

"No!" said a muffled voice. Still, it was a voice. Castang took her by the hair, which did not come away in his hand: it was hers even if it didn't look it.

"I've got her, Rob: loose her." Orthez, who had taken his time on those goddam steps and arrived fresh as a daisy, took hold of her wrists and cuffed them. She tried to spit but her mouth was too dry. When her bottom half got disentangled Le Goff stayed where he was and there was a lot of blood. All over his head: Christ. "Still, boy, still. You'll be all right."

"I'm not fucking all right," in a loud angry groan. Castang, sitting crosslegged, jumped as a car with a loud noise stopped what seemed a bare inch from his shoulderblade; he cringed automatically and then realised it was Maryvonne. Who'd had the wit to take the car and drive round, instead of engaging in the cross-country lark.

"Is he? – oh my God."

"Shut up," said Castang briefly. Rob was not that badly hurt: he was talking too much. Maryvonne was fumbling cotton-wool out of the first-aid box.

"Pull me," said Rob. "My leg's blocked." It was only then that they saw he had a knee round the upright of the handrail.

"He's only scalped," said Castang. "I hope." Orthez took him by the shoulders and heaved him to a sitting position. Thérèse, handcuffed to the rail, lashed out and caught him in the ribs. Orthez slapped her face as quick as a snake, would have given her another but Castang stopped him. One couldn't see past all that blood and hair. "Scissors," he said, like Doctor Kildare operating.

"Don't cut my hair," howled Rob.

"He's been clonked," said Maryvonne.

"I'll give him another if he doesn't stay still."

This explained the absence of Thérèse's pistol, which Orthez had been looking for everywhere. Her shot had not gone off because there was no cartridge in the breech. She hit him instead with the barrel – lucky it was not the butt, they all said fervently – and as he took hold of her feet she dropped the gun, which slid down the embankment.

"You're a fine shot, I don't think," said Rob, feeling a bit spiteful once the dizziness wore off. More cross about his hair than anything else: Castang had cut off much too much.

"If I'd fired to hit her I might have hit you, from below like that." It was a nasty long scratch, and with his exertion had bled a lot. Castang finished work with a big strip of sticking plaster.

"She's your pinch, chap, and very well done. Drive them both home, Maryvonne, and come back for Orthez and me. You set her to

171

cool, Rob, and take some aspirin, and call off the man hunt. Salviac," reflectively, "won't be pleased, but it'll be a comfort to him," grinning a bit, "when he sees your head." Thérèse, feeling the handcuffs beginning to stop her circulation, had sobered down. She was no longer the centre of attention and submitted to Maryvonne shoving her into the car, without struggling.

The two that were left leaned their elbows on the parapet of the bridge and surveyed the still-deserted parking lot. The truckers were preferring discretion to valour. Enthusiasm for the real-life-television had been damped by that cracked window. They would be out in a little while, ready to complain about damage done by the other bullet to their precious paintwork.

"I'll go and sort that lot out," said Orthez, vengeful from being tripped.

"Let them go – more trouble than it's worth."

"Pity: I'd have liked to baptise those two into the true faith with a dose of total immersion."

"Save your energies. Who sheltered her, where did she get those clothes, the gun, money? – there'll be work, tomorrow."

"Liliane's arm, Lucciani's balls, Rob's head – not bad work for a fourteen-year-old."

"And you and me both biting dust. Solace yourself – think of Maisonneuve's face. Let's go," said Castang, grinning, "and get ourselves a good press write-up. And be grateful," meaning it, "that it was all no worse."

Richard had said one day that Commissaire Maltaverne was a troll. A mistake, because he'd had to explain about Henrik Ibsen, whom nobody in the department had ever heard of. Probably there was no one in the department capable of finding Norway on the map, said Richard.

The gentleman was ushered in now by Fausta with her nose wrinkled, for he had taken recently to a pipe and had one now stuck in his trap. Was it in imitation of Fabre, his chief? Was it a projection of some new statesmanlike image? Was he just giving up cigarettes? As usual with Maltaverne it was impossible to tell.

Most people getting ushered by Fausta cheered up, when they did not get a gleam in the eye (she was a very pretty girl), but not ol' lobster-eye there being impervious.

A smell came out of the pipe: Richard, uttering hospitable words, lit one of his cigars and turned on the thing that extracted fumes.

"Fabre mentioned this affair to you?"

"Correct."

"The Minister wants to feel that the department is sound."

"Yes."

"No, uh, extremist views being held or promulgated."

"No."

"It's been suggested that you might co-author a confidential report."

"So I understand."

"Because the Inspectorate . . . mention of which . . ." This was sticky going.

"Creates agitation."

"Quite so. They've enough to do. Nobody wants another ostentatious clean up. People wishing to make political leverage would start talking about witch-hunts. So we're all politically reliable, okay? You. Me. Joe. All these dossiers are snow-white. Nobody getting bad marks. The Minister, being a prudent man, wants to be able to read between the lines a bit. He knows all about the syndicate of commissaires in Paris. All about the corrupt civic functionaries in Marseille. Now his beady eye falls upon the provinces – even ours. Why, d'you think?"

"Municipal elections coming up. Fewer unpleasant surprises the better."

"That is a pretext sufficient to satisfy us, wouldn't you say?"

Maltaverne took the pipe out of his mouth just long enough to say "Why me?"

"Consider Joe. Joe's dossier says he's politically reliable. Who knows, that might even be true. But the best way he can prove it is to have friends who can vouch for him. You have friends like that: or so a fellow I know tells me."

"I don't suppose he has any name, this fellow-you-know."

"He has, but only within certain walls. Not mine." Nod. "You like Bordelais food?" Nod. "There's a restaurant in the town where you get it quite genuine." Third nod.

"Just to make sure of him, what sort of car does he drive?"

173

"Swedish. They place a lot of emphasis on safety."

There was a silence. Smoke drifted towards the extractor fan, powered by a little electric motor, such as is said in espionage fiction to help bewilder electronic insects. But who believes what they read in espionage fiction? Not policemen . . .

"One has to look ahead," said Maltaverne. "There's such a thing as prudent foresight."

"Very true," said Richard. "However, to speak frankly, your name on a report of this nature wouldn't be in any sense compromising. Sort of thing that goes into the shredder when a ministry changes hands, you know."

"And yours is the other name."

"Politics has never interested me much."

"Yes. Due to retire soon, aren't you?"

"Pretty soon."

"You've been here a longish time, haven't you?"

"I've been fairly comfortable that way," said Richard. "It could be said that I lacked ambition, maybe? Or was too prudent: there is such a thing as being too prudent. I'm rather looking forward now to retirement. Yes, a longish time, now that I look back. I suppose that probably that's why they asked me; my local knowledge ought to be pretty fair. But I don't imagine it will run to being consulted over the choice of my successor."

"I'd have thought you'd have earned a reward by now – deputy directorship in Paris, say."

"Paris has never tempted me all that much," said Richard reflectively. "My wife likes the country. Great gardener. And I've no children, alas. Yours must be growing up, now I come to think of it. School-leaving age?"

"Anxieties around that time," agreed Maltaverne. "One would like to see them make a good career. Sciences Po, or the National School of Administration. Trouble is, those places are all in Paris and one needs to have a flat there. And the prices have run wild. Not the sort of money a provincial commissaire commands. Even a divisional, like yourself."

"I'm well aware of it," said Richard, sympathetic. "Nothing more expensive than children at student age. Well, I don't want to hurry you. Perhaps you'll let me know. A tiresome job, I agree. A bit of

174

prestige and not much else. Still, when your name was brought forward I thought yes, that would be seen as reliable."

"Well, one always wants to oblige a friend. Whenever that's possible."

"That's for you to judge," said Richard getting up. "But with your family responsibilities I'd have thought the chance of making your number in Paris wouldn't exactly do you harm."

"Like to take counsel with myself."

"Naturally," said Richard. "Just don't be too long. Those municipal elections are due within a couple of months."

Castang had been at home for several days. Hell, he was a Commissaire; he didn't – shouldn't at least – have to ask. The Serious Crimes Brigade had solved homicides, numerous homicides, and weathered a lot of comment in the press, most of it flowery though all highly unwelcome. He had been generous with credit for his subordinates but he was bloody well going to be first in the queue for days off. He was hysterical about the telephone, refusing to answer it, refusing to let Vera answer it. Well if she insisted on answering the thing then he was out, and remaining so. She wasn't knowing where he was nor when he would be back.

Since it kept raining all the time he hardly set foot outside but carpentered away; very nervous the first day and all his work had to be done afresh, not to speak of dropping nails and wounding himself quite painfully with a screwdriver: as though he wasn't still black and blue all over.

And Vera of course had to go and say these homicides weren't in the least solved: qué, SOLVED? They'd caught a child, and a Buddhist, and did anybody have the remotest notion how such things came about? – no of course they didn't and –

These homicides have been put a stop to, interrupted Castang with much annoyance. Id est, solved; and now put-a-sock-in-it.

Vera spent much time with Judith: women changing the world. Castang did not refuse to listen but was too tired and irritable to absorb any of it. You're as bad as Richard blithering on about the north wind; in fact much worse because you go on and on so. You tire me. You bore me. He shut himself crossly up in the attic and

175

discovered that several sections of tongue-&-groove boarding had been sawn three centimetres too short by some fatuous and malevolent cretin bent upon sabotaging him; cretin named Castang.

"Moron," screamed Castang, flinging the hammer.

He had no book to read, and sat pressing buttons on the television set, appalled to find the whole population of France as moronic as himself. Something had to be done. Put all the morons in a very large concentration camp, and pass me the death ray, would you. Vera became highly thin-skinned and steadily shorter in language, and he went back to work. 'Jolly good job' she said, looking round the attic, but the phrase had a double meaning. He had broken the television set she said, with that perpetual jabbing at it: not that she cared; she never looked at the thing, but it was an expensive toy and it was stuck on that oafish First Programme and oh god why do we live in the centre of this frightful hexagon, why don't we live on the Normandy coast where people are civilised, probably because they can get the BBC on the box . . .

"I'll send you Lucciani," said the Commissaire in a lordly way, and stalked off to the office.

There was nothing much to do, bar confusing the staff who were working stolidly through La Bande-à-Thérèse as the papers called it; much hampered as usual by the Proc, the Judge of Instruction, and a great array of lawyers; and now himself: leave us alone, will you, to get on with it.

And the North Wind syndrome had entered an acute phase.

"Now, Castang," said Richard annoyingly, "concentrate, will you." It was still raining, outside.

"This business of being a carbon copy of Fabre; the pipe all the time and here, have a fill of my tobacco. He's really revoltingly glutinous."

"Maltaverne," said Richard thoughtfully, "is extremely ambitious. He wanted a transfer to the PJ some years ago and was blocked, nobody seems quite to know why. So he concentrated on being in everyone's good book, and I wish you'd do the same. Now he sees a way to unblock – and the way open to Paris: he's sick of this dusty little hole. Biron's chosen his man pretty astutely. Now I'm the key – Maltaverne will be round bringing me flowers for my desk."

"Yes, well, I hope he brings some better cigars while he's at it."

"You're unaccountably nervous and irritable, boy. Good, I've a very quiet job for you. Biron. I can't go following him about in a disguise; it's only a matter of minutes before I get rumbled. I detach you. We'll fiddle your subsistence allowance. Go to Paris, anywhere, but I must have more information about this network he's getting ready for Der Tag. It's virtually a holiday. Apart from having to stay here anyhow, I've got to handle Maltaverne with a silken glove, or a bowstring or whatever it is."

"I can't make out how he came to pick you. You grumbled enough about the Ancien Régime while it was in power; in fact you were rather Popular Front."

"Don't be obtuse. I'm a good time-server like most policemen, and Biron finds me simply a defter coat-turner and sail-trimmer than most. If I'd really been a Pop Front militant, a) I'd be in Paris now and, b) I wouldn't have held this job for ten years and more. I'd have been sent to Marseille to get shit upon: every time an American undergraduate took an overdose of heroin my incompetence would be the cause.

"Now, seriously, Castang, what has changed since the eleventh of May?"

It was the question everybody kept asking. The date was that upon which Uncle François, known to all as 'Tonton', had been elected Socialist President of the Hexagon. Terrible goings-on there had been. But now that the dust had settled, and the so-called state of grace was finished, what difference was there?

Some querulous chap in a crowd had flung a complaint at a politician.

'On the television nothing has changed!' A journalist had cooked the book in time-honoured fashion by suppressing the first three words on a tape. Been caught, and the trivial detail had acted as catalyst to all the boredom and frustration of all the journalists. What, really, had changed? That wasn't merely cosmetic, like Richard's disguise?

He put on his lecturing voice.

"Castang, you've only to look at the television: it's a parallel. Two people got sacked – two – with maximum uproar. For the rest, all the old soldiers are back; shuffle a few jobs but they're all still there. Magnanimous? Not really: it was discovered that however mediocre they were they knew, at least, the job. Over the last twenty years, how much socialist talent gained experience through holding a position of responsibility in the system? None at all. The artistic Reds don't know a cathode tube from a hole in the wall.

"Anything about the police that strikes you as similar? Ninety-nine per cent of cops are right-wing by definition, and they're all like me, grovelling coat-turners who on the twelfth of May woke up discovering that really they'd had left-wing sympathies all the time and just hadn't realised it. So now you know why the people's flag is palest pink, and not as red as you might think, end-of-quote. So buzz off, boy, and find out for me who it is that Monsieur de Biron decides he can really trust. Because I might think I'm having him on, and he might think exactly the same."

"All right," said Castang, "that's anyhow a clear instruction at last."

So here he was. And what had he found out? Nothing much; not enough, anyhow. Biron was rich; had inherited money, married money. Owned property around the place, houses, ground, all sorts of lush comforts. He knew that already. And what interest could it possibly have?

Castang disembarked thus, in this foul little town, in a bad frame of mind. All very well for Richard, saying 'Find out' in that airy-fairy manner. Find out what, and how? Be as discreet as he had been told to be and you find out nothing. Be a Nosy Parker in a town as small as this one and you'll still find out nothing, because you might just as well seat your bare behind upon a wasp's nest. In both instances you will leave more rapidly than you arrived. The problem is invariably dodged by fictional detective-agents. There is too much leg-work and it is too difficult, and they will not shine. They tend thus to have a friend who owes them a big favour, some doctor or lawyer or journalist who knows everything, and is only too happy to blab it all out.

Anyway he loathed small towns. Once many years ago he had been left (with a totally green Lucciani and greenish himself; it had been his first totally independent enquiry) in a small town like this one and had sat in several wasps' nests, to – apparently – the vast amusement of Commissaire Richard. And that had been only a local squire, a notability in nobody's eyes but his own. This was a much trickier personage. Politically – Castang was well aware – real power belongs to persons whom one has never heard of: power means not having your name in the paper. It is not a riffraff of Deputies and State Secretaries, nor the bank-president, and least of all the spokesman for this-or-that. That good word 'mouthpiece' . . . Power in France may be the Inspector of Finance who inspects nothing whatever and enjoys a comfortable salary for so doing, or the Master of Requests, or the Referendary Counsellor – surprising numbers of these obscure medieval dignitaries are knocking about and what do they Do? Nobody has ever found out. Biron was an excellent example of the power that isn't just behind the sofa but is stretched out there horizontally, at full length, on a lot of cushions, and never even utters: unperceived, but if it were one would merely wonder idly whether it were asleep or dead.

He was surprised – agreeably – at this small town being (at least, looking) much nicer than expected. There were even remnants of Frenchness about it, rare now that the whole of France looks and behaves like a bad copy of America and admires itself greatly for so doing. What has happened to that French countryside now so vile and so sterile, with never a bird or a butterfly, never a flower, producing nothing but oversized watery vegetables and undersized watery meat; both tough, both tasteless? We have to go to the back of the north wind, said Richard with indignant incredulity, to find a decent meal. Is this – rhetorical after another drink or two – the country of Montaigne, of Renoir? This is the desert of Giscard, boy, and don't count on Tonton to change any damn thing.

A town though, recognisably lived in by three or four people recognisably human beings. A few old houses; a hideous, immense, ludicrous but wholly delightful cathedral; a few crooked streets going steeply up and down – and even some slippery cobblestones. Rain-shining slate roofs. Perhaps there is a baker who actually bakes bread, a butcher miraculously knowing the meaning of the word 'andouille'. Castang cheered up.

To work. Now was this fellow even at home, and if not, who was? What did the household consist of? A cop on an enquiry often proceeds by means of bogus enquiries.

"Telephone engineer here," in a thick singsong accent. "Something wrong with this line, is there then?"

"Not as far as I know. Who said there was, then?" Something South European: Portuguese maybe.

"Jesus, mate, how should I know? Gets passed on. How many lines you got there then?"

"Two but there's nothing wrong with either of them."

"Unlisted line maybe?"

"We haven't got one. Don't you know that?"

"Think I carry the book around with me then? Got it wrote down here, complaint of fading on local calls: if you didn't call, who did?"

"Well, I'll ask. Monsieur is not here this morning."

"Ask Madame then."

"Madame is in Paris but I will ask the secretary: hold on."

"Who's this then?"

"This is the house man; it's possible that the secretary . . . hold the line . . . hallo? No the secretary knows of no complaint, what number are you ringing?"

"Thirty-two seventy-four twenty-five and there's nobody else there, no?"

"My wife and she's the housekeeper, she'd have mentioned it. It's correct, this is Monsieur de Biron's house. Very odd."

"Baron, right?"

"No no, Biron."

"That's not your name?"

"No no, this is Andrés the house man. I told you."

"You're not Baron?" with the disbelieving tone of invincible cretinism.

"No no, Gonçalves is my name, I told you; Biron."

"It's those stupid girls, mate, that's what it is; they're always making these cock-ups. Sorry to have troubled you, mate."

"No, that's all right."

"Don't say nothing, okay? Like to get me into trouble. Those cows try to put the blame on me, see?"

"Okay. I understand."

Right. House man, probably doubling as gardener, and a cook-parlour-maid wife. And a secretary – probably following Biron around. And he was in residence, but out this morning. Fair enough.

The local police.

"Commissaire in? Castang, PJ, tell him wouldja . . . don't bother . . . morning, Commissaire. No trouble, not 'sfars I know; you got any? Routine thing; passing by, thought I'd have a word. Some stuff about a burglary outbreak. No more than usual? I see it all then: there ought to be a note in the margin, complaint from a notable and go easy. You've had no backlash? Subprefect's brother-in-law strikes again. These big isolated villas ugly as hell, stuffed full of art objects: there's a lot of them round here. If there's nobody there, d'you have an alarm link? Biron, never 'eard'vim, some Parisien? Oh I see, a big shot, all is now clear. Well if the place is lived in what's he fussing about? Secretary? Manages local affairs, property-like? Well in with the mayor I suppose? Well look, fill me in, wouldja? Then I can make a report for the city, a golden syrup job they can shut his mouth with: word probably came down from Paris. If you know any local dirt put me wise, so's I don't put my foot in it. Yes, thanks, a cup of coffee would go down well."

Quack quack: glug-glug.

"Well, well, say no more. I'll keep my mouth shut and so will you. Neither of us want the Préfecture on our neck. Nor RG, ha ha. No local power structure, huh? One never knows with these types from Paris where the influence got put in: if it isn't the Cour des Comptes it's the frigging Académie Française. So we'll just make like this never happened, okay? The mouth sewn up, stop any black marks flying about. It's natural enough since the scare down in Marseille; the Minister eats crackers in bed and if there are crumbs it's our fault."

Once out of the door, this cheerful imbecile was translated into a very different personage.

It had been a very great actor who had first taught him how to play this rôle: indeed it had been the Louis Jouvet of *Quai des Orfèvres* who had chalked the first arrow on a Paris pavement which led by odd movements of instinct and intelligence towards a life in the half-world: the twilight world too of black comedy ('Bizarre – you said bizarre?' – he could still hear clearly that extraordinary voice – 'how bizarre I find that!'). The moving, appalling composition of the down-at-heel routine cop; poor and shabby, humble and sarcastic: black cloud of corrupt cynicism and the sudden sharp light of purity. Lesson; that the anaesthesia of vice can and does co-exist with the most exquisite sensitivity. Outrageous Jouvet, vinous and deadly, in one twitch and intonation moving from the highest moral seriousness to the grossest farce.

He himself had not known that world of the prewar Préfecture of

181

Police, of squalid little offices that stank, of greasy insolent clerks with satinette sleeves, sitting on round leather pads in underclothes that were never changed, a filthy cigarette butt glued to an unshaven lip, exhaling a reek of black broken teeth and stale coffee warmed up with rum. Every little crim-brig cop an executioner's assistant; misery-existence racked between the urine-scented basements unwhitewashed of the Quai des Orfèvres, and the never-aired garret in the Rue du Roi de Sicile. Not even Richard had known that life of dirt, disease and ignorance; eczema and tuberculosis omnipresent and equi-not-distant . . . made bearable only by alcohol. Clock marked in sections by the morning rum giving way to the nukey-red and in turn to the cheap sticky commercial apéros.

He had known, though, someone who had been brought up there, and his whole day was dogged by the two figures of Louis Jouvet and Monsieur Bianchi.

The enquiries on behalf of families! The petty bourgeoisie, mostly, emptying their bowels of their mingy mean secrets. The battered babies and the violated daughters and aborted sisters, and worn-out collapsed fat smelly mothers: the ether-sipping and cocaine-sniffing, the never-ending alcohol, 'la goutte': the petty peculation of greasy black paper and paper money, backstair blackmail, the manipulator manipulated. It is just the same today, even if the Bank of France now keeps its paper whiter and crisper, and the underpants are changed once a week . . .

The discreet and confidential enquiries were mostly done by the girls nowadays. But the shadow of Monsieur Bianchi still lay like his finger (brown and ragged-edged like the maize paper Gitane that lived in his mouth, perpetually relit from an old petrol storm-lighter; dry-knotted, pointing always accurately) on those dossiers. Nothing could have retired him but force, and it was a bullet in the lung that was needed in the end to do the job. Semi-literate and unable to spell; but nobody knew the human heart like Bianchi.

Castang had learned the technique from him. The tone slow and pompous, the words full of earnest clichés, but both essentially kind, and always superhumanly patient: ramble as you wish, we've all the time in the world. Shabby, humble to the point of diffidence, terribly grateful to be asked to sit down and rest the feet, overwhelmed by the offer of a cup of coffee. The insistence that all appearances (never mind realities) to the contrary every interlocutor is a balanced, sensible and reasonable being. This technique is very old and was invented by Inspector Bucket over a hundred years ago: Castang had been made to read *Bleak House* by Vera. In English too. It hadn't killed him because it was so utterly seizing – 'saisissant'! He was allowed to skip the boring Esther-bits with their sugary smirk. But Grandfather Smallweed and Mr. Guppy, Mr. Tulkinghorn and Mr. Chadband were French and he had met them in Paris. And Mr. Quale, with his shining knobs for temples and his concern about Africa – have we not known him in the Palace of the Elysées? And Bucket! – Bianchi to the life, buttonholing people with that dreadful finger, licking his pencil and margarining respectable tradesmen . . .

He was doing it right now to the combustibles merchant whose dealings in coal, wood, or domestic-fuel-oil all at keenest prices had brought him to a padded, satin-lined comfort opposite Biron's house. 'Now you're not a man to go gossiping over no card table, and your goodwife knows how to use her eyes while keeping command over the unruly tongue, as the Good Book tells to us, and a lifetime in this trade has teached me which there isn't better advice not nowhere. It's a nasty word for a nasty thing, is blackmail. Which you wouldn't want, supposing you was to confide in the discretion of the investigating officers . . . hush: no need to protest for you'd know was you just one day in these shoes of mine what the Archbishop himself has to guard against the evilthinker . . . of the officers, you'd be satisfied wouldn't you to know how that officer knows how to keep a secret and not go attracting attention among the neighbours'.

Much less crude was – had to be – the approach that afternoon to the secretary. Jouvet was needed here: no over-acting could be allowed to creep into voice or manner, because this was no puffed-up village magnate. This good lady had been in the bull-ring before: she shied even at the suggestion of a meeting in the local commissariat, and his efforts to get into the house were turned down flat before he was past the insinuation stage. She only agreed to the town hall after resistance. He had been brought out into the open a good deal more than he would have liked. She wasn't going to deal with any understrappers, it was made clear, and the Secretary of the Mairie, putting him in a little office back of the Births, Deaths and Marriages, confirmed that he had known the lady some years, and she wasn't one to get dust thrown in her eyes. She appeared exact to the minute of the appointment; fiftyish and faded but trim in a jersey two-piece; not an ounce overweight.

And started with a minute scrutiny of his identity.

"I'd like a photostat of this," tapping his official card with a polished nail.

Castang smiled. Cheek! but he felt some admiration. A counter-attack was also in order.

"As you know very well, Madame –"

"Mademoiselle."

"Noted – what you suggest is under no circumstances permissible, and to put the confidentiality of any exchange beyond question I will ask whether you have a cassette recorder in your bag. And we'll set that aside, with your permission, and I'll lay emphasis," his own fingernails might not be polished, but were scrubbed, "on the one immoveable condition attached to my speaking to you: no word goes outside this room. And that includes your employer."

"You can exact no such condition from me."

"I can and do. As you have had the opportunity of verifying, an officer of Judicial Police of my rank does not come here to turn up old birth certificates."

"You must indicate the nature of your interest."

Castang blew his nose lengthily and then said "State Security."

"Nonsense. As you must know, Monsieur de Biron holds no representative mandate, and any suggestion of dealings on whatever level with a foreign –"

"Stop. No such suggestion has been made. Nor will be – by me . . . You had better be very careful," making the finger long, white, dry. "I have no connection with the surveillance services. As my credentials make clear. The PJ's concern is with crimes definable by the Penal Code and within the competence of the Assize Court," scowling horribly.

"I ask," glacial, "how that could in the remotest concern myself."

"Blackmail, Mademoiselle, falls within these parameters."

"But you can't be serious!"

"If you are not yet convinced that I don't sit here," with a killing circular look at shelves of municipal archives, "to amuse myself, then you run the risk of being charged with outrage, if not rebellion,

184

towards a state functionary. It's not the Assize Court, but it is occasionally forgotten that the Correctionelle exists to correct. Very well? Then don't let's have any more invincible ignorance if you please." Jouvet knew well the art of bellowing in a whisper.

"But who – I mean whom . . .?"

"If you will listen; without interrupting." Lay your ship alongside that of the enemy and you cannot go far wrong, said Admiral Nelson: sound man. "A judicial enquiry is initiated. By the authority of the Procureur. Upon whose request? An anonymous denunciation? Upon the faith of a common informer? Or upon that of a citizen of high repute and blameless antecedents? Whichever it may be, and whatever credence we initially afford, greater as might be thought evident in the latter case, we are not credulous people, Mademoiselle. We sift," glaring. "Sift. And whom do we sift? Logically, the close associates – known or unknown – of the author. The instigator enjoys a presumption of good faith, of innocence. Particularly, we may say, in the case of a gentleman who has rendered services to the state: is placed to do so anew. But," the finger became supple, snaky, "a double prudence enjoins and imposes itself. May not such a person have an ulterior set of motives? An approach such as I describe; might it be designed to blunt enquiry, to disarm criticism? To enable it later to be said 'But I was the first to welcome and encourage investigation'? Beware, Mademoiselle, of those who claim they have nothing to conceal. We have all of us things we prefer to conceal." True, true, but keep going with those body-punches, and get one in below the belt.

"If these confidences were violated, Mademoiselle, the Court would show displeasure. The Procureur has punitive powers."

"No one, no one, has ever, in my entire career questioned my integrity or my discretion. I wouldn't be where I am."

"Very glad indeed I am to hear it," said Castang pleasantly. "Let's continue along these lines."

"What do you want to know?" she said at last.

"Everything." Tout: the monosyllable came out flat and hard like a small-calibre pistol shot; quite enough to knock over the opposition at quarters this close. She was biting her lips, had clutched her handbag upon her lap, hands folded protectively over it. Castang put a small cigar in his mouth and aimed it; eyes blue and horrid holding her in the sights over the flame of the lighter.

"Be it private or personal. Drain and disinfect every possible seat of

185

infection," tapping the lighter against his sinus. "The only possible way," restoring the lighter to his pocket; it was the colour of synthetic orangeade and spoilt the effect, "of safeguarding Monsieur de Biron, against any person wishful of bringing leverage to bear, is to identify and isolate the abscess. This has to include his wife and any other members of his immediate family. I wish to know about stimulants, which can be small boys as easily as amyl nitrate. The blade of the little penknife in a waistcoat pocket which scrapes white powder into a fine line."

"You don't suggest – " much shocked.

"I suggest nothing. If such a thing existed, as it can and does side by side with stamp-collecting, you are the person to know."

There was something, certainly. She was troubled, hesitant; she had localised the shred of fibre stuck so naggingly in her teeth, and in Maltaverne's teeth too, but worried at being caught in public working away with the safety pin. He kept silence and looked out of the window. A revolting sansevieria plant occupied the sill with its stiff spiky clump.

"Commissaire . . . I must get this clear. What connection have you with the other? Has he been working under your instructions?"

"The other?" bringing a bleak eye to bear and hoping that the extremely noisy alarm bell was inaudible.

"You approach me – or pretend at least to do so – directly while at the same time an indirect kind of a . . . I suppose that to you is a usual sort of technique. I'm expected to accept that as commonplace. In the world of politics a good deal of deviousness exists, but let me tell you I don't like it."

"No separate approach has been authorised by me. If such has been made or attempted be assured that I shall know how to deal with it."

"A man . . ."

"Kindly express yourself more clearly. A police official – or representing himself as such? Did you not give his credentials the same scrutiny as you did my own just now?"

"He came with a written word of recommendation," unhappily "from my employer. After that I couldn't very well . . ."

"Can you describe this individual?"

"A heavy, stocky sort of . . . lumpish way of moving."

"Aha, that sounds familiar; my esteemed colleague on the economics front. However, profoundly tactless of him not to have mentioned it. You are," with a thin smile, "the unwitting witness of a procedure fairly common in government service. Not doubtless the first time you've come across it. Known to the English as oneupmanship, and to the Americans as sticking it into your dear colleague and breaking it off short."

"That does sound familiar – to borrow your expression," laughing a bit over-heartily in an effort to break the tension: for a moment this official, a nasty piece of work at any time, had looked nastier still by far. Not an expression one liked to see on anybody's face.

"Very well," said Castang, making a fairly accurate shot at what was in her mind, "you'll have gathered that even enquiries upon a high level of confidentiality are not exempt from interference. You have observed the precautions I take and you'll begin to see why. I'll be the more careful still in consequence. I might add that I see no possible justification for viewing this matter from an economics standpoint." He was shaken, and she had seen it, and didn't like it: he was talking too much and too wordily. "There was of course a financial and fiscal check. Standard procedure, and to my eye totally irrelevant."

"He was asking too about – associates," scanning him.

"He was, was he? Exceeding his instructions." Forestalled, damn it. No, Monsieur Maltaverne, I won't under-estimate you: it doesn't do.

"So the Police Judiciaire," quite merrily now that she was beginning to enjoy a situation she had understood "has something of a flea in its ear." Just a little spitefully; getting her own back for his having frightened her.

He had lost his edge upon her, and it wouldn't be easy to recapture.

"Personal associates?"

"That too."

"Did he take notes?"

"He seemed to be relying more upon memory."

"Irregular, most irregular," snapped Castang. He had to discredit this bastard somehow. "Nor ask for your signature to a deposition? That won't do. As you must know, the debates before any tribunal must by law be oral and contradictory, and by exactly the same token in the preliminaries only the written word eventually duly signed and witnessed – confidential or not this won't do. If your words are not to

187

be taken out of context, even distorted or misquoted. For your own protection," paternal now, more gently, "or nothing would have evidential value and we're in the realm of hearsay. You need have no misgiving," holding up a hand. "Even at such hearings as might not be held in camera – agreement is always reached with the tribunal and prosecutor that sources be protected." His experience had taught him that even sophisticated persons who wouldn't for an instant be taken in by a political or financial manoeuvre were oddly naive about criminal-code bullshit, and could be overawed; even by nonsense as crude as this.

Whew, a close shave. It wasn't likely that Maltaverne would be hanging about dogging anyone's footsteps: the animal had, as an urban police officer, no standing hereabouts; could be challenged, and knew it. But he would have covered up, playing Castang's own game of having been requested by Biron himself to take a good careful look around. And he couldn't trust that woman. She was experienced, and would take every possible opportunity of verifying. For himself he wasn't worried since any enquiry she made would find its way automatically back to Richard. But if that animal had left her a phone number, and said something on the lines of 'anything you find a bit funny don't hesitate to clear with me; I'll check it out' . . . In which case he was burned, and had better beat it with what he had, because it would be wise to expect the worst.

"There's probably no harm done," said Richard comfortably. Castang had not come storming in dramatically crying 'I'm burned!' "So we know that the animal is prudent as well as tricky. And if he reaches the same conclusions about me; on the whole these conclusions are favourable. He'll be chuckling and saying 'Thought as much!' And that may help to put him off his guard, to think he's got me taped. All right, have a nice domestic evening."

So he did, and found Vera in a serious frame of mind. While in the daily routines of man-at-the-office and child's-mealtimes she could

188

be, and generally was, bristly with barbed grievances against society in general and the French in particular; but if, as had just happened, he were away for a day or two she liked to welcome him back with small sybaritic comforts. Nothing, she always said, inconsistent in her attitudes: the true equality of women was something he had not understood yet. 'How patient I am'.

"How patient I am!"

"How patient we both are," said Vera. He basked in all this mutual admiration and ate the lavish supper belonging to her best days: eggs scrambled with fresh mushrooms; in season but . . .

"Where did you get these?"

"Judith went out and picked them at the crack of dawn before the village children got there: aren't they delicious; she brought a whole basket and a book from Adrien." He couldn't get used to the dread Divisional Commissaire having another name. "North wind stuff."

"He takes this theory very seriously."

"So do I; it's very interesting, all about Oliver Cromwell."

"I don't see that it's anything but quite simple. The standard of public morality has always been higher up there in the north. Something to do with common law."

"And why – what is the origin of all that?"

"I don't know: their bourgeoisie is less grasping. They don't have all this," tapping that day's paper full, as every day nowadays, of yet another company-owner who had organised a fraudulent bankruptcy, smuggled a few million gold francs into Switzerland, or simply slaughtered a few employees by disregarding safety precautions.

"Oh, they had their share of that too. 'Professors who have been to school with Mr. Gripe-man in Love Gain, which is a market town in the county of Coveting, in the north'." Quote from a gentleman named Bunyan, whom she explained: he too was delighted with people like Mr. Two-Tongues (parson of this parish) and Mr. Facing-Both-Ways. "This fellow never visited France?" he enquired.

"I'm quite sure that in the past – I have to admit a rather dim past – women there were treated with far more respect and enjoyed a greater real equality. Even today they don't go rushing out to work with the same frenzied aggressiveness as here. More composed, more genuinely thoughtful and less idiotically intellectual. And less infected with the Teachings of the Prophet and all those frightful ayatollahs from Saint

Paul on: this detestable orientalism that has done Europe so much harm." She continued in this vein some little time. He was listening; he was interested; but his eyes were watering and he began to find the effort not to yawn unbearably hard.

"I really must have an early night."

"Whenever I speak seriously to you, invariably you discover within a very few minutes an unconquerable fatigue." Sorrowfully, but more pitying than spiteful. Men take such a very, very long time to unseal the eyelids towards anything at all new, reflected Vera, sitting by the fire – how nice to have a fire – long after he had gone to bed.

Burr burr. It wasn't the alarm clock but the frigging telephone. He had been so deeply asleep that he now knocked several things over with resounding crashes, including the alarm clock and a candlestick (Vera was not really making warfare upon Electricité de France: one must re-educate, she said, the eye. We don't need all that artificial light).

"Wah," he said; remembered who he was, and said "Yes, Castang – up to a point that is."

"What? Gendarmerie here. That Commissaire Castang? Message from Commissaire Richard and could you get out 's smart 's you could manage, sorry but that's the wording given."

"Where?" bleakly. (Imbecile . . .)

"Sorry. His house."

"What's the matter with his house?"

"'S on fire, 's all I know."

"What?!"

"Don't shout at me; 's not my fault. I know nothing, just passing the message on 's all I can do. Back at the switch-board, they don't tell me nothing. Just a frigging silicon chip's all I am." It sounded comically like Vera complaining that she was the electronic zzz, the programming relay, the minuterie for orgasms and soft-boiled eggs: after five minutes exactly your record will stop playing.

"Sorry," said Castang. "Collecting myself. That's all you know? Right, I'll be as quick as possible." Vera will certainly have been woken by all that racket: don't alarm her.

"Hell of a bloody noise," said a cross sleepy voice.

"Yes, well, I'm not happy either. Got to go out" striking a match and lighting the candle: slower perhaps but not so hard on the eye at –

190

hell, two-fifteen, near's made-no-matter.

"What a sodomity."

"Exactly. But go back to sleep."

"'Nother homicide?"

"I very sincerely hope not," tying a shoelace. Stopping in the living room for cigarettes, for one very quick very small whisky. Did one want a gun, might one enquire? No, one mightn't. And the car started at a quarter of a turn: Renault in making a good design for a mechanical donkey has at last made a real car. Winged donkey. Not much traffic this time on city outskirts.

Richard's flossy, eminently desirable village was on a spur of hill, a whaleback really, sticking out into the valley. But, thought Castang, it'll still only be the village fire-brigade . . .

And if Richard has asked for me urgently – what does that mean? Is this personal or professional? The serious-crimes brigade, or something new about north winds? Like don't light fires when a stiff one's blowing. The mistral too is a north wind.

'Mon Père disait

C'est le vent du Nord

Qui fait que nos filles

Ont le regard tranquille

De nos vieilles villes

Qui fait que nos belles

Ont les cheveux fragiles

De nos dentelles'.

Brussels Jack. Best poet we've got, still.

He could see the flames from a long way away. Too much of that house is wood, and once it got a hold . . . But Richard was a careful person, and while Judith might be a bit dotty . . . not dotty that sort of way, definitely. He couldn't remember when the Serious Crimes Brigade had last had a case of arson . . . the gendarmerie had them fairly often – farmers, with too much tied up in expensive machinery and needing to get liquid in a hurry.

It was the north wind, 'my father said', that broke England away from Zeebrugge. Did queer things to people. It was the sea bridge that made the English suffer from apartheid. From closer up the cop took over because it was clear at a glance that the house was a goner. The merry blaze was in its last paroxysm now that the professionals were

191

pouring it on from close quarters but down to its foundations the house was no more. The volunteer group from the village must have known from the start there was little they could do, and lost no time in alerting the city group from the North Station, but that was a good fifteen kilometres: a quarter of an hour's delay, and that had been quite enough to make the powerful equipment and sophisticated approach a merely formal academic exercise.

Castang sought for authority. There was much, altogether too much: a mayor and a court of village wiseacres: a lieutenant of gendarmerie: the captain of the Sapeurs-Pompiers, very military. All were voluble.

"Same problem as you get with these old farmhouses – too much wood. Tinder-dry and woosh, not a chance. And at least they have the old thick masonry . . ."

"Everything against one from the start. Like a bloody fortress with all these trees and high hedges: had to hack our way in. Too bloody well ungetatable."

"Windows left open – very good ventilation down there in the cellar – real helpful, oil and a nice big pile of logs. Proper feu de joie, went up there like a bonfire on Saint John's Eve. Ding dong merrily on high, invite the village to come and grill sausage."

"Where," asked Castang, "is Commissaire Richard?"

"Who's that?"

"That the owner?"

"Got out all right; cut it rather fine though, mucking about."

"That's the chap, middle-aged, silver sort of hair? Proprietor? Sent him for first aid; bit burned round the hands and arms. No, nothing very bad, but shock and all, send them automatically in the ambulance. Very easy to catch pneumonia or whatever on top, you know."

"Monsieur Richard? – took him straight off to hospital. There wasn't anything he çould do."

"Madame Richard?" asked Castang patiently.

"Went with him no doubt. But whether she just went along or whether she needed treatment, that I couldn't tell you."

"You'll be here for another hour or so?"

"Who're you?"

"Castang, PJ. Colleague of Monsieur Richard's."

"What's your involvement, hereabouts?"

192

"In the first place because he took the trouble to phone and ask me," containing irritability. "In the second because one never knows. May be more to this than meets the eye."

"Criminal origin, you're suggesting? Safely leave that to me. My field of expertise, my responsibility. Sort of suggestion always being made, gains too easily facile credence, the press there always like a flash of light, just the thing we needed for headlining page five. Goddam rumours spread quicker'n any fucking fire. Police officer, oh sure. Basque terrorists. Breton extremists. Corsican fanatics. The ecologists who blew up EDF's great big four hundred thousand volt pylon!"

"Yes, well don't let your imagination run away with you." Drily. A bit too drily.

"Look, Mister Castaing, you leave this to me, right? When it's properly cooled, have no fear, we'll go in there."

Castang sought the gendarmerie officer, whom he knew, and would incline less to bloodthirsty tales about ecologists. Anyway, had it been ecologists, even of the most loony sort, who'd stolen an air-to-air missile and popped it off at the nuclear power station? Hadn't made much of a dent, but created fearful havoc in the Prefecture – all the civil-defence people (sleepyheads, serve them right) had been getting neurotic nightmares ever since.

"Everybody packing up to go?"

"Not much left one can do, alas."

"You thinking of leaving a dogsbody on guard?"

"You think so? Not as though there were anything to loot, though."

"I've nothing to go on myself. In confidence, and it's just based on feelings, I'd be happier. Soon as I can get one of my boys I'll stick him on post. Matter of holding the fort, till then? You'd oblige me."

"Can do. Nothing abnormal."

"Richard might know something – know where they took him?"

"Polyclinic I should imagine in Saint Just. You fussed?"

"No. But he took the trouble to put a call to me through your switchboard, before they swept him off."

"So he did. My brigadier told me but it slipped my mind. Okay."

Poor Judith! They'd made a right Passchendaele of her garden. Hacking their way in was all too accurate a description, and putting it mildly at that. Everybody knows in theory that the Fire Brigade is twice as bad as the fire, but one has to go through the experience for it properly to sink in. Hm, a radical job, and it wasn't the moment to get emotional about that. Vera would, soon enough. Though Vera, bless her, was blessedly far from unstrung, in any real crisis. It was when he walked through her kitchen with muddy boots on that she became shrill.

What about insurance? Richard as a prudent householder would have one. And insurance companies would be quick to dart at any hint of an escape clause in their small print. Their expert might for once be a help to the police (all cops have the greatest hatred and contempt for 'experts') but that would not do Richard the human being any good. That's one dog we'll let lie. Have a little chat with that fire captain. This one we want kept in the family.

The gendarmerie lieutenant could be trusted to keep the press at bay. What else was there?

The night porter at the clinic was officiously helpful.

"Only an outpatient job. Be over there still, resting up, I dare say."

The night sister was coolly ironic.

"Quiet evening. The gentleman to be sure with the defective razor in the bathtub who shortcircuited himself – wasn't much we could do for him. Two overdoses of different drugs, three addicts with imaginative and ingenious pretexts for obtaining more, one accident with a tinopener, a miscarriage – oh yes, the gentleman who dropped the toothglass and trod on the shards, oo I'm BLEEding: nothing for the police in all this. Ah, the burns? Not to write home about, but they're painful things, no doubt about it, so I've popped him in for a day or two's observation; no, not the specialised unit. They'll quite likely want to take a patch off the thigh. No you can't, he's asleep and under sedation. I'm not about to argue the point, Monsieur Castang. The wife yes, she's resting over there in a cubicle and you can take her home whenever you like. Only the nerves a bit jarred as is very understandable. Excuse me – what? That's not broken it's only dislocated, pop that back for you in no time. What you been doing then with a finger at this hour of night, hey? ..."

"No," the switchboard girl was saying. "We don't take infarctus cases here. Cardiology unit, University Hospital. Not at all, pleased to be of service." He rescued Judith.

"I was just lying there wondering. No, one can't sleep, it's like the

194

Gare d'Austerlitz. Easy to phone a taxi, but where would one tell him to go, now that I've no home left?"

"You're coming with me."

She came obediently, in the tatty dressing-gown over her nighty. Her hair was usually in a bun, showing the good structure of the plain and beautiful face; now loose and long.

"Frightful woman that," in an undertone, catching sight of the night sister on an errand of mercy, "but undeniably, good at her job. Henri, you are kind. Oh dear, don't let me start talking; she told me to shut up, most brutally."

"No, don't talk," said Castang, though he was longing to encourage her. But it would stop her sleeping. And she might say extravagant and misleading things.

"I'm sorry," said Castang gently.

"No," said Vera getting out of bed, "don't be. I was only dozing uneasily, because my bones told me there was a catastrophe, and the ones I imagine are much worse. Leave it to me; I'll cope. And so will she. Women do, you know," looking at him wryly.

And so much better than men, thought Castang rolling himself in a blanket on the living-room sofa. It wasn't a thing he had succeeded in defining accurately. Their minds are more flexible; less material; less formal? Not thing-minded? This is exactly it – I lie here worrying about exact definitions, and they don't.

Undress, or not undress? And what time was dawn, this late in the year? Just unwind. When it's there, you'll wake up for it. He did.

Gave himself the time to brew some coffee amid the scatter of tea-cups and tisane packets on the kitchen table. Drank it quietly, thinking. The dog rapped its tail in sympathy, tock tock on the tiled floor. The kitchen clock – about 1830; they built good clocks around that agitated, tormented, revolutionary time – made its slow comforting noise. Stood up, buckled gunbelt, went out to where he had left his car on the street. Yes, there was the glimmer of easterly light beginning. Cloudy morning and still, with a faint southerly drift of mild air. No feeling of rain.

He parked on the grassy verge of the straight bit of road before the downhill curve above Richard's house; the laneway narrow with scrub woodland growing on both sides. He picked and ate three blackberries. Nice dewy morning; one could see the pattern now of smallish clouds huddling like sheep. Might be sunny, later. Not an impressive cloudscape, just a nice, pretty, painterly sky. He walked quietly down towards the scene of ruin.

There was no gendarme at the gate. The lazy pigs, thought Castang unemotionally. Well, he was here, and in time. But with a few hours to go . . . He had phoned last night to the PJ night-duty bird; told him to send someone out, didn't matter who; whoever was first in, in the morning. And of course he could go and stir up those coffee-drinking buggers but it meant going back for the car, and he couldn't be bothered.

The ruin was sadder still by daylight, looking foul and smelling sour. The broken trees, the deep-scored ruts in Judith's grass, the scatter of charred wood – didn't bear looking at. But the hedge at the end was there still, and in view . . . and the sun would come up just the same. It's recuperable, he thought. One has lost all that one possessed. But there is a deep tenacity in those two. And what had Richard said? – 'I hate this house, really'. Too much junk; one moved easier, less laboriously, when less loaded down with all that rubbish . . . And the soil was intact. Wood ash made quite good fertiliser . . . He stood there, grinning a little.

But there is work to do. The masonry walls were standing but everything else had gone through into the basement. 'Well yes' he could hear Richard drawling, 'it looks impressive but there was a lot of short-cutting'. 'For example?' 'Under these tiles' – in the hall – 'there ought to be concrete and there's only wood. Insurance company would insist on its being done but what the eye doth not see the heart doth not grieve over' laying a finger on his nose.

'Fuel store underneath see?' The fire captain had seen as much straight off. 'If it ate back there into those cellar stairs and caught a draught then it would build up and implode'.

He remembered the big porcelain-tiled stove. 'Burns anything' said Richard with satisfaction, 'and once you've got it built up – ever since oil got so dear we only use it really below freezing point'. The fire chief hadn't seen it, but guessed at its existence.

'Lot of people have these old stoves again, to economise. Some of them more picturesque than safe. Folk give the cinders a rake out at night and fill'er up to the top, being a bit sleepy forget to close the ash door, and go off to bed: an hour later the thing's red hot – if the sparks haven't already set the chimney alight . . .' They would find the carcase of the stove fallen through, down there at the bottom, and the hypothesis would satisfy everybody. Are you quite sure you closed the ash door? Yes, one was quite sure. But by the third time of asking, one was no longer quite so sure. A technique a cop used, practically daily. In fact the surer an eyewitness tended to be, the more likely he was to be wrong. Not necessarily far wrong. The small fat villainous 'dark-complexioned' Arab gangster didn't always turn out to be a great big fair-haired Polish villain. Just a bit off: the H on a number-plate of the bandit's car was an M or a W.

Castang had two choices. To be a good cop and disturb nothing, and especially no evidence, until the fire-brigade expert got here, which would be nine or even ten. Or go poke about quietly in the ruins. They'd poured in gigantic quantities of water in the effort to stop the oil tank going up, and in that greasy black mess somewhere: he felt quite certain . . . It wouldn't be hard to force that basement door. What was there to pinch down there? Logs, Judith's garden tools, old sacks and kindling wood, the plants that had to be kept from the light – who'd bother? The average bourgeois yes, but not Richard, who had got Lucciani to fit a delightful booby-trap on the door to the hall involving a nasty electric shock and a couple of New Year's Eve bangers. Alarming the evil-doer while alerting Maestro.

Memo, find the fireman who broke in that cellar door: likewise the lock, down in the débris. Meantime, what sort of trace did thermite or other small incendiary device leave? Castang didn't know, but the fire people's technician would. No, he'd better not go rummaging in anything. Would ruin his shoes, and probably his trousers, anyhow.

There were a lot of small noises. There always were, he supposed: even drenched to this extent there would be hot bits still cooling inside the pudding, but mostly it would be soggy water-noises, and the settle and slither of the unstable ruin. He paid no attention and went on staring – and looked up, and his guts made a loud heavy bang; hit by a battering ram. From the corner of the building, hitherto hidden by a lump of wall higher than a man, the sound of any prowlings muffled under the drip and suck of wetness, standing still and tall and massive, calmly studying his subject, a man: named Maltaverne.

Castang had noticed himself trembling a little; nothing very bad. About the way a glass of beer would on the ferry: a calm crossing when

197

only the vibration of the engines puts a shiver on the surface. You wouldn't notice till the froth went down. His hands had clenched into fists in the deep side pockets of his Canadian jacket, put on because an autumn dawn is chill as well as moist. He loosened them deliberately, moved his neck to get the stiffness out. Maltaverne's posture hadn't changed.

"Looking to see whether everything's all right?" Castang enquired lightly.

"On the same errand as yourself, I should suppose. When I heard about this I wasn't quite satisfied." The voice was the same as usual; a stickiness like an industrial lubricant that has not warmed up enough to flow freely.

There was no point in fencing, now.

"Or to see perhaps where things went wrong? Since they did go wrong." The face opposite didn't alter at all. It's no surprise to him, thought Castang.

"Did you send away the gendarme that was supposed to be here?"

"That is correct," moving now unhurriedly to bring himself to the same level, careful to keep the skirts of his overcoat free of debris. Bothered was the last thing you'd call him. "It wasn't a coincidence."

Maltaverne halted a few paces off, putting his foot on a lump of fallen masonry, resting an elbow on his knee.

"I pulled a bit of rank," he agreed, with a smile that was not sly. Attractively boyish, pleased at a scrap of innocent cunning. "He'll think nothing of it. Whereas you, of course . . . Yes," as though he had also made his mind up that any fencing was now worthless. "How much do you know about all this?"

"Condensing it, that you're friendly with a man called Biron."

"Oh. Ah. Richard told you that, I presume. Indiscreet," sadly, as though he'd always known that Richard wasn't really trustworthy. "And what d'you know about a man called Biron?"

"He's one of these people who understand that power isn't what you do, but what you get other people to do. He'll never make any headlines."

"Richard tell you that, too?" with something of a sneer.

"I spent a couple of days looking him up, in his little town over there. You'd been there too."

"Ah." Appreciative.

198

"Didn't really need to go as far as Paris." It had had to be brought to a head, and now it was there. "Reducing him to a formula, though he's a lot more complex than that, he's anticipating a swing back, a reaction in the country. 'Nother right-wing government next time. Something crisp and efficient; after all this well-meaning doctrinaire fumbling. So we get organised. We can't have any more of this crude, clumsy-footed fascist crowd. Like the Service d'Action Civique. Hopelessly discredited. Worse, old-fashioned. Marseillais gangsters selling building plots on the coast. The town hall fixers forging bogus invoices. So nineteen fifty, all that. Instead we have now Mister Clean, with ideals. No more crooked bankers with friends in the Vatican. No more drugs or prostitutes. Idealists. Like you. Very difficult to find idealists in the police. Cynical sort of business. But you'd be idealist, once you heard from Biron that there were more. You'd be even more idealist, in Paris, wouldn't you? And in a moment – misguided – of enthusiasm you even told Richard so."

"We may as well get to the bottom of this," Maltaverne in an indifferent voice.

"Biron had just a moment of impatience. I'm not boring you? I'm not wasting your time? Just the one error and that minute. He took a look at Richard and saw a very intelligent man, whose career had somehow petered out, on account of a spirit of independence that didn't please them in Paris all that much these last ten years. The error was to think that intelligence is all Richard cares for. Mistake we've all made, I suppose. None of us understood Richard. I did no better, so I suppose I don't blame you, all that much."

"Say your piece," said Maltaverne, "but don't get fancy. You've always been an over-decorative object, so don't peacock about."

"True. I'll try. I don't take any credit. In fact . . . but I don't want to get personal. You're very bright. Brighter than me. That's a mistake. Sorry," there had been a gesture that was irritation, no more. "There was one fact Biron didn't know, which was that Richard put himself back to zero, the way he did when he was twenty, in 1940. He started again from scratch. It's a thing that doesn't obey logic, or intelligence, which is why neither Biron nor yourself would understand it. Your bad luck."

"Castang," said Maltaverne deliberately. "You're not a person lacking in intelligence, and little as I like you I've always had a certain

199

respect for you. But there's a flaw in you – you're intolerably gabby."

The best way to show agreement with that, thought Castang, was to nod. He took the end of the cigarette he had been smoking and tossed it among the ruins. Some incendiary expert raking around might pounce upon it and decide that it was valuable. One clue, for the use of. Some sort of grin must have crossed his face because the other was stung.

"It's funny?" sarcastically.

Castang was full up with muddled feelings. A fatalism; it was too late for talk, for the tortuous approach: a sudden impatience with the deviousness. Growing fear, because there was no way out. He lit another cigarette with the threadbare nonchalance of the man knowing that the executioner is in the next room, waiting for a clock to strike. The English hangman, he had read, proud of his craftsmanship, made a point of beginning with the bell and having the job neatly finished before the last of the eight strokes had died away into silence. And the English had a phrase . . . about taking time by the forelock. He pointed to the ruins.

"There's something there, for whoever knows where to look. And you do. You came to look, and if need be to efface. Correct?" The brows tightened into a deeper V, the backsight of the gun, but Maltaverne did not speak. He took his foot off the support and faced Castang squarely.

"Richard made up his mind about you," Castang went on in a voice that sounded apologetic. The man was a colleague, or should one say a former colleague? "He laid some bait and you took it. You wondered for a moment whether Biron was setting you up. This way, you decided. Stop any leak at the source. Richard was a secretive man, and kept things to himself. He wouldn't have told Fabre. He would have said nothing to Paris."

"But he did say something to you." Maltaverne's voice sounded quite friendly, and the fear crept further towards paralysing Castang. He had never seen how quick this sluggish-seeming man was supposed to be.

"Richard, they tell me, is suffering a bit from burns. It'll be a few weeks in the clinic until they heal. You could visit him. Bunch of grapes; paperback book."

"Paperback crime fiction?" suggested Maltaverne, the big jaw bunching up in a wide smile. "There'll be no evidence, you see. Only you, and you've a bad cancer, and you don't know it yet."

Do it now, before the fear chokes you.

He leaned forward a little, to spit the cigarette out. Cop technique is that of any sleight-of-hand man; an action to distract a chap from another action. He drew his gun and fired it.

The chap knew the technique too. He was, after all, a cop. I am dead, thought Castang in mid-gesture. There'll be no more worries. A monstrous fist knocked him clean off his feet. There were not even little cop-human worries about hitting his head on a stone or getting his jacket dirty. The big hole.

It was not the next world. Assuming such existed, a matter to which philosophy gave as a rule more thought than the police, though without perhaps getting much further. Not that there was too much pain, but it was a physical pain. Pain that lifted him, danced him about, rolled him over and stood him on his head. Pain in immense waves, huge rollers breaking upon a rocky shore, that ground him upon coarse salt and sand and shingle and sharp-edged shell. Pounding and battering while the undertow sucked his lungs empty and he drowned in the pain.

Then he found himself washed up beyond a tidemark. Dead, at last? Not yet: he was the toy of vertigo and nausea. His lungs laboured; there was air somewhere. This world still; a horrible world but he was still in it and of it.

Castang assembled pointers: senses for instance; shouldn't there be five? He could not see but he could hear something past the noise of waves, of that snot-coloured whirlpool of sea and sand that had disoriented him utterly. A low keening sound, both sob and whine; an animal wounded. Himself.

Then he could smell, a sour reek that brought on more nausea: he retched awhile but now he had a bearing to follow. He was lying with a face in sand or dirt, and a side, left or right he didn't know – but left and right exist, top and bottom exist – was crushed, paralysed. However, there was a hand in front of him. He wriggled the fingers; they belonged to him.

Prone and supine likewise exist. Prone, prone. A brain had begun to work. He was alive, and must make efforts. He pushed at the hand.

201

Nothing happened but another wave of retching, but that cleared his mind. Come, there are elementary principles of engineering, such as leverage. Ropes, or pulleys. A fulcrum, that was it. Push yourself up. After a few shots with rests in between he found himself sitting. Swaying about, and a head as though he'd drunk a bottle of damned cheap schnapps, but sitting and no longer sprawling; no longer a disintegrating heap of incipient decay. He'd coped with that. Now there was this pain. He could not suppress it or alleviate it but there were things that could be done, for there was a mind, appearing intact: just a bit bashed about; but functioning.

He pushed hard again and this time got his eyes open. There was the large pattern of a jacket, called a canadienne; belonging to him. Checks, they're called; those colours are known as black, white, and grey. He looked about for the rest of himself and found another colour, this one red and present in large quantities: blood, you have lost large amounts of blood, had lost, were losing. Do something about that quick or you will pass out again and this time there'll be no coming back; it will be the end. Last chance: he forced himself to look at the smashed half of him.

To his surprise it wasn't as bad as expected: it wasn't half and it wasn't his body, but an appendage that had previously been an arm. The coarse wool of the canadienne was pierced and soaked in blood. He remembered then; there'd been a bullet. God knew what was under that; ripped-up mess of bones and bloodvessels, nerves and tendons in shreds judging by the pain. There is the source. Lose no further time. Need knife.

He had a right hand, which he was propped upon, so now came a hard bit of staying upright forcing this wobble-thing, this jellyfish chest and belly to stay balanced while he sought for the right-hand trouser pocket where the knife lived or should: there it was, solid and comfortable. Comforting? Big sharp competent affair; use your teeth. The deep-incised block letters 'Glandières Laguiole' danced before his eyes.

He fumbled with buttons and got to a pullover: under that there must be a shirt which cuts, rips: there is also a heart, which beat, as it seemed to him, quite strongly. Perhaps blood had congealed, or falling upon the smashed arm had arrested the haemorrhage somewhat. He was alive and intended to stay so, so he managed to tear enough of a

202

strip to wind round below this armpit thing and get it knotted, which loving-jesus took about an hour and a half. He closed the knife-blade, used the knife to twist the ring, wedged it in the armpit. Would do for a little while, as long as he didn't pass out or frig about. Do not do either.

He needed something to concentrate upon, to help with this. What was that, over there? A laborious process of mind concluded that it was Maltaverne, whom he had forgotten, truly; utterly. This person was not a pleasant, nor a helpful subject for thought but did help attain the desired result awhile, of thinking less about his own misery. Going over there to look was undesirable, but at last, too, needful. Creeping was not the right word. Humping? Slithering? If you turned a caterpillar or perhaps a centipede upside down would it advance at all? – he didn't think so: whereas the human being did quite well on its bottom, though the bottom appeared wetter and stickier than it should be: the word 'emmerdé' acquired new and literal connotations. There was a rueful meditation during the long journey, upon the frivolous phrase 'scared shitless'. More properly though no more primly is it the physiological effect of large-calibre bullets upon muscles. Maltaverne had shot him. And it looked as if he'd shot Maltaverne.

That much indeed was obvious, even though it had been against all hope at the time. Well before he got there he was aware that Maltaverne was dead: the local insect life had made the same discovery. This hillside was drier and more – as it were – wholesome than that dismal swamp where they'd found poor Lonny, but the results would be the same, for the same irreversible mechanism had been set going. At a distance of three or four metres he sat there a longish time and thought about it.

There are triggers in the human being that nobody knows anything much about; functioning normally enough on the whole, upon command, so that one did not think of them (the sphincter muscles while a cruder affair provided perhaps a parallel). Nobody knew why the Japanese gentleman had suddenly found himself unable to stop slaughtering Lonny. The police didn't: it could just as easily have turned out to be the Iranian or the Israeli. For all their brave talk the psychiatrists did no better. The judge and the jury would decide upon the material evidence. The phrase 'irresistible impulse' was absurd as a doctrine but it existed.

Nobody knew any better what dark impulse triggered a fourteen-

203

year-old girl like Thérèse Martin into killing men (and women too). A great army of experts would dissect her down to the last morsel of the poor child's body: they wouldn't find her soul.

On the face of things he'd killed Maltaverne in self-defence: it was an acceptable legal plea which no one would question for a second. Just a tiny bit more difficult were the numerous cops and other respectable citizens who couldn't say 'He attacked me' but could and did say 'I thought he was going to attack me' and it might even be true; perhaps generally was true. It is fear that kills. Fear of the other, fear of oneself, of society, of life itself: the word 'panic' had had a clearly defined meaning once, and talk about the death-wish made things no clearer . . . Saying that Maltaverne intended to get rid of yet another inconvenient witness was nonsense. I shot him; I was panicked. Pan had hold of us both.

Vera was groping for it blindly, blindly. Could a world exist without fear? Richard, more soberly, thinking of a world beyond the north wind in which people lived in respect for the plants, the animals, the people with which they shared it. That world had existed but had never been able to banish fear. Fear, surely, was the reason why that world no longer existed.

Even if I live, thought Castang, I will never again carry a gun. That is the best I can do for now. Meanwhile, you are still a cop, so that little as you like it you must look.

His bullet had been an ordinary nine-millimetre calibre from a standard police pistol: four-inch barrel; an efficient weapon and accurate to about twenty metres. The target had been twelve to fifteen, and taken slap in the throat; trachea on the way in, spinal column on the way out. He'd never known what hit him and had been dead before reaching the ground.

Maltaverne's pistol was there a few steps off. Castang didn't bother with it; knew it when he saw it: typical of the man to carry a .44 magnum, a charge that would send a bullet through three buffalo obliging enough to stand in a row, and I wouldn't put it past him to have loaded a Teflon bullet. He'd taken that somewhere round the elbow. Taking it just about anywhere sufficed to kill one. It might take a little longer and be a little more painful. And there, doubtless, was his death arriving. It had been sitting awhile there in a tree. There are no true vultures in Europe, but we manage.

A slow small wind had blown up upon the hillside; more north-east than true north. It ruffled the hair of the two men lying there.

Lucciani, driving out from the office, was grateful that traffic was all in the other direction and that he was making good time. Not that he was late: in fact he had been tremendously early in consequence of being late too often in recent weeks. Just his luck, to have been stuck as a result of virtue with a tedious chore. He had no idea what old Castang was yacking on about with this get-out-there-fast; but fast it would be, because a Castang in the early hours, exposed moreover to the foggy foggy dew, would not be at his most genial. He reached the bottom of the hill and started on the narrow winding bit. There was Richard's house all burned out, and ours not to reason why, and where was Castang's car? He parked, got out. Oh sweet Jesus God.

A closeish call, and a lot of hanging by a thread. 'C'est le cas de le dire', had said the surgeon, because what was left of that arm had been hanging by a thread . . . And what with the loss of blood things had been highly traumatic; the word was apposite. He pulled through it, a phrase chosen to be deliberately banal.

"No occasion just yet to leave Lady Hamilton to the nation," said Vera as soon as he was properly conscious which was not for some time. Once this historical reference sank in he found it suitable.

"No Kiss-me-Lucciani? – what a horrible thought." He'd made a joke at last and was living again.

There had to be a lot of surgery, from the sawbones viewpoint quite banal nowadays, even boring.

"We've loads of them," said doctors, students, nurses, all odiously nonchalant. "Farmers keep falling into the reaper'n'binder and get brought in mangled. Worse than you. If you have the choice between a bullet and a chain saw choose the bullet."

The surgeon though, when he got around to it, was pessimistic.

"Yes, yes, dear boy, can do; constantly do do. I'd like though to have something to work with. You catch your tit in the mangle or your zizi in the motor-mower I'll fix you up as good as new, but somebody has to bring the bits in. Now you, while standing off the People's

205

Army, I ask no embarrassing questions, get hit by a rocket. The bits got strewn over an acre of surrounding countryside, and the dustpan-and-brush were insufficient. We can put a hand back on nowadays, if it's brought to us quick enough, but mending a great big hole is something else, and I can't give you any guarantee. You want to know so I'll tell you; it's six-to-four on that I'll have to take the arm off. We can give you a marvellous Japanese arm full of electronic thingies: you'll do anything with that. Plenty left to hitch it up to.''

"I won't have any thingy," growled Castang. Perish the thought; we are more than enough robotised as things are. Even he would prefer to be one of those colonels blown skyhigh in Indochina or Algeria. France used to be full of them, hobbling about with black eyepatches and sewn-up sleeves, covered to be sure in medals.

An awful fate it is being cursed with imagination when you are a cop; a combination at its worst when you are pinned down in bed snivelling with self-pity.

"Just dip it in hot tar," he told the surgeon, who grinned and went away.

Not really like Admiral Nelson. More like the legendary cavalry officer who

Lost a leg at Waterloo
At Quatre-Bras
And Ligny too

– English of course. One arrived at the field attended by thirty servants all carrying crates of champagne: one then went into battle in full-dress uniform, armed with an umbrella.

He had to be 'prepped' for the operating-room: not very nice. He decided to have nothing further to do with this miserable figure being bundled about, but the scenes he found himself imagining, of a totally new life, afterwards, were not reassuring. Hard grains of cop-intelligence kept working grittily through the swathed layers of fantasy. The Vera whose lower half had been paralysed, whom he'd lifted and wheeled about and helped wash and dress, a year and more, would know how to deal with him. She'd be exceedingly down to earth about a man with one arm. A banal affair after all and always had been. One learned to do things with one's teeth, with one's toes like a fisherman or an Indian tailor: hell, he'd even seen (admitted only on television) an African blacksmith working with his toes.

The anaesthetist appeared, rather a nice woman smelling delicious, as a change from ghouls drowning one in ether-soaked sheets.

"I want my umbrella," he mumbled slipping away from all this.

" 'L'escalier de Jade est tout scintillant de rosée'," she said sliding in her needle. " 'Lentement, par cette longue nuit, la souveraine le remonte; laissant la gaze de ses bas et la traîne de son vêtement royal, se mouiller, aux gouttes brillantes' ". . .

"Li T'ai Po," she told him when she saw him next: he had remembered to ask.

A lot of sleeping; sixteen hours at one stretch.

Quite normal, said the surgeon when he came to look. You had, you see, several kinds of bash one on top of another and your whole nervous system has to recuperate: go on sleeping.

It was comfortable enough. Water beds, electric beds, and a teddybear-for-my-girl. Nice things to eat, pots of foie gras and so on, brought by people like Orthez. Dotty intervals. 'Nuvoletta in her lightdress, spun of sixteen shimmers, was looking down on them, leaning over the banistars . . .'

"James Joyce," said Vera. "I know sleep incantations too." They said you could feel the arm even when it wasn't there.

"Is there any arm there?"

"Of course there is," said the surgeon "and don't be so bloody wet. Not denying of course a lot of fancypants in along with it. I'll lay it out for you when I've time. Roughly what would go into a modern tennis racket – ask Rossignol. What did you expect – Paddy Doyle's pig? The important thing is to move it. Today's the day, so throw the ball up and serve."

"Hurts."

"Course it hurts; what's left of you has to get used to all that. Excellent sign that it hurts: if it didn't I'd start worrying."

"Stretch it," said the physiotherapist, after an interval of stupid nurses insisting that he play with stupid toys; Rubik cubes or Chinese puzzles. "What do you feel?"

"Tingling sensation, like when you've sat on it and it's gone to sleep."

"Yes yes, stretch it more."

"Ow. Hurts like hell."

"Good," said this abominable sadist, smelling of sweat rather. "More."

"This is foul."

207

"Ah, you'd like to be James Bond; have the little Balinese dancing girl walking on your spine. Blonde with a mink glove for effleurage, who'll finish the treatment by tossing you off. There's that big night nurse who might oblige you."

"La Gravosse?" asked Castang, interested. "The one with the enormous bosom and the very sickly perfume?"

"That's her," taking hold of the arm and breaking it.

"Christ," said Castang: even being tossed off by Big Marge the Tennis Queen would be better than this.

There was a water treatment. Hot, cold, salt or sweet, needle sprays or just running: all wet. A frightful painted blonde girl, singularly unsexy.

"Every time I stretch the arm," complained Castang "my dick does too."

"O, that's very good," said Vera. "Just a sec till I lock the door and I'll fix that for you."

They throw you out even earlier than possible. You are costing of course millions a day to the Social Security, but it isn't so much that; it's all those people who've had road accidents who need your space. He never did get around to La Gravosse, but Vera's therapy was better than all that water.

"Do you have any knickers on?"

"No I took them off in the car." Once he was allowed to go home there was no more foie gras, but she made him steak tartare. As James Bond said so pompously, 'There are moments of great luxury in the life of a secret agent' – his notions of what they were seemed poorish. 'You might lend me Solitaire for a week' said the elderly drunk Raymond Chandler: one felt so sorry for him.

"Mouth," said Castang greedily.

"No no," said Vera who was straitlaced, "if fan isn't good enough neither's my face."

But it was in this manner that he got his plastic and nylon, fibreglass and titanium, carbon and Dupont Rossignol ski-and-tennis racket arm healed.

"You are now convalescent," said the surgeon happily. "I congratulate you. I congratulate myself, naturally. Even more. I'm going to sign you a chit. Six weeks paid for by the Police Department in Biarritz at Louison Bobet's thalassotherapy centre," – what a

208

splendid word that is – "and a further three at Belle Ile En Mer."

"I've deserved every minute of it."

"The arm's perfectly free now?"

"When lavishly aided by sexual stimulus, on the whole yes."

"That I can't provide."

"Not to worry," said Castang lavishly. He missed that way the climax to the excitements. Anticlimax, Richard would have said.

Vera told him. Passed on from Richard to Judith to herself. That was one story. The other one came back up from the ground, meaning Orthez.

Richard's convalescence wasn't long at all. Some of the burns on his arms were second-degree, but the areas were not large. He disregarded his entitlement to sick leave, pretending that Commissaire Domenech had slackened the reins over-much in his absence. The department seethed with jokes of an incendiary nature, there was much talk of decarbonisation, and when Fausta bought a new frock everyone agreed that it was an elegant shade of gentian-violet. The truth was that Richard had determined to keep the affair from breaking bounds. In this he was aided by everybody knowing bits of the truth but nobody knowing it all: there is agreement among senior police officers that there are certain truths that nobody wants to know; and among the more junior it is important to recognise the truths it will do no good at all to know. This applies to the press, too. As for the public, even sex won't hold its attention for more than a minute or two.

There was one person though who knew too much of the truth already. He could prove nothing, for when policemen fall upon the field of honour, in defence of Republican liberties, no effort is spared, as the Minister says at the subsequent press conference, and when that much effort is unspared it is no great matter to make two police pistols vanish. The malefactors who had planted infernal devices in Commissaire Richard's cellar had not hesitated to add assassination to arson: that all three victims should be among the upper ranks of regional authority just showed that this was a grave attempt at destabilisation, and nobody would continue to be the dupe.

Certainly not Monsieur de Biron.

Fausta placed the phone call to his house, openly, for Richard had decided upon being perfectly open.

"Richard! My dear chap – no lingering ill-effects?"

"Ach, these things take some time to heal, so one has to give them a push."

"But no golf yet awhile."

"On the contrary; just what would do me good. Some of this infernal elastic strapping on the wrist still: I'm looking for a pretext to get rid of it." And a rather crude pun about being forearmed.

"Ha, that's not bad. Bit wintry though, no? Bit heigh-ho, the wind and the rain?"

"A nice change," said Richard blandly, "from being stretched upon beds of pain."

"I say, you sound in good form. But is this an invitation?"

"It is. For this afternoon. It's lovely out," more blandly still, looking out of the window at exactly the sort of nasty rain that would be snow on higher ground.

"I'm afraid I have to be in Paris this afternoon."

"Put it off," not at all blandly.

"That all sounds rather pressing."

"No need to say more on the telephone."

"Mm. Well. I'll see what I can do."

"Do!" said Richard putting the phone down.

For what between beds of pain, bureaucracy, arguments with the insurance company, rehousing (in a tower flat known as the airy eyrie) and official types of discretion known as letting the dust settle, the seasons had revolved quite a lot. It seemed a long time since the summer holiday in England, and was.

Winter comes early to the uplands of central France. The traditional vintage weather of the grape-harvesting season gives way to the equally traditional downpour of the Toussaint, when France makes pilgrimage to put chrysanthemums upon family gravestones on lst November. One hopes for a fine spell around Guy Fawkes Day, to enjoy the smell of burning leaves as well as the less military kind of rocket. Hallowe'en, Thanksgiving – it is a good time of year. Enjoy it because all too soon the snow will fall in the mountains and golfers think of skiing instead.

The golf club was closed and the secretary gone to sun himself upon Tunisian sands. The greens had been given a coat of top dressing and left to rest: the fairways of the windy plateau lay quiet this day under a centimetre of fluffy sticky snow. In the club house a little patina of dust lay on the furniture and the central heating had been turned down to save oil.

"But this place is shut!" said Biron.

"I know," agreed Richard comfortably.

"But then why did you? –"

"For exactly that reason."

"But where is everybody?" looking around.

"There's a maintenance man, who is reading a comic book in the boiler-room and has no intention of putting his nose outside."

"I fail to understand." It was not the feigned bewilderment with which he would have ticked off a slipshod typist, though the tone was the same. A genuine bewilderment masking a genuine anger. Why be bewildered? Because it is a vain man. Why be angry? Because it is now a frightened man.

"We're going to take a simple stroll," said Richard. "Walk, man. Step out. Open your shoulders; swing your arms. It will do you good so look as though you enjoyed it."

Biron crossed his arms over his chest and looked grim like Field Marshal Haig dressing down a nincompoop ADC.

"Richard, are you trying to make a fool of me?"

"Swallow it and look as though you liked it. Head for your car and you will be escorted back here by one of my men. Ignominiously, which would humiliate you further. Instead – observe. This snow fell during the night and nobody has been on it since. Mark my footsteps well, my page, as the English sing at Christmas in Oxford Street."

"Now what is the point?"

"I'll tell you if you'll stop shouting. It's that this is a large piece of ground affording a remarkable degree of privacy when nobody is there. There are no witnesses, and no microphones. I can do as I like with you."

"You can't think of offering me violence."

"I could, very easily. Even with bandaged wrists I could make a horrible mess of you without effort. Or I could whistle up my boys like Eddie Mars. They are stationed here or there around this perimeter. They have binoculars; they have also weapons. They have also a mentality. Violent types exist, you're aware, in the police. They'd like nothing better than to fall upon you and deliver a swift kicking where it would do most good. Bulldog Drummond style."

It was by no means a continuous monologue. In fact it was exactly like the usual golf course conversation, with intervals for concentration, for addressing the ball. Biron, who certainly did not lack intelligence, and it could now be seen did not lack selfcontrol, had decided to say nothing. A captive audience, thought Richard. Not often I find one. Not often, I suppose, that I'm in that much need of one!

"We'll talk about violence, si vous voulez bien meaning I take your wishes for granted. I've been in the police a long time, and violence of one sort or another became second nature to me.

"Look around you here: I'm about to draw a comparison. This landscape is that of a very old piece of violence in the earth. Volcanic rock. Quiescent all these years; further so eroded as to be planed smooth. People then picked it up cheap and smoothed and moulded it further for this ridiculous game; and even had to introduce a few artificial asperities to add to excitement.

"I found myself, last summer, in a different landscape. A hill, curling up steep on one side, dropping away in precipice on the other – nothing very different in its natural features to a good few more of the same sort all over Europe, but possessing a strange quality of violence of its own. One could very readily imagine thought and behaviour of great violence taking place there.

"This experience brought me face to face with myself in abrupt fashion. I'm here to administer the law, specifically the criminal law, and low as my opinion of these institutions is, that's my job and I do it: no escape or evasion is permitted me. Which leaves me with a personal problem concerning violence: it isn't to me at all academic.

"It has led my mind into some obscure paths, because having reached the age of sixty and done nothing but administer some very poor quality man-made regulations is to say the least a very feeble achievement.

"I know a police officer, a good one, up in Glasgow. It's one of the places like Palermo or Bogota where extreme violence is a commonplace, a way of life. His detestation, he says, of violence is so great that he'll go to any lengths to stop it, which is catch twenty-two. Ah, he's around forty; he'll either go completely off his nut which is very likely, plenty of cops faced with this problem do; or he'll learn to live with it, and with himself, since it's to himself he does the most violence.

"With the means, and the thought, at our disposal we don't get far. The means are lacking, because purely technical means, like more cops, better radios, faster cars, more powerful computers, are useless when the end is wrong. And it is, because it's simply power.

"There's some thought, but it is very far from lucid and it's very poorly shared or distributed in consequence.

"Then I came across you. Another person hungry for power, busily assembling the leverage to acquire it. Yet another political club anxious to build up a network. It's going to be child's play to dismantle all that – you'll give me all the information I need, and I'll see to it that you do – and in doing that I'm simply doing my job with the means at my disposal: if it comes to involve violence to yourself that's too bad.

"Remains the personal problem of what to do with you. You see, I don't believe Maltaverne did all that on his own. He was a dangerous man, because he wanted power very badly, was highly ambitious and greedy for money: a cop gone that way has gone bad.

"There's nothing you can do bar shoot them, the way you would an axe-murderer run amok. Castang knew that, and did.

"But would he have reached the stage of putting a fire-bomb in my house, without you? He was suspicious of me: you were suspicious of me. Alone, he'd never have done that. You saw a bad cop and leaned on his weaknesses. You ended up by killing one, and very nearly two.

"What will Castang do to you, when he gets out of hospital? Think about that, for five minutes . . .

"Knowing him as I now do, he'll leave you to me. And I am sorely tempted to leave you to my subordinates yonder. I've a couple there that would hang you up by the heels in the basement and love it. I'm tempted myself. A little blood on the snow would look good, don't you think? To let you lead the rest of your existence in terror. Not only clip Charlemagne's wings but make certain there's no recurrence.

"It would not be in the least clever because we've already seen what Maltaverne's fear did to him. That violence is fed by fear is the number one cliché in the trade. Not just cause and effect; the effect is the cause. That's gone on for thousands of years and I know of no way to turn the clock back.

"All that I can do is take my own responsibilities in the matter. I leave you here," said Richard, halting at the far end of the golf-course.

"You can make your own way back. I mean that both ways. You'll come to see me, and you'll turn over every item of information about Charlemagne, and that goes as a confidential file to the Ministry. Further I don't intend to do anything at all. You're a free man to go as you please and do as you wish." He walked away towards the conifers planted on the boundary close enough to discourage trespassers and sheep. On the rutted pathway beyond he picked up Orthez, who drove him back to the office. A slight grin there, Richard noticed, flickering round the chops: he asked what it meant.

"Ach, nothing much."

"I forbade – "

"Yes I know."

"Kindly tell me."

"Ach, put my knife – yes, childish. Only in the tyres of his stinking car." Shamefaced maybe, but quite unashamed.

Richard said nothing. Orthez changed down into second gear, for once without a lot of engine noise.

"If Castang had been gut shot," his voice, like the motor, was quiet, "then I would have put the knife – . . ."

"I'm aware," said Richard. The error in Maltaverne's shot had been a few centimetres, which meant that the error in his hand was a millimetre. That millimetre had just saved Biron's life. Orthez, and he himself, would have gone on breathing, but their lives too would have been finished. We make small errors in judgment every day, Richard was thinking. Maybe every half hour. The difference is in not holding a gun. An example: Orthez is a good driver who aims the car with extreme precision. An error there too of a millimetre is flagrant after ten metres and an enormity at thirty. But it isn't a bullet.

Over our heads is a satellite with a camera that is a technical marvel and can spy a lump of sugar from ten miles up. But if the camera told the computer, and the computer told the rocket 'Take out that piece of sugar' it could only do so by flattening a hundred square miles of shabby old Earth.

Each peak of violence tops the one before. Like the three jobs that coincidence had handed to Castang in quick time. That Japanese . . .

A people, thought Richard, about whom it is safer to avoid generalisations. The head of Toyota Motors had had the splendid idea of a memorial monument to all the unfortunates who had been killed

214

by his products. Costing, one was given to believe, some four hundred thousand dollars, to pacify restless ancestral spirits. What did that work out at per head?

Castang had caught something like a black eye in recompense.

Next had been a pubescent girl. More frightening still. Likewise, cost to the department still relatively trivial: a few cuts and bruises and Liliane's collarbone. Some alarmingly close shaves though.

And then Maltaverne. What had been the minute error there, at the start of a human being, that had turned him into a bad cop? Richard remembered his medical dossier, full of approving notations. But the most any shrink would ever have managed would have been a mumble that too much of him stayed blocked in adolescence, and hell, they'd say the same about Orthez.

"We're home," said that gentleman, putting on the handbrake. He glanced at Richard's closed eyes. Getting old, he thought.

Vera went to the station to pick the man up from his voyages. Social Security had rather grudgingly admitted the principle of convalescence, but was blowed if it would pick up the tab for air tickets. It didn't matter; Castang preferred trains anyhow. Coming off the platform, carrying the lighter of his encumbrances rather proudly under the left or tennis-racket arm (it hurt a good deal still sometimes; he supposed it always would; the main circuits got blown but secondary lateral nervous systems managed to take over and do the job; something rather similar to the happenings in Vera's spine; in this at least they were now on a footing of equality) he noticed that in the main concourse the scaffolding was still sitting there, that he had had put up to disguise cameras. Nobody had ever bothered taking it down: bets would be laid on how long it would now stay there.

Vera was double-parked outside. A cop was staring at her, wondering whether to overcome inertia long enough to give her a ticket: recognising Castang he was glad he hadn't and went all nonchalant. Lydia was there too, strapped in an aluminium frame.

"Will you drive?" asked his wife, just a thought over-casual but she'd do better with practice.

"Why not? Are there any new one-way streets?"

No welcome-home committee, for which he was profoundly

grateful. A singularly scrubbed hearth-and-home: flowers: champagne: all quite conventional and very proper. She would have mobilised herself strictly, with severe instructions to hold herself ready to serve every male caprice without a second's hesitation. He waited for this to wear off, in some trepidation. Surely within a day or two she would fidget, and King Charles's Head would reappear with disquisitions on how much better women would do everything: discontents and fits of the sullens, which had been his portion for a year and more. It didn't.

He went to work. Trepidation there too. Was he going to get put in the garage? Polished up and sent to the Museum of Antique Automobiles? Richard met him in a casual fashion and tapped the arm.

"As good as new?"

"As strong anyhow as the ordinary one; a bit eggshelly feeling. I'm frightened of getting a crack in it. That's like having a new car and will wear off. But I'll be permanently slow."

"Yes," said Richard turning over papers. "I've the medical report here."

"I suppose," defiantly, "I get sent to the archives or whatever. I don't care: I've made up my mind I'll never wear a gun again."

"Oh shut up" absently. "I've been in Paris, where as you need no telling there was a to-do. A small to-do. The upshot of this is that the Person goes back to Pau. He was always unhappy here, and is thrilled. You are going to take that slot. There was some muttering, since the slot belongs to a Principal, and you aren't."

"Christ I've only had this rank a year."

"And will have it a couple more. There was and will be some jealousy. You'll get the step when that simmers down. I made a fuss about keeping you, which was nearly the occasion for your being sent to the Cotentin Peninsula and left there commanding the Artificial Insemination Centre. However. Pau has already claimed its own, and I'd be grateful now if you'd get into your new office and learn something about staff work, because Fausta's already making jokes about Commissaire Thalidomide."

"Who gets the criminal brigade?"

"I'd have liked to have Williez but a woman in charge of that was too much for them to stomach. There's a lad coming from Sedan."

It was not the moment for personal enquiries, not even 'How's

216

Judith?". He looked around his new office desolately, but in the passage he had passed Davignon carrying a sheaf of papers, who winked at him and made him feel better.

When he reached home Vera was drawing: a good sign. She did not cry when told, though she looked out of the window in a tense moment of getting hold of herself.

"I haven't been very much good this last long while. I'll try and do better. I think now that it was me who nearly got you killed."

"Oh tra la," crossly.

Well, he'd have to risk it.

"What about the north wind?" hoping it didn't sound sarcastic. She picked up the stick of charcoal and concentrated on her subject.

There'll be something now about metaphysics, he thought with dread. One of those terrible remarks about immortality, or a man's incapacity to understand. For a long long time she had been so impossibly humourless. Almost the last time he'd seen her laugh had been after one of their frustrating scenes which led nowhere: after brooding in silence over one of her books she'd begun laughing uncontrollably and in the end had shown him. It had been the worried little man in the James Thurber drawing, saying 'With you I have known peace, Lida, and now you say you're going crazy'. He had laughed too, while not quite sure whether to laugh or not.

And what was the drawing? Another of those Imaginary Prisons, by a twentieth-century and psychotic Piranesi?

There was silence for five minutes. Then she blew at it, studied it awhile, went and got a cigarette, a thing she now did about once a week. She stood and looked at it some more, went to get her thing which blew fixative, so that the charcoal would not smear. Then she turned it round for him to see.

In a very few strokes, giving a remote, Chinese feel, there was an open landscape of stones and a tree. A man sat under the tree, in a loose comfortable way with a knee drawn up. He seemed old: his face was calm and untroubled. A vaguer, androgynous figure, its back turned, reclined on the ground, head propped against a hand. On the ground between them was a chessboard, pieces barely sketched. The reclining figure was concentrated, with anxiety in the line of the neck and back. The sitting figure was filled with serenity.

"I like this very much," said Castang. "Is this where it is, the

217

landscape? Behind the wind?"

"Perhaps," said Vera, holding the drawing so that the light fell right for him; wrinkling because of the smoke from the cigarette in her mouth; smiling at him.

Outside night was falling upon winter. Snow was stopping and starting again, unable to make its stupid mind up. Castang had the sensation of hot sun coming out from behind black cloud.

"If so tell them we'll be with them shortly."